DREW AND THE DETECTIVES SERIES

# SCANDAL
# BENEATH
# THE SKYLINE

ANDREW PACHOLYK

author of The Rhythm of Betrayal

Scandal Beneath the Skyline
by Andrew Pacholyk MS LAc
Copyright © 2025
Editor: Lucy S.

Fiona's dialogue a registered trademark of Fiona Says

The trademark for "The New York Post" is held by NYP Holdings Inc

ISBN 979-8-9985535-0-9 paperback
ISBN 979-8-9985535-1-6 ebook
ISBN 979-8-9985535-2-3 hardcover
Library of Congress Control Number: 2025901576
Know Publishing, New York, NY

Book Cover Design and Interior Formatting by 100Covers.

# Table of Contents

# Dedication

To my gypsy family: "True friends are the threads that weave the tapestry of our lives, adding color and warmth to every chapter."

Candela Alarcon

Debra Arditi

Israel Loreto Diaz

Vincent Dixon

Elena (Lani Ford) Everitt

Francesca Muia

James Palacio

Aisha Qandisha

Grace Redwood

# Chapter 1
## Park Avenue

New York, a city defined by stark contrasts, pulsed with an electric edge. Its streets, filled with the vibrant energy of summer, hummed with anticipation, even as the relentless traffic drowned out the lively buzz. The crowd ebbed and flowed like a tide in a concrete sea, each surge rising and crashing with the force of grand dreams, mirroring the city's impressive yet daunting facade.

New York held a special place in Drew's heart, reflecting his own world. His magnetic pull toward the city was undeniable. Having spent half his life here, it had become an integral part of his identity. It was more than just a city—it was his backyard, his playground, and the foundation of his successful dance career. Now that he called Miami home, a return to New York provided him a sense of renewal and an opportunity to reconnect with the experiences that had shaped him.

Drew's reverie was abruptly shattered by a chorus of catcalls and whistles. With a grin, he noted that the attention was not aimed at him but at Francy, who confidently strode along Fifth Avenue by his side.

Wearing casual shorts and a tricolor t-shirt, she perfectly displayed a dancer's form, her Italian beauty making even a paper bag seem alluring. Amused by the construction workers' playful banter, she swept her long, wavy brunette hair to one side and smiled broadly, as if her smile had activated a signal that spurred an even greater outpouring of admiration from the busy laborers. "I thought that trend was outdated," Francy teased in a slight Italian accent, casting a mischievous glance at Drew.

"Welcome back," he chuckled.

Francy's return to Manhattan brought back fond memories of her dancing days. For her, New York was a routine stop between shows—she would book a dance gig, tour for six months to a year, return to the city, and repeat the cycle.

But this trip was different.

"This is the address," Drew interrupted as Francy strode ahead.

"Here?" Francy looked up at the towering apartment building on the corner of East 60th Street and Park Avenue. "Phillip lived here?" Her eyes widened in surprise.

A tall, imposing doorman in a long green coat, dark suit, and matching cap opened the large brass doors. He immediately positioned himself between them and the ornate art deco lobby shining behind him. "Can I help you?" he asked authoritatively.

"Drew and Francesca here for Richard Belltone," Drew replied, matching his tone.

The doorman raised an eyebrow. "They're expecting you," he said. "Penthouse A."

They boarded the gilded elevator to the 35th floor. "How does a dancer afford to live here?" Francy asked, turning to Drew.

"I recognize the name now," Drew said, snapping his fingers as the connection hit him. "The Belltone building, the Belltone Theatre, the Belltone Art Foundation... But how are they connected to our friend Phillip?"

The elevator doors opened into a narrow hallway with just two doors. In an instant, the door on their left swung open.

"Drew?" a gentleman inquired.

"Yes, Richard?" Drew answered, puzzled by the caller's identity.

"Oh no," the caller replied playfully. "Jonathan Matthews. I'm the Belltone's art curator. Please, come in," he said with a smile.

They were met by a man in his early 60s. His jet-black hair and deep brown eyes complemented the warm, caramel tone of his skin. He carried himself with effortless charm. Standing tall with a confident posture, he moved purposefully, gesturing as he ushered them inside.

Drew and Francy entered an expansive foyer with black and white parkee floors. A large, gold-framed mirror stared back at them on their left, while an abundant floral arrangement sat to their right on a wrought iron and glass table.

"This way, please," Jonathan insisted. "The Belltones are waiting for you in the living room."

The living room of the Belltones' New York City penthouse was breathtaking. As they stepped inside, they found themselves in a world of pure luxury. The walls featured intricate gold leaf moldings that blended seamlessly with lavish oil paintings depicting scenes from the city's rich history.

A grand crystal chandelier hung from the high ceiling, its soft light casting a warm glow over the carefully selected antique furniture. A plush velvet sofa, accented with elaborately embroidered pillows, served as the focal point. On either side of the sofa were matching armchairs, upholstered in rich green and beige brocade material. In one chair sat Richard Belltone; in the other, his wife Veronica.

"Welcome to our home," Veronica Belltone said as she slowly rose. A distinguished woman in a celestial blue and white dress and three-inch heels, she looked younger than her years as she extended her hand first to Francy, then to Drew.

Richard Belltone followed, briskly rising from his chair to shake Drew's hand. His reputation preceded him—a larger-than-life figure whose face Drew recognized from frequent news appearances. As the iconic head of a famous New York family, he embodied the status of a respected financier and real estate mogul, a true product of Manhattan's Upper East Side.

"It's an honor, sir," Drew responded.

"We saw the headlines and photos in the Palm Beach Post and learned you were Phillip's good friends," Mrs. Belltone said excitedly.

"When we read that you solved that terrible double murder in Miami, we knew you were the right people," Mr. Belltone added, shaking his head. "We worked with that Miami shipping business and know the White family."

Drew and Francy exchanged a look.

"I'm sorry, please have a seat," he offered, motioning toward the sofa.

"Such a beautiful home, Mrs. Belltone," Francy complimented.

"Oh please, call me Veronica. And thank you. I love decorating," she said modestly. A woman of refined elegance, every move she made conveyed the polish of someone accustomed to the finer things in life. Yet beneath her polished exterior lay a deep sorrow.

"I'm sorry, Mr. Belltone... the right people for what?" Drew inquired as he settled onto the divan next to Francy.

"To solve Phillip's murder. And please, call me Richard." He unbuttoned his fitted jacket and sat back, running one hand through his impeccably styled silver hair.

"The police aren't doing enough to uncover what happened to our son. We want you and your detective friends to take the case. We will spare no expense!" Veronica Belltone pleaded.

"I did not realize Phillip was your son. He didn't have your last name. Was he adopted?" Drew asked.

"Phillip insisted on pursuing show business. He wanted to sing and dance," Richard replied, shaking his head.

"I can relate," Drew confirmed, noting Richard's sarcasm. His eyes slowly scanned the room. In one corner, a grand piano stood proudly, inviting anyone with a love for music to create harmonies. Drew recalled how skilled Phillip was on the piano.

"Phillip wanted to succeed on his own terms—not merely as a Belltone. He chose to change his last name to Wright," Veronica confessed. "I could respect that."

"Yes, Phillip Wright. That's how I knew him," Francy recalled. "Phillip always admired you because you helped him. You connected him with the right people for a dance scholarship and befriended him when he was just starting out. He never forgot that," his mother said, tears welling in her eyes.

Her words brought comfort to Drew. "Phillip was incredibly talented. He deserved every opportunity."

4

"We never truly realize how many lives we touch on our personal journeys," his father added sadly.

"Well, you're a perfect example, sir," Francy remarked. "Your influence is evident all over New York."

"Clearly, you were an inspiration to your son," Drew smiled.

Richard looked at Veronica and offered a subtle smile.

"What were the circumstances surrounding his death?" Drew asked gently. "It's important for us to know the details so we can better understand what happened and where things went wrong."

The conversation paused as a diminutive figure entered the room, her soft steps barely audible on the plush carpet. She was an elderly woman, short yet dignified—a reflection of many years of quiet service. Dressed in a traditional maid's outfit, her face, marked by time, carried the wisdom of her early eighties, etched with lines that spoke of smiles and sorrows witnessed in silence.

"Oh, Bayya, just in time," Veronica Belltone exclaimed. "Bayya makes the best lemonade."

In her hands, she balanced a tray with the poise of an experienced ballet dancer, each glass of lemony refreshment glistening through ice cubes like miniature jewels against the polished silver. She distributed the refreshments with practiced ease, her movements nearly choreographic in their precision.

Drew noticed pockets of silver hair peeking from beneath her cap, framing her ebony complexion with hints of a once raven hue, now a dignified reminder of her years. On her finger, a blue sapphire set in a simple silver band caught the light.

Upon reaching Richard, her soft, mellifluous voice—harmonizing with the clinking ice—asked with genuine concern if there was anything else she could provide.

"Francesca, Drew, I'd like to introduce Bayya Jenkins. She has been with us since I was a young man," Richard said with a warm smile. "We need nothing else, my dear."

Bayya offered a crooked smile and tucked her tray under her arm. Despite her age making the task more challenging, she moved diligently as she headed back to the kitchen.

It was then that Drew began making further observations within the room. The expansive windows across from him provided a breathtaking view of the city, with floor-to-ceiling silk drapes cascading down their sides. They framed the vibrant New York skyline and the enchanting vista of Central Park, offering a picturesque backdrop to the living room.

"Phillip was murdered in cold blood and we need to know why?" Veronica said, standing to ensure the maid was out of earshot. "The police have not offered any clues or explanations for what happened." Her eyes filled with tears.

"We need your help. You knew Phillip and he admired you. We can't sleep without knowing what really happened, and we believe you and your team can solve this mystery."

Francy and Drew exchanged a knowing glance.

Veronica then walked over to an ornate fireplace. The mantle was lined with family photographs and fine porcelain collectibles, showcasing the Belltones' cherished memories. She removed a picture from the mantel and handed it to Francy.

"This is you and Phillip," Francy said while holding the photo and then turned to Drew.

"I can see his attitude was much like yours," Veronica observed. "This must be why he admired you so."

Drew glanced at the photo. "This was backstage at one of our shows together. Yes, I remember." He looked closely and noticed something in Phillip's hand, but said nothing.

"Well then, I'm sorry to have to rehash the past, but we really need some details," Drew said, already determined to help the family. He recalled Phillip and knew how he died. "How did Phillip die?" he asked, feigning forgetfulness.

"He died backstage during his performance," Richard replied as he accepted the photograph back from Drew. "He was about to step on stage when he collapsed. The theater quickly called paramedics, but he was gone by the time they arrived." Richard recounted the story once more, each retelling deepening his pain.

"I'm so sorry for your loss," Francy told Veronica.

"The paramedics determined it was a heart attack, yet Phillip had no history of heart problems and was in excellent condition. He was a dancer, for God's sake!" Richard slowly walked over to his desk, opened a large drawer, and retrieved an autopsy report from the hospital, handing it to Drew.

"What makes you think it was murder?" Drew asked while flipping through the report. He noticed the letters "LX" enclosed in a circle on the last page and waited for an answer from the Belltone family.

"He was poisoned." Veronica slumped in her chair and burst into uncontrollable tears.

"Poisoned?" Francy echoed.

"I don't see a toxicology report," Drew observed, looking up from the papers.

"After his body was returned from the hospital, I had a private autopsy and toxicology screening performed at the city morgue," Richard said sternly.

"I assume you have the capability…"

"And the resources to perform this," Richard interrupted. "No one will give me the final word without my own investigation." There was a spark in his eyes, a relentless ambition that suggested this leading figure in industry was as dynamic and determined as ever.

"Do you have a copy of this second report?" Drew asked, standing and returning the papers to Richard.

"No!" he exclaimed. "It was sent to my work computer, but our system was breached and the report deleted. However, the examiner I hired from the city morgue, Dr. Foster, found traces of poison in his bloodstream."

"Did he specify the poison?" Drew pressed.

"No. The examiner said he needed to conduct further tests."

"Surely the examiner, Dr. Foster—who performed the second autopsy—must have had a report?" Drew said, confused.

"No!" Richard replied again. "Dr. Foster was murdered."

"And the report he sent you?"

"It was wiped clean from his computer." Richard sat down, sweating and appearing as if he had just run a marathon. He was mentally exhausted, drained of every reserve. "I'm at my wit's end," he managed to say.

"The coroner who performed the second autopsy…"

"Dr. Foster suffered a heart attack, just like Phillip," he interrupted Drew. "There's no doubt it was the same poison."

Francy and Drew exchanged a look of disbelief.

"Of course, I had a detective friend on the case, but he found no evidence to support these claims. In fact, he encountered obstacles at every turn. I knew he regarded me as a crazy old man, yet I felt powerless."

"Sir, your artwork is all displayed in the study," Jonathon Matthews announced from another doorway. The art curator approached Veronica Belltone, kissing her hand, then shook Richard's hand. "Everything is pristine, sir." His eyes met Francy's as he turned and nodded to her and Drew.

"Nice meeting you," Drew said.

Jonathon blew a kiss to the maid as he left the penthouse.

"Do you have any suspects in mind?" Drew asked, turning to Richard.

"Detective Jameson, who is handling the case, focused on the theatre and questioned the cast and crew of the show Phillip was in, yet he wasn't convinced there was more than a heart attack." He paused and looked at his wife. Finding no further evidence, he confirmed that the hospital's autopsy had ruled Phillip's death as a heart attack, effectively closing the case.

"Did Phillip live here with you?" Francy asked Veronica.

"No, he had an apartment in the West Village. He would occasionally visit us—sometimes staying overnight if it got late—but he always cherished his West Village home," Veronica sighed.

"Have the police investigated his apartment?" Drew asked Richard.

"No. The investigation focused on the theatre, and Veronica didn't want the police disturbing his apartment and making a mess."

"I was trying to preserve his memory," Veronica cried.

"Did your detective friend, Detective Jameson, visit Phillip's apartment?" Francy asked quickly.

"He did not." Richard replied and then sat in the nearest chair, looking overwhelmed.

Overwhelmed by grief and anger, Veronica collapsed into an armchair, covering her face with her hands as she wept silently.

"We knew this would stir up pain and sorrow," Richard consoled his wife, gently placing a hand on her shoulder. "But we want answers, don't we, dear?"

She paused and looked up. "I just want my son back," she whispered.

"We understand," Francy interjected. "We're going to do everything we can to help."

Richard attempted to steer the conversation. "Drew, if you don't mind me asking—it takes a special person to be driven to do this kind of work. What inspired you to take this on?"

Drew cast a subtle glance at Francy for silent encouragement. Taking a deep breath, his voice steady yet heavy with emotion, he said, "Sir, when I was a teenager, my aunt was tragically murdered in Los Angeles. Despite our efforts, her case remains unsolved."

Veronica's gaze shifted toward Drew, her eyes filled with sympathy and understanding.

"I think it has always troubled me—the helplessness I felt when I couldn't do anything about it," Drew said, glancing at Richard Belltone. "This drives me: the need to secure justice for others, for the justice I never received for myself."

Richard nodded in understanding.

"Our recent case in Miami compelled us not only to prove our innocence but also thrust us into a situation only we could manage."

"That's incredible," Veronica said, placing her hand on Francy's arm. "Destiny charts its course."

Richard rose and walked to a teak desk on the far side of the room. He bent over, opened a drawer, and retrieved a checkbook. He scribbled a number in his ledger while his wife looked on.

He slowly straightened up and walked briskly toward his guests. "All the resources of this family are at your disposal," Richard affirmed, handing Drew a check.

Drew hesitated to look at the amount. He glanced down, swallowed hard, and passed the check to Francy. Her reaction was noticeably less restrained.

"Sir, this is an obscene amount of money. We can do our best, but we can't guarantee the results," Francy said nervously.

"Oh, we have great faith in all of you!" Richard affirmed.

Richard moved to his desk and wrote down an address on a piece of notepaper. "When I said we would spare no expense, I meant it. We want answers, and we know you are invested in this case—after all, you knew Phillip and understood what kind of person he was." Then Richard lifted his chin and approached Drew.

"Your son was an upstanding citizen, a superb performer, and an extraordinary talent," Drew confirmed.

He was also inquisitive, tenacious, and exceptionally diligent. He worked tirelessly to obtain whatever he desired and fought relentlessly against injustice. Although stubborn, he could not tolerate unfairness— he always seemed to be on a crusade.

"This is where you and your crew will be staying," Richard said with a smile as he handed Drew the notepaper.

Drew read the address. "The Waldorf Astoria? But sir…""It's Richard. Yes, we have an apartment at the Waldorf Astoria that will comfortably accommodate all of you. Although the hotel is closed for renovations, there are current residents in the building, making it centrally located and more comfortable than a typical hotel."

Francy, still in shock, turned and thanked the couple for their generous offer.

"I'll take you to Phillip's apartment tomorrow so you can begin your investigation," Veronica confirmed to Drew.

"Is there any way we can access the theater to see Phillip's dressing room?" Drew asked.

"We'll figure out a way," Richard affirmed. "When will the rest of your friends arrive?"

"They'll be here tomorrow," Drew replied, glancing at Francy for confirmation.

"You can move into the Waldorf right away," Richard said with a smile. "The building manager will give you the keys—he's waiting for you."

Drew nodded to Francy, and they both stood up.

"Listen, there's one more thing I'd like you to do," Mr. Belltone said in a lowered voice. "I left an envelope for you at my Central Park office; please pick it up."

"I will," Drew agreed. "Again, we can't thank you enough," he added as he shook Richard's hand.

"We'll get you answers," Francy confirmed, kissing Veronica Belltone on the cheek.

As Francy and Drew descended in the elevator, an overwhelming feeling washed over them. "It's unbelievable what money can do," Francy said, shaking her head. "I'm in complete shock."

"I feel so grateful for their confidence in us, yet at the same time, I feel obligated to deliver answers—it's a precarious position to be in."

"We'll put our heads together—all seven of us—and get to the bottom of this," Francy declared proudly. "Hey, is that your phone buzzing?"

Lost in thought, Drew ignored the phone vibrating in his bag. "Hey, it's Detective Vincent from Miami."

"Drew, did you make it to New York?"

"Detective Vincent, how are you?" Drew smiled as if his old friend could see his grin. "Yes, sir, we just spoke with the client and they really want our help." Detective Vincent and Drew had known each other for a long time; they had grown closer during the exciting case they handled in Miami.

"Good. I want you to talk to Detective Conor Jameson. I called the 140th Precinct, and he was the acting detective on the Belltone case. He's an old friend and is available to speak with you now," Detective Vincent said in his Jamaican accent.

"Okay, so he's aware that we'll be working on the case?" Drew asked, uncertain how readily Jameson would provide details about Phillip's death.

"Well, he knows about you and your Miami case. I'm not sure he's convinced that your team will uncover any new details, but I assured him that your lack of experience is balanced by your determination."

"I understand," Drew confirmed.

"He's straightforward and to the point—kind of like you. But he's a bit more hard-boiled, a real straight shooter. So, go in there knowing exactly what you want to ask," Detective Vincent advised.

Drew nodded in agreement. "I understand," he repeated.

"Despite his gruff exterior, I've seen a glimmer of compassion in his eyes when interacting with victims or witnesses. I'm speaking frankly with you," Detective Vincent stated without any sugarcoating.

Drew began to question whether it was a wise decision.

"Jameson is a man of few words, but each is carefully chosen and reflects his unwavering commitment to seeking justice in the city he loves." Drew recognized the relaxed tone in Detective Vincent's voice; he trusted his friend.

"Alright, Detective Vincent, I appreciate your candor," Drew said, thanking him before hanging up.

"That sounds promising," Francy said with a slight smile.

They walked briskly down Park Avenue, completely engaged in conversation about the new case. Unbeknownst to them, a black Mercedes had been tailing them for several blocks.

Drew felt a prickling unease. When he looked back, he saw a suspicious vehicle quietly approaching and pulling alongside them, as if it had been following unnoticed. With a subtle gesture, he grasped Francy's arm and brought them to a stop.

"What is it?" she asked, slowly turning to look at him with one eye.

"Black car on my left," Drew replied.

She glanced over his shoulder and noticed the polished gleam of the vehicle's tinted windows. After a quick check of the street sign, she whispered, "Take a right here. It's 52nd Street. It runs east—one way, so they can't follow us."

"Smart," Drew replied. "Even numbered streets run east!" Their hearts raced as they carefully planned their escape route, making split-second decisions to confuse their pursuer.

"Maybe we're just being paranoid?" Francy asked as they continued moving. They crossed three blocks of Madison Avenue, then turned west onto 49th Street. Believing they might have lost their tail, they stopped to catch their breath.

Suddenly, Drew caught sight of the black Mercedes, intent on catching up. They stood frozen, realizing their earlier suspicions might have been true. The Mercedes screeched as it accelerated and maneuvered through traffic, racing toward them as if tracking every move. Gripped by fear, they understood that their lives were in peril. Without warning, they watched as the tinted driver's side window lowered, revealing a glint of metal.

# Chapter 2
## South Street Seaport

Two bullets were fired in quick succession, their sharp sounds reverberating off the surrounding buildings. The projectiles sped through the air, aimed with deadly precision at Drew and Francy, who dove for cover behind a parked car.

Adrenaline surged through their veins. They ran down the street as though floating. "Look," Drew pointed, "The Waldorf Astoria."

"We shouldn't go in there. Then they'll know where we're staying," Francy yelled.

"Come on… I have an idea," Drew urged her.

They sprinted to the corner of 49th Street and Park Avenue and then up another two blocks, hoping their rapid movements would lead them away from the pursuer stalking them.

At the center of the block, St. Bartholomew's Church rose impressively. As they approached, its massive dome—crowned by a gold cross—caught the sunlight, glowing against the New York City skyline.

"Let's hide in here," Drew suggested.

The vast interior of the cathedral became their refuge. The thick stone walls were adorned with detailed patterns and carvings. The stained-glass windows cast a shifting array of colors, bathing the space in a warm, inviting light. They collapsed into one of the pews.

"We should be okay here," Drew said, panting. His lungs felt as though they were ready to burst. Sweat dripped down his forehead and pooled near his eyes.

"What's happening?" Francy asked, looking around while trying to catch her breath. Her heart pounded like a time bomb waiting to detonate. "Could this be connected to where we just came from?"

"That's a fair assumption," Drew replied as he slowly stood up. He gazed down the long aisle toward the shimmering marble altar. Gradually, his breathing steadied. "Someone seems to have anticipated our arrival. We have to be cautious about whom we share information with."

"Let's start with the people we just encountered," Francy said as she stood, still trying to steady her breathing.

"Phillip's parents, Veronica and Richard, Jonathan Matthews, the art curator, the doorman…" Drew rattled off the list.

"And the maid, Bayya," Francy added.

"They all seem to be people determined to guide us toward answers," Drew mused. "Maybe our path was set even before we reached their home."

They sat in silence, reflecting and thankful simply for being alive.

"If Phillip uncovered something so shocking that it cost him his life, we must go back and retrace his steps," Francy said, her gaze fixed on a radiant statue of the Virgin Mary—a sight that stirred thoughts of Phillip's mother. "I want to get Mrs. Belltone some answers."

Francy's disbelief was evident as she struggled to accept the latest news about the tragic loss of their dear friend.

"It's ironic—the last conversation I had with Phillip was a heated debate about life after death. He was afraid of what awaited him after he died," Drew recalled. He glanced toward the altar while Francy slowly turned, casting a long, perplexed look in his direction.

"Is that why he always invested his time and energy in signs and symbols?" Francy said slowly as she began to understand.

"Yes, and how other cultures viewed death and dying," Drew confirmed. "If he couldn't control it, he was determined to make sense of it logically and rationally."

Before they knew it, the sun had disappeared through the windows, and the sacred statues cast a shadow along the center aisle.

"I think we've lost them. Let's go," Francy exclaimed.

They passed through the large wood and glass doors at the front of the church, searching for their attacker up and down Park Avenue. "Looks like the coast is clear."

They walked downtown, constantly glancing over their shoulders. A car honked in front of them, startling both of them.

"Okay, just breathe," Francy whispered. "It's rush hour."

As they crossed the busy street, Drew caught sight of a black car. "It can't be," he said softly, hoping his instincts were wrong. A lump formed in his throat. He had no time to warn Francy when the driver of the Mercedes, unwilling to give up, maneuvered right past them, almost clipping Francy's leg.

"He's back," she screamed.

Without a second to lose, Drew and Francy sprinted along Park Avenue, narrowly dodging oncoming traffic. The driver of the Mercedes screeched to a halt, causing the car to slide sideways in the middle of the street. Other drivers reacted quickly—some coming to a full stop, others just grazing the vehicle to prevent a collision. The driver rolled down the window and opened fire, the sound of bullets piercing the air.

The crowds on the sidewalk scattered in every direction—women screaming and others ducking for cover. Dodging gunfire, Drew and Francy dashed at full speed, zigzagging between pedestrians and obstacles as they ran for their lives. They crossed the median in the middle of Park Avenue while desperately searching for an escape.

"Quick," Drew yelled as he spotted the entrance to the Lexington Avenue subway station. Summoning their last bit of energy, they dashed toward the entrance and raced down the steps.

They jumped over the turnstiles and ran down the platform. "Hold the doors," Francy pleaded. With seconds to spare, they leaped onto the departing train just as the doors closed, leaving their attacker behind.

Gasping for breath, they collapsed into the seats, their hearts pounding. Several passengers looked at them as if they had just robbed a bank. "It's okay," Drew gasped. "It's all okay."

As the train sped away, they locked eyes, relief and triumph mingling in their expressions. It was a close call, but they had successfully evaded their dangerous pursuer.

"That's the first time I ever mopped the train!" Francy exclaimed with mixed emotions as she caught her breath.

"Well, we were running for our lives," Drew reminded her. "I'm sure the MTA would understand that we didn't pay the fare."

The two sat silently as the train whizzed through the dark tunnel.

"Are you alright?" Drew asked, studying the blank expression on Francy's face. His skill at reading a room, understanding what others thought, and analyzing decisions was something he continually honed.

Francy shot him a look. "I know you're trying to read me," she smirked. "I'm okay, really." She leaned back in her subway seat and stretched out her legs.

"It's not every day you get chased by a car firing bullets at you," Drew reminded her. "If it weren't for the adrenaline and your dance and fitness classes in Miami, I wouldn't have made it." Drew did his best to reassure her.

Francy was far from her classes. "I have my classes covered," she replied nervously. "I told management I was going away for a work con-ference." She shifted in her seat as throngs of people disembarked at 34th Street while another group merged onto the train.

Drew lowered his voice. "Well, this definitely counts as work. Clear-ly, there's some information worth killing for. Someone doesn't want us to find it."

"If Phillip was killed and the independent coroner Mr. Belltone hired was also murdered, then someone is covering their tracks." Francy's thoughts turned back to the information Richard Belltone had shared.

"I say we crash at our current hotel tonight and head to the Waldorf Astoria tomorrow when the team arrives." Drew wiped the sweat from his brow and leaned back as the subway train barreled downtown, its rhythmic sway soothing his racing mind.

★★★

There was nothing more beautiful than a summer morning in New York. That beauty was not just seen—it was experienced. From the cozy confines of their hotel room, nestled near the vibrant South Street Seaport, the day's opening scene unfolded through the expansive windows in Francy and Drew's hotel suite. A range of soft pastels spread across the horizon, announcing the sun's arrival.

South Street Seaport, one of New York's oldest historic districts, centered around where Fulton Street met The East River, with the water—a quiet guardian of the city's slumber—reflecting the gentle hues of the awakening sky. From this viewpoint, the city seemed to pause in a moment of calm anticipation. The river shone with the promise of a new day. Boats, both small and large, began to appear along the waterway, their bows catching the first hints of the morning breeze.

Francy and Drew made their way to a quaint café near their hotel along the cobblestone streets of the Seaport. The air was crisp and refreshing, carrying a trace of salt inland from the vast Atlantic beyond the harbor.

"I did not sleep very well last night," Drew confessed. "I kept thinking of what the consequences could have been." The lingering taste of coffee on his lips suddenly shifted his mood.

"I kept seeing that car in my nightmare with the gun protruding from the driver's side window. It was awful," Francy admitted.

They sat in silence, watching the world around them.

Over the water, the Brooklyn Bridge stretched into the growing daylight. Its renowned network of cables and stone pillars stood as a clear sign of human ingenuity and perseverance. The towers, reaching toward the sky, were outlined by golden sunbeams that revealed its intricate design.

This was New York City at its calmest—a brief pause before the city's heartbeat quickened. It granted them a moment of serenity before the rush of urban life resumed.

Seated and absorbing both the roughness and refinement that gave New York its shine, Francy wiped the sleep from her eyes, removed her light sweater and stowed it in her bag before changing into a tank top and spandex shorts—ready to start the day. She downed her coffee and croissant. "I've resolved to move on and not dwell on yesterday's events," she stated matter-of-factly. "If I think too much about it, I'll end up trapped in my own thoughts."

They both stared into the distance, lost in their own reflections on what might have been. Suddenly, the familiar rumble underfoot caught their attention.

At regular morning intervals, a stream of downtrodden commuters emerged from a small opening in the sidewalk that served as the subway entrance. Most bore the marks of life's hardships on their faces. Occasionally, a few young, determined individuals broke through the crowd, carrying an air of possibility with them.

Francy and Drew exchanged a knowing glance, remembering their friend Phillip.

"That used to be us too," Francy managed to say.

Drew gave a somber smile and nodded.

These morning warriors were armed with two essentials: a steaming cup of coffee and the day's headlines. Known for its over-the-top, jaw-dropping 35-character headlines, the NY Post was a New York institution. Almost tabloid in nature, it sharply contrasted with the refined New York Time. Yet often, you'd see New Yorkers carrying the Post. Even in a digital era, things were different here. This was New York—where scandal, sensationalism, and blatant tongue-in-cheek humor always found an audience, and the Post never disappointed.

"Well," Drew began hesitantly, "first things first." As he rose from his chair to start their day, he noticed a guy in his late 20s with brown, tousled hair and black-rimmed glasses racing toward them on roller blades. He swerved in and out of traffic coming off the Brooklyn Bridge, barreling in their direction. "Now, what could this be?" flashed through Drew's mind as his body tensed for any possibility. That skater picked up speed during his chaotic descent down the off ramp, waving both hands to attract attention.

"It's Israel!" Drew exclaimed.

"What? Where?" Francy asked, scanning every direction. As she did, the skater zoomed past her, tossing half of a cream cheese bagel wrapped in foil into her hands.

"Good reflexes," Israel called out as he circled back on his skates.

"You expected anything less?" Drew shouted. "She's a fitness goddess!"

"Let me guess," Francy said as she watched Israel perform tricks around them. "You flew in from Miami last night, hit a party in DUMBO, and decided to join us for breakfast?"

"Why, you must be a detective, amiga." Israel skated up and over a cement partition, pausing in a perfect fourth position like a trained professional.

"It doesn't take a detective to pick up on your M.O.," Francy remarked, scrutinizing him.

"Drew, check your text." Israel then sat on the edge of a fire hydrant, wiping the sweat from his forehead. He pulled out his phone, and Drew scanned several messages before opening one from Israel. Drew watched a video—seemingly shot from Israel's perspective—skating along the pedestrian walkway on the Brooklyn Bridge. "Did you record this on your phone?" Drew asked.

Israel raised his right finger to the tip of his glasses and shifted them up and down as though they were eyebrows.

"You recorded that footage with those Ray-Ban glasses?" Drew marveled. "You really are the gadget king. That could come in handy someday."

"Pretty cool, huh? AI-enhanced, wearable tech. We're living in the moment, my friends," Israel said as he embraced his two besties.

They shared a history—their bond growing stronger when they united in Miami to solve the notorious case that secured their place in detective lore.

Israel was the group's tech-savvy whiz. His inquisitive mind was always two steps ahead, and he often voiced his thoughts, a habit that only added to his charm.

"That's why we love you." Francy smiled. "Your adventurous spirit always guides our group in the right direction."

"It's a team effort," Israel laughed.

"Well, guess who just texted me?" Drew asked.

"Elena and Debra," Israel answered quickly.

"How did you know?" Drew inquired.

"They're already in New York. We tried reaching out to both of you late this afternoon to check on the interview with the new client."

Francy wrapped her arm around Israel. "We have a story to share with you."

"Let's discuss it on the way. I texted the girls to meet us at the entrance to Central Park. Mr. Belltone also has an envelope for us at his office across from the park."

★★★

Debra stretched her arms overhead and took a deep breath. "Ahhh, New York mornings. I love them," she said with a smile, twirling in the middle of Fifth Avenue. Her bright yellow Max Mara summer dress swirled as she spun. "My dear, Manhattan is the catwalk of the world!" she declared, strutting along the avenue like a runway model. Though small in stature, she radiated boundless energy.

The Argentinian heiress, Debra, with a flair for drama and fashion, danced through life with the grace of a "petite ballerina" — a nickname Drew had given her in homage to her classical ballet roots. Bold and forthright, her view of life was as unique and cherished as her heart of gold, earning her the role of the group's guardian and spirited protector. Being back in New York made her feel alive; after a successful career as a dancer in the city, the urban rhythm pulsed through her veins. She started jogging in place. "Hello? Are you awake in there?"

Elena, still half-asleep, reluctantly pushed her Wayfarers down to the tip of her nose so Debra could see her eyes. "You have enough energy for the both of us," she replied, plodding alongside her.

Elena embodied a mix of charm and cleverness unique to New Yorkers. With her wholesome look, blond hair usually styled in pigtails and a radiant smile that masked her biting New York sarcasm — what Drew affectionately called her humor — she was an intriguing paradox. A jaded New Yorker, she took life with a grain of salt, accustomed as she was to its unpredictability and exaggeration; lessons learned from show business. Her singing gig at the Blue Note the night before was now her excuse. "Morning meetings are not something I enjoy scheduling."

"How was your show at the Blue Note last night?" Debra asked.

"Bad sound check — great show. And a full house," a small smile touched Elena's lips.

"I would have loved to come, but it was past my bedtime!"

"Are you sure Drew wanted to meet uptown?" Elena asked. "He usually gets a nosebleed above 23rd Street."

"He said he had something to show us," Debra said with a shrug. The girls then headed to the corner of Central Park and Fifth Avenue, passing by the Plaza Hotel. They quickly crossed the street to stroll along the cobblestone path lining the Park.

"I'm not sure what's worse—the faint scent of urine in the air or the overpowering smell of horse manure assaulting my nostrils." Elena said as she turned, gesturing toward a horse dressed in royal blue velveteen from bridle to saddle. A striking black top hat, adorned with feathers, crowned the animal's noble head. Its owner wore a matching outfit and top hat. He busily shooed pigeons away from the horse's feed bucket while trying to sell rides to tourists through Central Park. Pacing back and forth, he struggled against the persistent pigeons. Elena watched the absurdity of the scene with an awkward smile.

The girls reached the far side of the park. "Drew, Francy, and Israel are on their way and asked us to meet here," Debra announced. She looked up at the impressive Maine monument overseeing the west side of Central Park South. Stepping into a poised stance, she bowed slightly to the three golden, gilded horses and the rider atop the stone structure. Her dancer's grace remained evident.

"It's almost time for my third cup of coffee," Elena said as she tried to mimic Debra's bow with half the enthusiasm. She tugged at two belt loops and bounced up and down, pulling her snug black jeans further up before sitting on a bench to fasten her boots. Her black cut-off t-shirt read "Sautee the Rich."

"There you are!" Francy called as the trio crossed Central Park West. The five friends embraced with hugs and kisses before settling on the monument's tiered steps while Francy and Drew updated the group on their new client's request.

"Where did you just come from?" Debra asked, shading her eyes against the sun.

Drew pointed across the street to 2 Columbus Circle. "This is our new client."

"The Belltone building?" Debra asked, uncertain of what Drew meant.

"How does that tie in with Phillip's death?" Elena asked, knowing her friend was the main reason she was back in New York.

"Our friend Phillip Wright was the son of Mr. and Mrs. Richard Belltone," Drew explained.

Debra gasped, covering her mouth with both hands as she absorbed the news. "The Belltones?"

Francy explained the details of their meeting with the couple. "They believe their son was murdered."

Her words were met with disbelief.

Drew continued, "They insisted that we are the ones who can uncover the truth—and they're offering us a substantial sum." He pulled out a pen and paper and wrote the number down for everyone to see.

"That's a lot of money," Israel remarked.

"How are we going to deliver?" Debra asked quickly.

"Mrs. Belltone is taking us to Phillip's apartment today, and Mr. Belltone is working on getting us backstage access to his son's dressing room—two locations the police never bothered to investigate, assuming Phillip died of a heart attack."

A heavy silence fell over the group. Drew studied his friends, noticing their doubts in the way they shifted and avoided eye contact.

Elena pressed on, "But didn't his death occur almost six months ago?" Her skepticism was evident.

"That's correct, but we made a promise to Mrs. Belltone, and I know we can deliver," Francy interjected. She couldn't shake the image of a grieving Veronica Belltone from her mind. "We just have to find some answers."

The group agreed knowingly; Francy always had a persuasive way about her.

"Besides," Drew added, "Francy and I were used as someone's target practice, and I'm going to figure out who was behind it."

"What do you mean?" Debra asked, her expression shifting from excitement to concern.

"After leaving the Belltone home, we were chased by a car that opened fire on us," Drew explained.

Debra's face went pale. "Seriously?" she said, looking at Francy in disbelief.

Francy confirmed with a nod.

"Listen… this is now completely real for me. Are you sure this isn't a matter for the police?"

Drew saw the genuine concern on her face. "Yes, it is a matter for the police. But—not just yet." Phillip's death was ruled a heart attack. "The parents believe he was poisoned. A coroner's autopsy initially found nothing, allegedly. Then Mr. Belltone hired a private coroner who, after a second autopsy, discovered that Phillip was indeed poisoned. The private coroner relayed this information to Mr. Belltone over the phone, but before he could provide further details, he suffered a fatal heart attack and his computer—containing the proof—was wiped clean."

"Well, doll, there it is," Elena agreed. "We have to avenge our friend's death. This just got real for me!"

"Hey, Aisha and Grace just texted me," Israel relayed. "They've landed at JFK."

"Tell them to meet us at our new digs," Drew replied. "The Waldorf Astoria."

★★★

An Uber pulled up in front of 301 Park Avenue. Elena and Debra stepped out with shocked expressions.

"Drew, the Waldorf?" Debra exclaimed, giving him a double kiss on the cheek, unable to hide her joy. "I thought you were joking. But I deserve this address," she said with a raised chin. "I can only imagine what we must do to earn digs like these." Elena caught Debra's offhand remark.

"You know it's never what you expect," Elena replied. "Not like the old walk-up apartments we once lived in, right, Drew?" She hugged him and swung her travel bag aside.

"Ah, those East Village days," Drew reminisced.

As promised, the Waldorf Astoria manager was waiting to meet the dancers. A short, stout, cheerful man wearing a red Pullman coat and black trousers greeted them at the door. His green eyes sparkled as he welcomed them warmly. "We're so glad you're here," he said in a broken Irish accent. "My wife already feels safer."

"We're grateful for your generosity," Drew replied with a smile.

The manager signaled the doorman with an "OK." "Don't forget these faces; they're our new tenants. Let me take you up. I'm Liam," he said, gesturing. "You're expecting two more friends, aren't you?"

"They're on their way, Liam. Traffic, you know," Drew reassured him.

Liam gathered everyone and led them through the beautifully restored Art Deco lobby into the large elevator. He pressed the button for the 25th floor, and they ascended. Anticipation filled the air as they exchanged glances. When the elevator doors opened, they stepped into their suite.

Morning light bounced off the marble floors and lofty windows. The spacious suite exuded a cozy ambiance paired with breathtaking views of the city's iconic skyline.

Exiting the elevator, they entered a grand foyer adorned with elegant artwork and subtle spotlights. The design blended classic sophistication with modern conveniences, creating an opulent living space.

"Well, I'm impressed," Debra whispered to Drew.

The living room was a spacious area meant for relaxation and entertainment, featuring plush seats arranged around a stylish fireplace. "I know which room I'll spend most of my time in," Elena remarked.

"All right," Liam led them through the expansive apartment. "Right next to the living room is a fully equipped gourmet kitchen with top-of-the-line appliances and elegant countertops—my favorite room in the house," he smiled. "This kitchen has everything you need."

"Look at these rooms!" Israel shouted as he moved ahead. The suite featured multiple bedrooms, each exuding tranquility and comfort. Adorned with elegant linens, soft lighting, and tasteful furnishings, they provided a serene haven.

"That's a great view to wake up to," Israel exclaimed. The blue sky visible through the windows beckoned him towards the bedroom. "We have views of the city that never sleeps."

"The bathrooms in the suite are pure indulgence," Liam explained as he led them through each room. "With marble finishes, spa-like showers, and deep soaking tubs."

"This is my favorite room," Aisha commented.

Everyone turned to see Spain's most beloved movie actress leaning in the entrance, arms raised, striking a perfect red-carpet pose.

"Aisha!" everyone exclaimed as their friend made a grand entrance.

"I need to indulge in luxurious toiletries and enjoy a soothing bubble bath," she cooed playfully. Aisha's long blond, wavy hair framed her bright smile and expressive eyes. She was dressed in a black bodysuit paired with thigh-high patent leather boots, and a layered gold chain around her neck. Known as the "Spanish Brigitte Bardot," Aisha was everything one would expect from Spain's most cherished actress.

"Just give me a bed!" Grace declared as she entered the room behind Aisha, laughing in disbelief at her surroundings.

"Grace!" the group exclaimed once more at her arrival. With her entrance, the circle of friends was complete.

"This is stunning," she exclaimed. "So, where are you guys staying?" Grace beamed, her high cheekbones aglow like polished apples. She set down her matching Louis Vuitton bags and swept her long emerald green braids over her left shoulder. She removed one of the many layers of material draped around her waist and shoulders. As the group's most cherished caregiver—even in her mid-thirties, she projected a wisdom beyond her years—she added, "I have to make sure you're all taken care of," while shaking her head and running her hand over the plush bedspread.

"Hello ladies," Liam introduced himself. "My wife is a big fan."

"She was so sweet," Grace confirmed. "She was waiting for us in the lobby."

"The Sexy Seven are all here," Liam clapped.

"Oh, you've been reading those newspapers again," Grace observed.

"The Miami press gave us that nickname," Debra scoffed. "It's so silly." Then, turning on her heel, she opened the sleek doors to the private balcony, already planning to relax while enjoying the breathtaking view of the city.

"From blazing sunrises to glittering city lights, this view transforms throughout the day and never ceases to enchant," Liam confirmed in a rhythmic brogue.

"This is an exquisite accommodation, Liam," Drew said as he shook his hand.

"The Belltones rarely use this place, but they are delighted you can," he admitted. "Well, I'll let you settle in." The group turned to face him, waving a cheerful goodbye.

Liam pivoted swiftly. "Mrs. Belltone asked me to confirm your arrival and inform you that Bayya is delivering the keys to Phillip's apartment in the West Village. She prefers not to go. Meet Bayya at Phillip's apartment at 1 pm sharp." He waved once more. "Someone will text you the address." Dropping seven sets of keys on the marble foyer table, he vanished behind the closing elevator doors.

Drew tapped Francy on the shoulder and motioned her to follow him into the living room.

They sat on the spacious sofa as Drew retrieved the envelope from his bag—the same one he, Francy, and Israel had picked up from Richard Belltone's office at 2 Columbus Circle.

"I was wondering when you'd open that," Francy remarked as she sat beside Drew.

Drew carefully unglued the envelope's seam, then opened it to reveal a photograph of a doll. For a moment, he and Francy exchanged puzzled glances.

The French doll in the photo appeared exquisitely crafted, evoking old-world charm and mystery.

"It's almost lifelike standing upright like that," Francy observed.

"Porcelain?" Drew asked aloud.

The doll's delicate expression was accentuated by painted blue eyes that held an unsettling intensity, as if hiding a secret. Her cheeks carried a soft blush.

"I've never seen a doll like that," Francy remarked, pointing to its muted red lips adorned with three X marks.

Drew quickly flipped the photograph to check for any writing, signature, or explanation on the back.

"What about the envelope?" Francy asked, a chill running down her spine.

"Nothing," Drew confirmed.

"The dress resembles a vintage French gown—perhaps from the late 19th or early 20th century," Drew observed. "Look at the detail; the gown is crafted from lace, silk, and velvet."

"They are beautiful shades of cream and lavender. The ribbons and tiny floral patterns on the material appear hand-stitched," Francy added.

"It exudes grace, yet something about the doll's cold, unfeeling demeanor unsettles me." Drew slid the photograph back into the envelope. "All in due time. We'll need to follow up with Richard Belltone."

"Should we gather everyone?" Francy asked, looking up at Drew.

"Everyone, gather around. We need to discuss a plan." Drew was now fully invested in the case they were about to tackle.

Israel, Grace, Aisha, Elena, and Debra meandered into the spacious living room and spread out over the sofas and chairs.

"What are you thinking, amigo?" Israel smiled as he munched on a bag of potato chips he'd found in the kitchen.

Drew cleared his throat. "Several of us knew Phillip." He nodded toward Francy, Debra, and Elena. "You worked on the stage with him, shared private moments, and confided in him."

"Some of us didn't know him," Grace admitted, raising her hand sheepishly. "But that doesn't make his story any less important," she added with a smile as her empathy shone through.

"Your selfless acts of bravery go beyond mere self-preservation," Drew said with a smile. "That's not typical behavior."

"We were born for this kind of work. I found my second calling because of you and the events in Miami," Aisha gushed, referring to their first case that thrust them into the spotlight to clear their names.

"I have a feeling we're headed for a darker, more dangerous path." Drew scanned the faces of his loyal friends, his pride and their devotion making him even more protective.

"We appreciate you looking out for us," Israel said, licking his fingers. His expression turned serious. "I can't speak for everyone, but you gave me the strength to face my fears instead of run from them. Now I stand firmly committed to justice."

Everyone nodded.

"It's the firefighter who rushes into a burning building to rescue a stranger," Drew explained, "or the bystander who pulls someone from the path of a speeding car…"

"Been there, done that!" Debra added.

"I want you to know that every one of you has an extraordinary capacity for self-sacrifice, and I'm so proud of you."

"Ah, shucks," Elena said with a smile that broke the tension. "We're a great team, thanks to you!"

"I want to ensure that we're all on board to proceed with this case. Of course, if anyone wants to step aside, we will understand," Drew said as he shook his head, making eye contact with each friend.

A round of applause confirmed their unity as a team.

"Alright, everyone, here's the plan," Drew began, crouching among the scattered group. "Francy, Debra, and I will meet Belltone's maid, Bayya, at Phillip's apartment. Aisha and Israel, you're assigned to search Richard Belltone's office. Phillip's second autopsy report was stolen—the physical copy is missing and the digital file was deleted from the office computer. I need to know who did it and how."

The pair exchanged determined glances, their nods sharp. Israel crumpled his empty chip bag and tossed it into the trash. "Let's roll, girl."

"Elena, Grace," Drew continued gravely, "the coroner from the city morgue hired by Richard, Dr. Foster—died suddenly, just like Phillip. He supposedly suffered a heart attack. I need you to investigate everything you can about his convenient demise."

Elena gave Grace a sharp smile. "You're with me, doll."

Grace glanced down at her Celadon-green jumpsuit paired with perky heels. "Looks like I'll have to change for this one," she said with a smile.

At that moment, the elevator sprang to life, its doors abruptly opening. A disheveled Liam stumbled out, gasping for air. Sweat beaded on his forehead, and his eyes were wide with fear as he staggered into the suite, his face etched with terror.

He couldn't speak. He managed to reach the foyer before his legs buckled, and he collapsed with a groan. That's when they noticed the knife hilt protruding from his back, his jacket blooming red around the blade.

# Chapter 3
## Murray Hill

A chilling scream tore through the air as Debra and Grace's terror echoed off the penthouse walls.

With his heart pounding, Drew dashed to Liam's side, his fingers trembling as he dialed 911. "Operator, we need help now! We're at 301 Park Avenue, the Waldorf Astoria Towers, penthouse B. A man's been stabbed in the back!" he shouted into the phone.

"Is the knife still lodged in his back? Can you tell me exactly where it is?" the operator asked calmly amid the chaos.

Drew's eyes fixed on the motionless body of the building manager sprawled on the cold parquet floor. "Yes, the knife... it's still in him. It's on his right side, just below the scapula, close to the spine." His words made his stomach churn as he knelt beside Liam, checking for a pulse.

Debra's voice was barely audible as she whispered, "Aisha, is he... is he going to die?"

Aisha did not answer. In a swift motion, she rushed to the bathroom and returned with a towel, tossing it to Francy, who handed it to Drew. His hands shook as he pressed the towel against Liam's wound. "He has a pulse, but it's very weak," he told the operator.

"If you have a towel, apply pressure around the knife and hold it steady until the EMTs arrive," the operator instructed.

Drew glanced at Aisha, who stood frozen by his side. "You already knew that," he said with a subtle edge.

At that moment, the elevator doors jerked closed and began descending. Israel reacted on instinct, sprinting to catch the doors. "What if the killer's coming for us?" he called, panic in his voice.

"It's probably the ambulance!" Drew shouted back, though doubt crept into his tone.

Elena's voice was laced with skepticism. "That was fast, wasn't it?"

The elevator doors slammed shut, plunging back toward the lobby at a terrifying speed.

"He's bleeding," Drew barked into the phone, panic rising. "There's blood soaking through his coat."

"Just keep pressure on the wound," Francy urged, echoing the operator.

Grace stood still, her eyes fixed on Liam's unmoving body. Debra moved to her side and wrapped an arm around her. At her touch, Grace snapped out of her trance. "It's happening again," she whispered, her voice trembling.

Debra pulled her closer. "He'll be all right," she whispered, striving for conviction. The memory of their first case—the last time they'd been powerless to stop a tragedy—hung heavily in the room.

"It's coming back up!" Israel warned, his voice tight with tension.

Elena and Israel took positions on either side of the elevator, prepared for what might come. Elena gripped the heavy fireplace poker and assumed a wide stance by the doors. "You ready for this?"

Israel flashed a grim smile, his skateboard held back like a baseball bat. "Born ready."

The elevator arrived. The sound of its arrival drew every eye to what was set to be the next explosive moment.

The elevator doors slid open with a jolt, depositing two EMTs into the penthouse with coordinated precision. Leading them was a whirlwind of a woman whose bright Irish brogue cut through the tension.

"Darling, is he breathing?" she demanded, her eyes locking on Drew.

Startled by her intensity, Drew could only nod. Undeterred, she dropped to her knees beside him, her plaid skirt swirling around her as she worked. A faded blue and white apron, dusted with flour, contrasted sharply with the chaos. Grey curls framed her round, flushed face.

34

"Pardon me parts, dear," she said with a wry smile, referring to her outfit, "I never thought my meek old husband would find himself mixed up in something like this today."

"Is the assailant still in the apartment?" one EMT barked as he scanned the room.

"No," Francy replied steadily.

"He was stabbed in the lobby," Liam's wife explained, her grip tightening on his hand. "I overheard two men asking him where the detectives were living. Our apartment is just off the lobby."

"Why didn't he come to you for help?" Drew asked, trying to piece together the events.

"I'm sure he meant to warn you, the daft eejit," she murmured, shaking her head. "My crazy old man."

"We've got it from here, sir," an EMT interrupted, gently prying Drew's hands away from Liam's wound.

As one technician took Liam's vitals, the other got to work removing his jacket to expose the knife. Liam's wife watched with quiet intensity, her gaze shifting to the old scar on the opposite side of his back. "Not the first time he's been stabbed in the back, you see," she noted with a wry smile. "Bar brawl, back in Ireland."

Drew stared at her, stunned by her composure. "Did you see the attackers?"

She hesitated, her brow furrowing. "No, dear... but I heard them. Their accents were foreign. One had a deep, gravelly voice; the other, a high-pitched tone."

"Anything else?" Drew pressed, knowing time was of the essence.

"It all happened so fast...Well," she said as she rose, her eyes fixed on Liam, "it's in God's hands now."

With Drew's help, she watched as the EMTs loaded Liam onto the stretcher and whisked him away. "You can ride with us, ma'am," one offered.

Liam's wife turned to the stunned group, her gaze burning with determination. "Catch these monsters," she urged, her voice low and deadly. "I'm counting on you."

As the elevator swallowed her, the group exchanged shell-shocked glances.

"I wish I had her nerves of steel," Grace breathed, her face still pale.

"As much as I love this penthouse," Drew mused, his mind racing, "we need to split up and lay low in different parts of the city."

"Someone's always one step ahead," Francy agreed, collapsing onto the sofa.

"We need to disappear," Grace added firmly.

"Feels like we're being hunted," Aisha said, her eyes darting to the windows.

Drew nodded, urgency rising within him. "Time to fill the Belltones in. They need to know what's happened since we left their place yesterday."

Francy met his gaze with a silent nod. It was time to come clean—and hope they weren't sealing their own fate.

They were interrupted by the sound of the elevator opening into the suite once again.

"Is there no security in this place?" Aisha blurted out!

"The security guard is on a stretcher downstairs. I'm Detective Jameson." He flashed his badge as he walked slowly into the apartment, surveying the scene. "The security guard and doorman were assaulted along with Mr. Liam."

Detective Jameson had a weathered face etched with the stress of years spent solving crimes on Manhattan's streets. His deep-set eyes revealed keen intelligence. A strong jawline—dusted with a day's stubble—framed his face, and his salt-and-pepper hair was slightly unkempt. He slowly surveyed the seven friends trying to make sense of the situation and locked eyes with Grace.

In a moment, her fear gave way to intrigue. Something about this man captivated Grace.

"Alright everyone, listen up: I'll be investigating the attempted stabbing of Mr. Liam. I know you're all shaken, but I need to ask some questions. Let's start with you, miss...?" He fixed his gaze on Grace.

"It's Grace. I'm a Taurus," she murmured, uncertain why she mentioned it.

All heads turned in disbelief at her answer.

Detective Jameson offered a half-smile as he noticed her charm. "Grace, how are you? Can you describe what happened?"

"Well, it was chaotic. The elevator doors opened, and poor Mr. Liam staggered out. We turned, and before we knew it, we saw the knife in his back." Grace gave a clear and concise account.

"So, no one saw the attacker because he was stabbed in the lobby—is that what you're saying? Was he able to warn you or give any indication of who attacked him?"

Aisha stepped forward, matching the detective's stance. "No, but his wife heard two men. They had foreign accents—one high-pitched, the other low."

"So, let me ask you, why do you think they stabbed Liam?" Detective Jameson moved closer to the group, making eye contact with each one.

"Those guys were looking for us," Drew explained. "Liam tried to protect us."

"You have blood on your hands," Detective Jameson said as he turned to look at Drew.

"What?" Drew snapped, misunderstanding the comment—until he noticed Liam's blood on his hands and shirt.

"If they were looking for you, why didn't they follow Liam into the elevator?" Detective Jameson was determined to piece together the situation.

"Because Liam's wife frightened them," Francy assumed. "Her husband didn't reveal our location, so they stabbed him."

"His attackers had no idea he was planning to warn us," said Drew, equally perplexed.

"I'm sorry, what is your name?" Detective Jameson asked.

"Drew. And this is Francy, Aisha, Grace, Elena, Israel, and Debra."

"Yeah, I know who you all are," Detective Jameson said matter-of-factly. "You see, Mr. Belltone informed me of your reasons for visiting New York. I called him to relay the message about the attack on his employees, and I spoke with Detective Vincent in Miami."

"Our old friend!" Israel blurted.

"And mine," Detective Jameson said as he circled the room, taking in the opulent surroundings. "You are living large, aren't you?" He slowly turned to the fireplace, playing with the fire poker. His imposing build lent him a formidable air that reinforced his authority. "I need to be very clear," he paused. "I don't need nosy, wannabe detectives sticking their noses where they don't belong. Understand?"

The group exchanged glances. Aisha, who was about to retort, was quickly silenced by a glance from Drew, who shook his head slightly, preventing her from snapping at Jameson.

"Furthermore, if you get any intel from your inner circle, I want you to run it by me first. Capiche?"

Drew squared off with Detective Jameson. "We hear you—loud and clear. We're not here to obstruct your work. But there are some facts you need to be informed about…" His voice trailed off as he gained support from his friends.

"Oh yeah? What is it?" Detective Jameson raised his head and faced Drew squarely, adopting a challenging stance.

"We heard many good things about you from Detective Vincent and Mr. Belltone," Drew said, though he was lying. "They both said you would be very helpful and that we could count on you."

The answer caught Detective Jameson off guard. He stepped back, tilting his head as he regarded each witness. "That's true," he conceded while rubbing his stubbled chin.

Grace stepped forward. He offered a half-smile as he watched her, waiting for her input.

Enchanted by the intriguing man, Grace fumbled her words. "Will the doorman and security guard be alright?" she murmured.

A faint smile crossed his lips. "The doorman has a concussion, and the security guard took down the attacker who had the knife. You know what I'm saying? He mentioned that the other guy must have struck him over the head with something, knocking him out!" Detective Jameson gestured with both hands. "They'll be alright. Don't worry about it."

Grace could only nod in response.

"Did you work on Philip's case?" Drew asked.

"I did. I know Mr. Belltone's story, but we never found any evidence to support his claims."

"But don't the circumstances seem suspicious?" Drew pressed.

"Yeah, but I can only rely on the facts. The facts are, I don't have any definitive proof that Philip was poisoned, nor do I have evidence that the second coroner—who also died of a heart attack—was poisoned. Frankly, none of this appeared to be foul play at the time." Detective Jameson ran his hand through his hair again. "It just seemed like a chain of events."

Jameson's phone started to ring. "Yeah?" he paused. "It's your boss," he told Drew as he handed over the phone.

"Hello, Richard," Drew replied promptly.

The group watched as Drew listened to Mr. Belltone's lengthy apology.

"Thank you, sir. We're all okay. We appreciate your call." Drew hung up and returned the phone to Detective Jameson.

"So, what's your next move?" Francy asked.

He pursed his lips in thought, furrowed his brows, and turned on his heels. "I'm heading to Bellevue Hospital to get a better description of the two men from the doorman and security guard—and to check on Mr. Liam," he declared with determination. "By the way, you all shouldn't stay here. Your location has been compromised. I suggest finding a different place." He then turned, winked at Grace, and disappeared behind the elevator doors.

★★★

It was exactly one o'clock. Francy, Drew, and Debra stood in front of Phillip's apartment building at the corner of Jane and Hudson Street. The long green canopy at the entrance shielded them from the hot midday sun as they waited for the arrival of Belltone's maid.

"I've always loved this West Village neighborhood," Debra said, admiring the tree-lined sidewalks and cobblestone streets. "So quaint."

"Mr. Drew?" Bayya appeared behind them, greeting them with a warm smile.

"Bayya, thank you for doing this," Drew replied, grasping her hand. He noticed the blue sapphire ring catching the sunlight—the silver band clinging tightly to her finger. "Beautiful stone, Bayya. Is that a sapphire?" he asked knowingly.

She glanced down at the ring and quickly retracted her hand. "Yes," she affirmed.

"Family heirloom?" Drew inquired.

She clasped her hands together and massaged her fingers slowly while silently nodding. "Mrs. Belltone could not bring herself here," Bayya added quickly. "It's still too painful."

"We understand," Debra interjected, noticing the sadness in Bayya's expression.

Bayya moved to the front door and unlocked it, allowing them to enter. The prewar brownstone walk-up was typical of West Village architecture. They stepped into a round central foyer with stone tile floors. Sunlight streaming through the door refracted off the stained glass Tiffany lamp suspended from the ceiling. They ascended the stairs to the third floor, where Phillip's apartment was one of only three. Bayya used one hand to unlock the top bolt and then released the door handle lock before slowly pushing the door open, as if expecting someone inside.

The tiny one-bedroom apartment was orderly and pristine. A long black leather sofa sat against an exposed red brick wall, opposite an immense, gold-leafed beveled mirror. A mauve rug separated the two, laying snugly on polished hardwood floors that ran the length of the apartment.

Drew, Debra, and Francy walked carefully through the space, admiring the museum-quality artwork displayed on the walls. The art was meticulously arranged above an angular metal desk.

"Oh my God," Debra gasped, pointing toward the paintings. "That's a La Croix!"

"It's a what?" Francy asked, moving closer to an obscure mural.

"They are three modern pieces by the French painter La Croix," Debra explained matter-of-factly, as if everyone should know.

Drew and Francy exchanged glances and then scrutinized the images, trying to decipher their meaning.

"But this painting, along with another from the La Croix collection, was reported stolen from the Prague Museum years ago," Debra recalled, racking her brain for details. "It's called 'Three Chromotones.'"

The trio stood staring at the artwork. One painting was divided into three sections, each displaying formless, bright splashes of color arranged in a random sequence. Bayya approached them from behind.

"I never understood modern art," she said while shaking her head, then turned and walked into the small kitchen behind them. She opened the refrigerator door slowly, as if expecting something inside, murmured a soft "huh," and closed it.

Drew turned back to the paintings. "If this painting was stolen from a museum years ago, what is it doing here?" His eyes widened as he nudged Francy. "Look at the bottom right-hand corner of the center picture."

"An LX in a circle. Is that a signature?" Francy paused and bent closer. "I feel like I've seen that symbol before."

"The last page of the autopsy report," Drew softly reminded her.

"What? What are you two whispering about?" Debra asked, not wanting to be left out.

Drew leaned in to whisper in her ear.

After scanning all three paintings, Debra said, "I see nothing."

"Focus on the center painting—the bottom right," Drew directed.

"That little LX in a circle?" she queried. "Yes, that's La Croix's signature. I believe the X represents a cross."

Drew again whispered about the same symbol mentioned in the autopsy report.

Debra then peeked into the kitchen to ensure Bayya was still there, out of earshot.

Drew noticed a closed door to their right near the bathroom. He turned to Bayya. "May we see inside?"

With an approving nod and a wave of her hand, Bayya allowed them to enter. She approached the countertop and ran her fingers slowly across its surface, as if checking for dust. "Huh."

Drew turned the knob on the door as it creaked open. "The room is impeccable. A place for everything and everything in its place," he whispered to himself. He observed the immaculate room, evidence of its owner's obsessive tendencies. "Except for that," he noted, pointing to a stack of books in the far corner.

"This feels intrusive," Debra confessed as she slowly looked around the room. "I sense we are invading his privacy."

"I feel the same way, Debra," Francy agreed. "This is uncomfortable."

"I understand," Drew attempted to comfort them. "But if Phillip was indeed murdered," he gulped, imagining the worst, "he would be glad we are here to bring justice for him."

Francy circled the small bedroom, impressed by its neat organization. She peered out of the window opposite the door. "Great view," she commented.

Debra looked out through the cage-like gate, which appeared half-open from the outside. "Yes, a brick wall. Typical New York," she huffed.

Drew paused and glanced at the window. His eyes drifted down to the sill where he noticed a slight brown smudge along the lip of the frame. "Tell me, if you had OCD, would you allow that gate to be open?"

The girls exchanged a glance.

"Maybe it's stuck?" Debra suggested.

Drew's eyes traveled from the light brown smudge along the sill to the floor beneath it. The dark stained hardwood displayed a light coat of dust over its polished surface.

"Francy, can you see if the window opens? Try not to disturb the smudge."

She cautiously approached the window, keeping an eye on the smudge Drew mentioned. As she shifted her position, she noticed the faint mark across the window threshold.

"Francy, which way does the mark seem to have been made?" Drew asked.

She studied the soft mark. "Left to right?" she replied hesitantly. "So, he's right-handed," she concluded.

"Why?" Debra chimed in. "Who's right-handed?"

"Because the broader part is on the right," Francy explained.

Drew turned from the window and stared at the floor. His eyes darted from a closed closet door along one path to a tall bureau on the far side of the bed along another.

"What is it, Drew? What do you see?" Debra asked with anticipation.

Drew remained silent. He knelt and aligned his cheek with the hardwood floor. Slowly, he twisted his head, closing one eye to focus on one direction and then the other.

"Will this help?" Francy suggested as she switched on the bright flashlight on her cellphone and handed it to Drew.

"Spectacular," he said, shining the light along the path from the closet to the bureau. "Phillip preferred to walk barefoot at home to avoid bringing in germs and bacteria from his shoes," Drew recalled. "There are two sets of prints here. One clearly shows a pattern from bare feet, while the other lacks a pattern, indicating someone was wearing socks. The sock prints extend from the window to the closet, then from the closet to the bureau, and back toward the window.

"So, someone entered through the window, removed their shoes, and began searching around," Francy observed.

"Correct," Drew replied. "If you look outside the window, there might be traces of shoe prints or signs of the dirt left on the sill."

Debra looked at them, impressed by the observations. "Francy, who are you?" she marveled.

"What?" Francy replied, shrugging. "He influences you," she said, gesturing toward Drew, who was already crouching under the bed.

"Spotless," he murmured, inspecting the bed made with crisp sheets, neatly tied hospital corners, and four perfectly aligned pillows.

Debra walked to the closet and carefully opened the door. The closet was tidy, with clothes organized by color and properly folded or hung—from short sleeves to long sleeves and then pants. Not a single item was on the floor. "Even his shoes have their designated places," Debra observed.

Francy, curious about the security gate outside the window, stepped onto the lip of the glass pane. The window slid upward easily, and she noticed that the gate was half open. She moved through it and onto the wrought iron fire escape before peering over to the street three stories below. As she turned, four star-like symbols imprinted on the metal flooring caught her eye. The same pattern appeared on three slats facing the window. She scanned the remainder of the fire escape as she made her way to the stairs leading down to the street and descended the steep steps, following the recurring star-like symbols every few rungs.

"Where is that girl going?" Debra asked as she watched Francy leave via the fire escape.

"She's like a bloodhound," Drew replied with a smile.

"Thanks to you," Debra said, straightening up from her crouched position at the window. "We've discovered our second calling, it seems."

"Apparently," Drew echoed, though his attention had shifted to the misshaped pile of books in the corner. "Debra, if you were as neurotic as Phillip, would you leave a pile of books in such disorder?"

Debra turned to inspect the books, which were twisted in every direction. "The spines aren't aligned; the fronts and backs face different ways. Something isn't right."

"Maybe this is what the intruder was after," Drew whispered as he pulled the third book from the pile.

"The Book of Sacred Signs and Symbols," Debra read aloud from the cover. "Why?"

"You were right, Drew," Francy interjected, poking her head through the window. "I followed a shoe print from the bottom of the fire escape all the way to Phillip's window and snapped pictures with my phone."

"Francy, now look at the smudge mark in front of you," Drew suggested.

Francy examined a light brown brush mark from her position at the window, now facing the interior of the apartment. "Oh," she murmured as if a sudden idea had struck her. "He's left-handed, not right-handed. He saw the mud outside, turned, and tried to brush it away before fleeing."

"Or she," Drew added. "Great observation."

"He, she, right, left?" Debra shook her head in confusion. "Who?"

"Whoever snuck up the fire escape, entered through the window, removed their shoes, and started searching for something in Phillip's apartment," Drew speculated.

"Hey," Francy exclaimed. "There are two distinct fingerprints here!"

Drew slowly rose and scanned the room. "Debra, do you have brown or black eyeshadow in your purse?"

"Is my makeup smudged?" she asked.

Francy chuckled.

"How about a makeup brush?"

"Well, you can't have one without the other," Debra replied.

Remembering the metal desk in the living room, Drew opened the glass drawer and retrieved what he needed. He walked over to Francy and handed her a white piece of paper and some clear tape. "Debra, can Francy borrow your eyeshadow and brush?"

Perplexed, Debra questioned, "Francy, since when do you wear eyeshadow?"

Francy smiled, though her focus remained on the task. "Okay," she began, "I'll sprinkle a small amount of eyeshadow onto the surface. Then, using the brush, I'll lightly sweep away the excess powder, making sure the print stays visible."

"That's it," Drew confirmed.

"I press the tape over the fingerprint gently, and now… I peel it off," Francy said, pausing before pulling.

"You got it," Drew encouraged. "Great job. Now, stick the tape onto the paper and repeat."

Debra, slightly embarrassed, mused, "I must have missed that class."

"There wasn't enough of a print to determine the shoe size, but there was definitely a star pattern," Francy observed as she examined the image on her phone. She quickly snapped additional photos of the smudge marks and the bedroom. "What did you find?"

Drew held up the book. "Do you recognize this?"

Francy tilted her head as if trying to remember.

"It was in the photo of Phillip and me that Mrs. Belltone showed us. He was holding this book and always seemed drawn to its contents."

"Oh yes," Francy recalled. "The signifier resembles the signified."

"Yes, that's it," Drew said, his eyes lighting up as if he'd made a breakthrough.

Debra's head swirled. "What are you guys saying?" A playful expression crossed her face as if she were being teased.

"That's the phrase Phillip always used: 'The signifier resembles the signified.'" Francy beamed with delight at recalling the information. "It means the signifier represents physical or material content…"

"And the signified represents the overall concept or idea," Drew finished.

Debra contemplated the phrase. "You mean, like a stop sign?"

"Exactly!" Drew replied enthusiastically. "The sign itself is the signifier. So when you see one, you immediately understand its meaning."

Debra grinned proudly, raising an eyebrow.

"Phillip always said that!" Francy added, smiling from ear to ear. "Especially when he had this book in his hands. He was fascinated by signs, symbols, and riddles…"

Drew carefully opened the creased book and thumbed through its pages. Dog-eared and crowded with notes on nearly every page, he quickly tried to decipher some symbols.

"What's that?" Debra asked as a triangular piece of paper floated to the floor.

Drew bent down and picked it up. "It looks like the corner of an old black-and-white photograph that has been torn off," he said.

"Can you see any image?" Francy inquired as she stepped from the windowsill to get a closer look.

"I just see the sky and what might be tree branches," Drew replied, pointing to the long lines in the fragment. He turned it over. "Da," he read aloud.

"A name?" Debra suggested. "Danny, Daphne, Darrin?"

"Or perhaps a location?" Francy offered. "Dallas, Daytona, Dakar?"

Drew shook his head. "There's not much to go on." He slowly thumbed through the book. "These back pages are bookmarked. Look at this," Drew said as he pointed to the handwritten messages near the end.

Signifier:

In ancient times, a ruler, wise
Used letters as secrets, hidden from eyes.
A number was chosen, neither too high nor low,
A shift in positions, a code to bestow.
Three steps forward, the answer is near,
But only a leader can truly appear.
What's the key, a clue you must see,
To unlock the message that's been set free?

Signified:

PB
JUDQGIDWKHUV
RWKHU
VRQ

"Now what is this? It looks like something Phillip wrote in this book." Debra and Francy gathered to examine the odd limerick.

"Look, he noted the signifier and its signified. Was Phillip leaving clues?"

"It appears he was trying to conceal information. But how could anyone decipher the code without a key?" Debra observed.

Drew flipped to the next page. "Here's another riddle!"

Signifier:

Behind the curtains, secrets hide,
Where actors wait and plot their stride.
A guardian stands, its mouth held tight,
Unveiling magic, out of sight.
Turn the knob a click will sound,
A box of mysteries to be found.
What place am I, where stories begin,
With hidden spaces and tales within?

Signified:

JV
YXZHPQXDB
TXOAOLYB

Drew repeated the rhyme outload. "Behind the curtains, secrets hide, where actors wait and plot their stride. - What is that? A stage?"

"A rehearsal room?" Debra asked.

"He's written several pages of concepts, riddles, and symbols in the back of this book!" Drew said as he flipped through the final pages to reveal a trove of handwritten notes. "These are all in Phillip's handwriting."

"That appears to be a broken chain, a key in a lock, an eye symbol?" Debra traced her finger over the inked images.

"The scale of justice, a snake…" Drew continued.

"An hourglass! Francy, you have to see this," Debra said, her eyes wide with surprise.

A sudden crash came from the kitchen. The three exchanged glances. Francy, closest to the door, sprinted into the living room. "Bayya!" she yelled.

The Belltone's maid lay unconscious on the kitchen floor, sprawled and curled in a fetal position. Francy quickly bent down and checked for a pulse.

"Oh my God! Twice in one day? Is she breathing?" Debra cried.

Francy held her hand to Bayya's nostrils as she observed her chest slowly rising and falling. "Yes, her breathing is labored, but she's alive."

"Debra, grab that pillow off the sofa," Drew called.

"Drew, help me turn her over." Francy grabbed Bayya's ankles and slowly rolled her, while Drew slid his hands under her shoulders. At the same time, Debra placed the pillow under her head. The trio stood silently, watching the fragile form of the woman before them.

"Did she faint?" Debra inquired.

Francy and Drew said nothing. In an instant, Bayya slowly opened her eyes, realizing she was lying on the floor. Her body jerked as she recognized her vulnerable position.

"Stay still, Bayya. You just fainted, but you're okay. We're here for you," Drew reassured her, more concerned that she might have broken a bone or her hip.

Carefully moving around Bayya's form on the kitchen tiles, Debra reached for a glass of water. She stretched precariously, her fingertips barely brushing a glass in the upper cupboard.

She then decided on another approach and found the light switch on the bathroom wall. Turning on the light, her eyes quickly surveyed the room. A glass sat on the sink, so she filled it with water. As she did, she noticed a clump of dark hair on the floor beneath the sink. "That's odd," she thought, turning off the tap swiftly before bringing the filled glass into the kitchen. She offered it to Bayya while Francy and Drew helped her sit up.

"Nothing appears to be broken," Drew said reassuringly.

"I'm so embarrassed," Bayya confessed, her voice tinged with a Jamaican accent.

"Did you eat today, Bayya? Do you have low blood pressure?" Drew suggested.

"I had a roll and coffee this morning for breakfast," she replied between sips. "My doctor says my blood pressure tends to run low."

"Has this happened before?" Drew asked.

"This is the second time," she admitted, lowering her head.

The trio gently helped Bayya to stand. "You can lean on me," Debra offered.

Drew bent down and picked up the book of symbols. On the back page was a hand-drawn LX inside a circle.

"Debra, could you help me with this?" Drew said, handing her the book so she could see the symbol clearly.

Debra's eyes widened as she looked at Drew in confusion.

"What is it, Debra?" Francy asked, as she helped Bayya settle on the sofa.

Debra walked over to Francy and pointed to the LX in the circle sketched on the back of Phillip's book.

Francy reacted silently, anxious that she might reveal information that could compromise them in front of Bayya. "Come on, Bayya, let's get you downstairs. I'm taking you home," she reassured the maid. "Go ahead, I've got this," she added to the others.

Drew concealed the book in his bag and assisted Francy in guiding Bayya out of the apartment. Debra hesitated. "Hold on," she said as she returned inside. Hurrying to the bathroom, she used a tissue to collect the stray hair from the floor and slipped it into her bag.

After securing the door, the trio helped Bayya down the stairs to the apartment lobby.

"Where are we going?" Debra asked eagerly.

"To the one place that might have information about the La Croix painting on Phillip's wall," he said while hailing a cab. "We're going to The Whitney!

# Chapter 4
## West Village

The West Village, rooted in New York City's counterculture history, exuded a distinctive energy on a sweltering summer afternoon. Nestled along the Hudson River, the neighborhood stretched toward the waterfront piers, standing in stark contrast to Greenwich Village, bisected by 7th Avenue. Here, the streets deviated from the city's grid system, meandering and curving with names that recalled stories of the past rather than simply designating locations.

As the day waned, the West Village came alive with a vibrant blend of old and new. Historic brownstones—once homes to artists and activists—stood alongside trendy boutiques and upscale eateries. The sidewalks pulsed with an eclectic mix of longtime residents, young professionals, and tourists drawn to the neighborhood's unique charm. The air was heavy with the aromas of savory roasting nuts and street food, mixing with the exhaust of idling taxis.

A cab stopped in front of the Highline's steps. "We have to take a stroll down that beautiful, elevated park sometime soon. It's been too long," Debra said, looking up at the tiered gardens built on the tracks of the old elevated El train.

The elevated High Line, a former railbed turned park, throbbed with activity in the late afternoon. Locals and visitors alike sought refuge from the summer heat in its shade, taking in a unique view of both the Hudson River and the surrounding cityscape. The park's design—blending native plants with modern elements—added a touch of greenery amid the concrete jungle. Yet even in this calm setting, the city's hum persisted—a constant reminder of the West Village's role in the broader urban sprawl.

"Let's see if we can learn more about the artist with whom Phillip was so infatuated," Drew remarked as he pulled open the glass door to the Whitney, catching a glimpse of the Hudson River beyond.

The Whitney Museum of Modern Art, located in the heart of Manhattan's West Village, was a treasure trove of American art and culture. Stepping through the doors, they were immediately embraced by a sense of artistic energy and creativity. The stark white interior was both intimate and inspiring, with natural light streaming through large windows and highlighting the works on display.

"I don't think the information booth would have any in-depth knowledge of La Croix. Let's stroll through the museum and see if we can find an expert to speak with," Debra suggested, readjusting her pink and yellow scarf around her neck.

The museum's collection spanned centuries of American art—from the 18th century to the present. They wandered through the galleries, greeted by a striking array of paintings, sculptures, photographs, and installations.

"Look, there's someone who might be able to help," Debra said as she pointed to a security guard on patrol. She approached the young man in a burgundy blazer and black pants, accented by his shiny work boots and a holstered club.

"Good day… Isandro?" Debra smiled as she read his name tag. "Oh, hola—eres Argentino?"

The security guard looked slightly surprised. "Sí, ¿en qué puedo ayudar?"

Suddenly, Debra became flustered, her cheeks turning a bright pink. She lost her train of thought but quickly recovered, switching back to English. "I hope you can help. Can you tell me whom I should speak to about some of the curated artwork here? I have specific questions and need a professional. We are here on behalf of Mr. Richard Belltone, one of the museum's largest donors," she asserted.

The man paused for a moment. "Ahh, yes…" his deep voice echoed among the vivid paintings. "You should speak to Marcus Larson. He works in the offices on the top floor and is the museum's Chief Art Curator."

Debra shot a look at Drew and beckoned him closer.

"¿Están juntos?" he asked, gesturing toward Drew.

"Yes, we are together. I mean, we're not… well, together," she stammered as her face turned from pink to red. "Can you help us?" Debra asked, hopeful yet unsure.

"Follow me. I'll take you to the offices," the security guard said, motioning toward a large elevator across the room. Debra and Drew followed.

"Isandro is also from Argentina," Debra informed Drew with a wide smile. "He's going to help us."

The extra-large, steel-encased elevator, seemingly built to accommodate huge works of art, ascended slowly to the museum's top floor. The two hopefuls trailed the security guard, who hurried toward his destination.

"What's wrong with you?" Drew nudged Debra.

"He's so cute," Debra whispered.

As the security guard opened the door to the office suites, a man greeted them at the entrance.

"Oh, Mr. Larson," the guard said, somewhat surprised. "I have two very important art dealers here, sent by one of our largest donors, Mr. Belltone."

"Gracias, Isandro," Debra said with a coy smile.

"Ah, good day," he said, peering over his wire-rimmed glasses at the two who had paused him from his task. "Marcus Larson," he introduced himself, extending his hand. "Did we have an appointment?"

Drew observed a slim, well-dressed man in his mid-70s, standing at an imposing 6'4". His distinguished gray hair added to his aura of wisdom and experience.

Drew quickly introduced them. "I'm sorry, we don't have an appointment. We were just in the neighborhood and thought we'd find you here today," he explained.

"Mr. Belltone sent you?" Marcus inquired.

"Yes," Debra replied confidently. "We had some questions about La Croix and his artwork."

Marcus looked down, as if consulting his mental notes for the right words. "Like other famous street artists such as Banksy, Lady Pink, and Keith Haring, La Croix remains an enigma," he remarked, shifting his stance as he searched for the right phrase.

"Are they featured in the museum's art collection?" Drew asked.

"Usually not," Marcus answered with a half-smile before clarifying, "While they are recognized artists, we generally treat their work as 'special exhibitions.'" He mimed air-quotes with both hands.

"And La Croix?" Debra pressed.

"La Croix has an exhibition scheduled to open in a few weeks," Marcus said proudly, as if redeeming himself. "Like Banksy, he uses a pseudonym, and his true identity remains unconfirmed, sparking much speculation. His art appears suddenly in the streets, and the public reacts with great excitement!" he exclaimed, throwing his hands up.

"So, no one knows his identity?" Debra asked skeptically. "How do you create an exhibition if his art just appears on the streets?"

Marcus smiled. "Private collectors," he confirmed. "They acquire most of these unique pieces and occasionally donate them for an exhibition, with the donors receiving most of the praise and recognition." Leaning closer, he whispered to Debra and Drew, "It's all about ego. Some works are even obtained illegally."

Drew glanced at Debra. "La Croix is from France?" he asked.

"Well, you would think so from his name. His work first appeared in Paris and the South of France, though now it can be seen in Japan, Mexico, Brazil, Australia— even in Los Angeles and here in New York."

"Do you have any images of his early works?" Debra quickly inquired.

"I can look that up. Please, follow me," Marcus said, turning as he walked back through his office suite doors.

Marcus led the pair to his glass-enclosed office, which overlooked the Hudson River. The low sun cast a warm glow over the space. He indicated their seats. "Spring water? Coffee?" he offered.

They declined and took seats in front of the curator's desk.

After a pause, Marcus looked out over the space. Reflecting on his knowledge, he began, "La Croix means 'the cross.' The artist first gained recognition about twelve years ago when his initial work appeared in Montmartre, on the wall beneath Sacré-Coeur in Paris." He turned his laptop so that Drew and Debra could view the image.

The photograph showed a curved, weathered wooden door painted on the wall beneath the cathedral. A red carpet led through the door, with French words inscribed: "Ton destin est entre tes mains."

"Your fate is in your hands," Debra whispered.

"Coming through an open door," Drew added.

Drew examined the photo closely, searching for a clue.

"What is that?" he asked as Marcus advanced to the next image.

"The government defaced the painting days later, washing it off the wall. This photo shows the piece after being marred by turpentine," Marcus explained, shaking his head. "Thankfully, local photographers captured the image before the cleanup. No one knew then how valuable the work would become. You can now buy postcards of the original image all over Montmartre."

Drew met Marcus's eyes. "Did you know a Phillip…" he began. "Wright? Phillip Wright?" he repeated.

Marcus paused. "No, but in what context should I know him?"

"Phillip was a collector of modern art," Debra clarified. "He lived nearby."

"I'm sorry, I'm not familiar with him," Marcus replied quickly.

"Do you know of any La Croix paintings that have gone missing?" Drew asked, watching Marcus's reaction.

Before Marcus could respond, he exclaimed, "Oh, of course!" A concerned look crossed his face. "The Three Chromotones," he repeated. "One of his paintings was stolen from Prague. I can't recall the name of the other, though."

"I've noticed the artist uses a distinct signature or autograph," Drew added.

Marcus turned back to stare at the computer screen, his eyes scanning the information before him. "Oh, yes," he answered matter-of-factly. "He always signs his work with an L and a cross."

Debra leaned toward Drew and whispered, "Are we trying to make the pattern fit the scenario?"

"Oh, but I thought it was an X in a circle," Drew corrected.

Marcus smirked. "Yes, I know that's what most people believe. It's actually an incomplete circle representing a scripted L, crossed with an X. But it isn't an X—it's the cross of St. Andrew." Marcus then turned his computer screen to show Debra and Drew a painting titled "Hidden Spaces."

"Ahhh," they chorused as they leaned in to examine the artist's signature. The white canvas featured seven black circles painted randomly across its surface, with the signature in the bottom right corner.

"Do you see?" Marcus asked. "Now look at the first image painted on the wall of Montmartre." He flipped back to the artwork on the wall.

"Sure enough," Drew agreed. The meaning behind the signature became more apparent. "Do you know why an X?"

"I can't really say, but many art critics have their opinions."

"Such as?" Debra interjected.

Marcus cleared his throat. "Many suggest that the artist's X can have different meanings depending on the context. Some say his name might be Andrew. St. Andrew was martyred; like the saint, many see La Croix's symbol as a sign of resistance, rebellion, or a call for change. Perhaps it functions as a brand identity or represents a target or point of focus."

Debra cast a sidelong glance at Drew.

"It's also been suggested that the artist himself may have intended his signature symbol to indicate something forbidden or rejected." Marcus took a long sip of ice water through a straw and wiped the sweat from his brow. "Maybe his art was dismissed by a teacher when he was a kid or he was mocked."

"So, becoming a provocateur who hides his identity gives him more clout, more intrigue?" Debra ventured.

The two men shook their heads in agreement.

"An astute observation, Miss Debra," Larson smiled.

"Has La Croix done other art besides paintings on objects?"

"Yes. That period of his work seemed designed to attract attention. Several years later, small dolls began appearing with X's across their lips."

Drew swallowed hard.

Then there were oil paintings on canvas that grew larger, free-standing installations, and finally his obelisk series.

"Obelisks?" Debra asked, unsure if she'd heard correctly.

"Yes," Marcus replied, scrolling through his images. "Here are a few of the dolls—quite distressing, I might add—and here are some of the free-standing installations. There's a bronze sculpture of a pregnant woman, a phone with octopus tentacles, and something that resembles a wall of Egyptian gods etched in gold leaf…" Drew observed the eclectic range of work.

"They were discovered in different locations around the world, each carrying its own statement depending on the setting. Quite brilliant," Marcus assured them.

"Do you know much about the dolls?" Drew asked, fishing for a clue as to why Mr. Belltone had given them a photo of one.

"It was during La Croix's Angry Period," Marcus stated matter-of-factly. "Clearly, it was early in his career when he was furious and had something to say."

"Were there many of these around?" Debra inquired, curious about Drew's interest.

"Many were stolen, and some were found broken… I know of one in a private collection."

"Who would that be?" Debra pressed.

Marcus straightened up from his position in front of the computer screen. "That's privileged information, I'm afraid." He took another long sip of water through his straw and changed the subject. "Was there anything else you needed?" A half-smile crossed his face.

"Well, we've taken up too much of your time."

"Oh, yes—thank you so much for your time, Mr. Larson," Debra said as she stood.

"Of course. Please give Mr. Belltone our regards. We always appreciate his patronage." Marcus opened the glass door to his office and gestured toward the exit.

"We'll see ourselves out," Drew confirmed. "Thank you."

Once they reached the elevator, they exhaled collectively.

"Hey, look," Drew noted, pointing to a grand marble staircase leading downstairs. "Come on, let's take the stairs."

They descended silently one floor before Drew mentioned the photo of the doll Mr. Belltone had given them.

"There was no explanation? He never said why he gave you a photo of one of these dolls?"

"That's going to be my first question next time I see him."

★★★

Francy helped Bayya exit the cab at East 60th Street and Park Avenue. The large brass doors swung open as the attentive doorman—still in his long emerald green coat, dark suit, and matching cap—rushed to the curb to assist. "Are you alright, ma'am?" he asked as Bayya looped her frail arm around his waist.

"Much better," she sighed, glancing up at Francy, who was now supporting Bayya opposite the doorman. "Thank you for accompanying us," she added, addressing the doorman, who then guided them to the elevator doors.

"Shall I take you up, ma'am?" he offered.

"No, no," Bayya quickly replied. "I have this fine girl to help me, thank you."

They ascended in silence.

"I was a dancer too, my dear," Bayya said, giving Francy another squeeze around the waist before regaining her balance. "I hate having to depend on anyone for these things. It's embarrassing."

Francy stepped aside and stood beside her, shaking her head. "I understand. I'm much the same," she replied.

"I was a ballet dancer. Dancing on pointe made me feel tall and alive."

Francy sensed that Bayya's thoughts drifted among images of taffeta tutus and pointe shoes. She noticed Bayya extend her arm in a graceful arc, her fingers executing a delicate gesture reminiscent of feathers.

"I was a prima ballerina in Jamaica," she said with a smile, meeting Francy's gaze. "Then I came to New York and was relegated to the corps de ballet."

Francy searched for the right words before simply shaking her head in dismay. "That couldn't have been easy for you," she managed.

"Well, once you're the star, it's harsh to be demoted back to the corps," she said, looking away. "Other opportunities came along."

Francy noticed Bayya glancing down at her sapphire ring and caressing it gently. "Was he special?"

"Oh, yes. Very much so," Bayya replied.

Suddenly, the front door of the Belltone residence swung open with a force that startled both women. "Bayya!" Jonathan Matthews called from the doorway. "Are you alright? What happened?" His face was etched with concern.

"Oh, my dear… I'm fine," Bayya replied as she pushed past him and entered the apartment.

"She fainted again," Jonathan said, directing a knowing look at Francy.

Francy nodded silently.

Jonathan firmly grasped the maid's shoulders and looked her straight in the eyes. "I told you, you have to eat. Carbs don't count." He shook his head.

"We discussed on the cab ride up about increasing her protein intake," Francy confirmed.

Jonathan waved her off as he exited the room. "Perhaps she'll listen to you."

Bayya quickly turned away and busied herself with work, then offered Francy a drink.

"Just some water, thank you, Bayya." Francy smiled as she was about to sit down when she heard a disturbance from the next room. She turned to listen.

"Why is there modern impressionism amidst this classical collection?"

"Apparently, Mr. Belltone is home," Bayya replied without looking up from peeling potatoes.

"Oh, great. I need to speak with him." Francy set her glass down on the counter and walked into the adjoining room. Bayya glanced up as she watched Francy pass by with determination.

"Francy," Richard Belltone greeted with a smile. "I'm sorry—I didn't realize you were here." He approached, taking her hand in both of his. "Perhaps you can share your thoughts on this art?"

Francy gave a polite, embarrassed smile. "Oh, I'm probably not the person to ask about art. I don't really know the difference between Picasso and a pickle." She settled into the chair between Mr. Belltone and Jonathan, trying to make herself less noticeable.

"Don't be silly," Mr. Belltone said, crossing the room while running a hand through his unruly hair to clear his forehead. "You don't need to be an art critic to know what you like."

Jonathan interjected as he released one of the hooks holding a framed impressionist piece, letting it swing precariously from the remaining fixture.

"Jonathan!" Mr. Belltone exclaimed in surprise.

"Sorry, it just slipped," he said, concealing the truth. "This belongs here," Jonathan asserted as he removed the modern art painting from the center, flanked by two classical masterpieces. "Besides, Mrs. Belltone loves it." He pursed his lips and glanced back at the artwork.

Francy slowly stood and gazed at the trio of paintings. "I really like the two on either side."

"You see," Richard quickly explained. "Classical art has endured for centuries, depicting ideals of beauty, realism, and storytelling." He gestured toward the hanging masterpieces.

"Modern art, though its peak lasted less than a century, represents significant artistic evolution in a changing world. And let's not forget, it was driven by the rebellious spirit of the era!" Jonathan declared passionately, while Richard Belltone listened intently.

Francy noticed a slow trail of sweat trickle down Jonathan's smooth brown skin. He radiated determination. "Your passion for modern art is admirable," she told him as she approached the impressionistic painting now lying on the floor. "This artist captured elements from both eras," she added with a warm smile that seemed to calm his charged emotions.

Mr. Belltone recognized Francy's maneuver as his expression shifted. "If you believe this is suitable here, let's proceed. And if Mrs. Belltone approves, that's an added bonus." Richard observed Jonathan relaxing his posture as he assisted in rehanging the painting.

"Voilà. My work here is finished," Jonathan declared. "Thank you both for your help. I'm late for a meeting." He adjusted his plaid vest over his oversized trousers and headed for the door. "Tell Mrs. Belltone I'll return at the end of the week to continue working on the art in her study." He grabbed a straw summer hat from the coat rack in the foyer and left.

"He can be a bit of a twister," Mr. Belltone remarked, apologizing on Jonathan's behalf.

"Artistic temperament. I understand," Francy said as she settled into a chair, her smile fading as she prepared to broach a delicate subject. Unsure how to proceed, she glanced at two large portraits hanging at the hallway entrance. "They are beautiful portraits," she remarked, diverting the conversation.

"My father, Damon Belltone, and my mother, Marie Belltone," Richard replied proudly.

"You look like your father," Francy complimented, then hesitated. "Are they…"

"They are both deceased," he confirmed.

"Well, I'm sorry," Francy said, at a loss for words.

"Thank you. My father was a prominent real estate developer, and my mother was a caregiver."

"Impressive," Francy nodded.

Though she had more to say, she chose to remain standing, finding herself more efficient on her feet. "Sir, I believe your trust has been breached," she began.

Silence fell over the room.

"Since our arrival, our safety has been compromised. Someone appears to have anticipated our every move," she asserted as beads of sweat formed on her brow.

She paused and sat. "Do you know how Liam is doing?"

"He will be alright, and so will my security guard, but the doorman sustained a concussion. The doctor expects a good prognosis."

"That's a relief," she admitted hesitantly. "But there is something else you need to know. The day we met you, after leaving your apartment, Drew and I were shot at."

Richard's expression changed.

Her voice trembling with urgency, Francy rose abruptly from her chair. "We were being followed—a black Mercedes trailed us all the way down Park Avenue, as if it knew every step we took. No matter how many turns we made, they remained on our trail like shadows."

Richard's gaze fixed on her, eyes wide with shock and disbelief. He leapt to his feet, his posture rigid. "A black Mercedes?" he questioned. "Did you catch a license plate? A description of the shooter? More importantly—were you hurt?" His body tensed, ready for action.

Francy's frustration was evident. Clenching her fists in anger, she said, "It happened too fast. We didn't have time to gather details. All I know is that there were two individuals—a driver and a shooter."

Richard's mind raced as he connected the dots. "Could these be the same two who attacked my staff at the Waldorf?" Without waiting for an answer, he grabbed his phone. "I'll have my security team review the hotel's footage. We'll find them."

Francy's face darkened. "We can't stay at the Waldorf. We've been compromised."

Richard ended the call, his thoughts racing. He sank back into his chair, his expression hardening as he considered the situation. "Alright. Here's what we'll do: Your group needs to split up. I'll arrange three safe houses among my properties in the city. Don't worry about a thing."

Francy nodded, relief flashing across her face. "Thank you," she said gratefully.

"Were you able to access Phillip's apartment?" Mr. Belltone's tone grew more serious.

"Yes, thank you. Bayya was very helpful," she replied.

"Did you find anything?" Mr. Belltone asked, leaning forward.

Francy hesitated, feeling her palms grow sweaty. How could she say it?

"We discovered a partial footprint inside Phillip's apartment. It appears someone entered through the window, seemingly searching for something, though we are not entirely certain what that was," she explained.

"Did you photograph the print?" he asked.

"Yes," Francy replied, quickly flipping through the photos on her phone. "Here it is," she indicated.

"Maybe I can identify the type of footwear. Text me the image, and I'll send it to Detective Jameson," he suggested.

"We also collected two fingerprints," she added.

"You're kidding? I'm in shock—someone was searching for something in Phillip's apartment?" He shook his head in despair. "I always suspected there was more to this."

Francy retrieved the two fingerprint images from her waist pack.

"I can send all this evidence over to Detective Jameson," Mr. Belltone said carefully. "And thank you for sending me the photos of the boot print. You are delivering in record time."

"Richard," Francy paused, "the photo you had us pick up..." she exhaled, "the photo of the doll? There was no information accompanying it."

"Francy, I'm going to say something." He paused and reached for a glass of whiskey on his desk. With one gulp, he swallowed the brown liquid and returned the glass. "I am a good man. But I am not perfect. I've made decisions in my life that I regret. I want you to know that."

Francy sensed that the whiskey had given him enough courage to speak.

"I have taken steps to address my past actions and protect my interests. Regarding the photo I gave you, consider it my insurance policy. That's all you need to worry about."

Francy nodded. "I get it… your ace in the hole. Very good. I won't bring it up again."

"Hopefully, I won't have to either, but if we need to make a move, we'll be covered."

His cryptic words sent a chill up Francy's spine as she wondered just how much protection that image gave him.

"Tell Drew I have a way to get four of you backstage at Phillip's show. You'll get in without drawing attention."

Francy's eyes lit up. "Are you serious?"

Richard gave a cold smile. "The show holds replacement auditions every six months. I have a theatrical agent who submitted four candidates for this round. You'll have the perfect cover. You decide who goes, but it's the best way to get backstage, check out the theater, or slip into Phillip's dressing room unnoticed. Maybe you'll find something there."

Richard noted the audition details on a piece of paper.

Francy's breath caught as she grabbed the slip of paper Richard handed her. "This is in two days…" she said, her eyes a mix of excitement and determination. "We'll be there."

# Chapter 5
## Theatre District

"Before the Nederlanders and the Barrymores, there was the Belltone family. They built a magnificent homage to Broadway on the corner of Eighth Avenue and 46th street in what was once affectionately called Glitter Gulch. Now known as Broadway's Great White Way, due to the many billboards, posters, and brightly lit marquees - the dream of Damon Belltone was realized."

"Is that what the tourist book says?" Drew asked as Israel thumbed through his new find from the bookstore.

"Is Damon Belltone, Richard Belltone's father?" Debra turned to Drew.

"Yes," Francy chimed in. "I saw his portrait in the Belltone's penthouse when I was there last. Richard confirmed that."

"Well, we are here."

Francy, Drew, Israel, and Debra approached the Grand Theater. Their footsteps echoed along the alley toward the stage door as they passed beneath the towering façade. The building loomed before them, its grand architecture serving as a silent reminder of the secrets it had witnessed over the years. The ornate doors, adorned with intricate carvings, stood slightly ajar, inviting them into the darkness beyond.

Yet none moved. They stood silent, their eyes fixed on the imposing structure, their bodies immobilized. The silence was heavy, and a sense of dread crept into their minds.

Francy's breath caught as she watched the ornate columns soaring above them, while a gentle wind whispered through the morning air. Her fingers twitched, eager to open the door and step inside, yet hesitation and unspoken fear kept her rooted.

Drew broke the silence with a whisper, as if the theater's walls could overhear their thoughts. "This place... it feels like it's holding its breath."

His words echoed among them, intensifying the tension already in the air. His eyes narrowed and his heart raced as his mind flooded with the questions that had troubled him since they vowed to avenge their friend's death.

Israel stood aside with his arms crossed, his gaze distant and lips set in a thin line. He seldom showed fear, yet even he couldn't ignore the uneasy feeling gathering in his stomach.

Debra, the skeptic, shifted nervously. Her eyes flitted among them, her lips parting as if to speak, yet silence prevailed. She tried to dismiss the unease crawling along her spine, but even her characteristic bravado couldn't hide the palpable tension.

Then, as if on cue, the silence broke with a distant, low note from unseen instruments drifting on the wind. It was almost imperceptible—like a remnant of a long-forgotten song. The audition had begun.

The tryouts for the show took place in the very spot where they had lost their friend. Now, it was their chance to investigate what had happened to Phillip. Auditioning was the only way to gain backstage access, but the pressure was overwhelming—exacerbated by the watchful presence of the dance director and the stage manager. They needed to be cautious and strategic.

"The audition is on the main stage," Drew confirmed.

A vast space with polished wooden floors gleamed under bright lights. Dancers filled the stage as they warmed up, stretching carefully. Some practiced on the staircase, others near backstage props, using nearly every inch of the stage. The air carried the scent of sweat, resin, and the old velvet curtains lining the back of the theater.

"Thank you for coming," boomed the dance director. Katherine Goossens—a renowned Broadway choreographer with decades of experience—was both beloved and respected, though she was known as a tough taskmaster. "We need one boy and one girl as cast replacements for the show," she announced.

"Let's get everyone on stage to learn the combination," called a voice from behind her, with only a shadow visible in the back.

Katherine swiftly demonstrated five sets of eight-count choreography. "Keep your shoulders back on the turn and mark that last count with an accent!" she called over the crowd, her voice reverberating off the seats in the balcony. Her tall, lanky stride added to her commanding presence, highlighted by her form-fitting black bodysuit.

"OK, let's get fifteen people on stage to do the combination," the mysterious voice from the side wings called out.

The first fifteen dancers dashed to center stage and arranged themselves evenly on the boards facing the seats, while the others moved back against the wall.

"What a cattle call," Debra murmured under her breath to Drew.

Katherine turned and signaled the piano player. The music began—a classical piece that started bright and bold, setting the rhythm for fluid movements.

Katherine stood at the front of the stage with a clipboard, her keen eyes scanning the dancers as they moved. Her gaze was critical and calculating, as if assessing each dancer's value. She pulled her auburn hair back into a bun and turned to signal the stage manager.

The stage manager, once only an unseen voice echoing throughout the theatre, emerged from the shadows to assert her presence. The fiery, short-haired redhead stepped into the spotlight; her assertiveness was matched by the large headset around her neck. Wearing a tight tank top and well-worn blue jeans, she projected authority as she strode onto the stage, her voice slicing through the air. "Get back in the wings or press against the wall, people. You'll have your moment," she snapped, her gaze sharp and unyielding.

"Ava," Katherine called out, her gesture signaling the stage manager to move on.

Ava adjusted her headset and barked, "Next fifteen dancers." She and the choreographer moved swiftly across the stage, their eyes alert, detecting even the smallest misstep with uncanny precision. Every movement was noted, each breath synchronized with the rhythm of the rehearsal.

Francy, Drew, Israel, and Debra took their places on stage. Francy, naturally graceful and confident in her dance, moved through the audition with ease. Drew, with a knack for rhythm, followed instinctively. Israel kept his movements relaxed, mirroring the dance director exactly. Debra executed the balletic steps as if she were born for the stage, her grace capturing Katherine Goossens's attention.

"OK, people, stop, stop, stop," she commanded. "What's your name?" she pointed at Debra. Without waiting for an answer, she ordered, "Step forward."

Debra stepped to the front of the crowd, visibly nervous.

"Okay, people—do it just like this." She signaled the piano player to repeat the phrase.

Without hesitation, Debra executed the combination as if she had created it herself. She finished her turn with a smile.

"Perfect! Just like that, everyone—without the smile."

"Happy now?" Drew nudged Debra as she slunk to the back of the line.

Debra could only roll her eyes. "Where are Francy and Israel?"

"Francy and Israel slipped down that narrow corridor. I think it leads under the stage," Drew said, nodding toward stage right.

As the audition continued, the dance director barked commands, guiding the group through a series of intricate steps. Everyone performed a set of pirouettes, arabesques, and fouetté turns. The music shifted to a more challenging, faster-paced piece.

Debra and Drew moved to the back of the stage and observed the space, noting that the stage manager frequently glanced at the clock in preparation for the session's end. "She really wants to get out of here," Debra observed.

"Okay, we are taking a 15-minute break," Ava announced, stepping out from her podium backstage.

Drew motioned to Debra. With a quick exchange of glances, they slipped away from the remaining dancers, careful to remain unnoticed.

"Where are they?" Debra whispered.

Drew nudged her, "Look." His head turned toward the end of the narrow corridor where Israel beckoned them to follow.

"We think we found Phillip's dressing room," Israel muttered. "Francy noticed the direction of the dressing rooms earlier, so we went searching for it."

Francy appeared at the top of the stairwell and quickly motioned for them to follow.

"You see, I told you… bloodhound," Drew mumbled.

Drew and Debra followed Francy and Israel, slipping silently through a side door and descending a narrow staircase into the lower part of the theatre. Their movements were deliberate, footsteps barely audible on the creaking wooden floor, as they moved through the dimly lit hall toward the dressing rooms. The doors bore only the cryptic initials of the performers inside, each a silent secret. Then, without warning, Israel stopped. "This is it."

"How do you know this is Phillip's dressing room?" Debra blurted. "Wait a minute."

"It's the only room with the initials PW."

"Phillip Wright," Drew managed to say.

"Who else could it be?" Israel deduced.

Francy tried the door handle quietly, but it was locked. Israel, thinking quickly, removed a bobby pin from Debra's hair and carefully picked the lock. The tumblers clicked in the quiet hallway, and the door slowly opened.

"I can't imagine where you learned that trick," Debra huffed, half appalled yet still intrigued.

"A trick he learned from years of sneaking around places he wasn't allowed to be," Francy assured her.

Drew scanned the hallway as he pushed the door open wider.

"There's nothing here." The words hung in the air as his face flushed with frustration and disbelief. The room was barren, its cold walls facing them like a void, except for a single mirror that distorted their reflections, its dusty surface a grim reminder of neglect.

Debra glanced around, her voice uncertain. "Maybe we're in the wrong room?"

Drew's eyes narrowed as his gaze drifted to the mirror. "Wrong room?" he repeated, his tone more thoughtful than dismissive. "Or maybe this is the right room... and we've just forgotten why we're here." He stepped closer to the mirror, his fingers lightly tracing the surface, although he never actually made contact.

"What do you mean by that?" Israel asked, unease creeping into his voice.

Drew's lips curved into a knowing smile, yet a shadow of something darker lurked in his eyes. "I mean, we're all here for a reason, aren't we? Perhaps we've been looking at this all wrong."

Francy frowned as a shiver ran down her spine. "All wrong?"

Instead of answering immediately, Drew fixed his eyes on the mirror, as if waiting for something. A long silence enveloped the room, and then—

Debra gasped. "Look at the mirror," she urged, focusing on a message etched in the dust.

"Ava is toxic." Israel's voice trembled as he read the message.

Drew quickly scanned the room. He walked slowly along the walls, pressing his hand against the wood panels and examining the seams on the cement floor. "There doesn't seem to be anything else here for us."

"Did Phillip write this message?" Debra questioned, studying the mirror to unravel its meaning.

"If this was his dressing room, then perhaps he did," Francy concluded. "I agree with that message."

"That woman is definitely headstrong," Debra added.

"Listen! The music. They've restarted the audition," Israel reacted. "We need to go."

Israel snapped a photo of the mirror as the four raced out of the dressing room and ascended back up the stairs to the stage.

"We just want to see the girls do the combination," Ava's voice trailed off in the backstage area as Debra and Francy hurried toward the stage. Drew and Israel hung back. Kathrine signaled to the piano player, who immediately began repeating the audition song for what felt like the umpteenth time.

"What was Phillip like, Drew?" Israel asked, seeking a clearer picture of his friend.

Drew paused, then whispered over the stage music. "He was a lot like you. Ambitious, a go-getter, and curious. He had a solid sense of self," Drew said, smiling warmly as he recalled his friend. "He was around your age – late 20s, and remarkably mature."

"I get the sense that he enjoyed proving people wrong," Israel suggested.

"Phillip wouldn't tolerate injustice. He fought for fairness every day. If someone wronged another and Phillip found out about it," Drew shook his head, "you'd better believe he wouldn't let it slide. I'm sure that's why he chose 'Wright' as his stage name." Drew chuckled to himself.

"Now we want to see the boys," Ava declared with determination. "Let's move!" she added, fixing her glare on them.

"Come on," Drew urged Israel, "let's show them how it's done."

Francy and Debra quickly moved to the rear of the wall. "This might be our only chance to check out this theatre thoroughly," Francy said, trying to catch her breath.

"I know," Debra replied, wiping the sweat from her brow. She scanned the area, wondering where else evidence of Phillip's horrific demise might be found. "Ohhh," she moaned in frustration. "I wish this theatre could talk."

"Well, if that mirror left us a message, there might be other clues around. The boys are busy on stage; let's finish our search," Francy said, pulling Debra away. "We need to explore this level."

Debra hesitated, glancing around. "Ok, vamos."

The girls slipped out of sight. Watchful eyes from some of the dancers in the wings met Debra and Francy with curious looks, though they were ultimately more focused on the casting process.

"Do you have your cellphone? I can't see two feet in front of me," Francy quipped.

"Hang on." Debra reached into her Alo dance bag and pulled out her phone. She fumbled with the buttons, and suddenly a beam of light revealed their surroundings. "It looks like we are between the back curtains and the theatre wall."

Looking upward, they saw shadows of the scenery suspended above them. Debra moved her light first to stage left and then to stage right, sensing a presence from an uncertain direction. Long shadows from the rigging gear and curtain ropes seemed to dance as she adjusted her phone's light.

"Mr. Belltone said Phillip collapsed backstage before coming on stage," Francy reminded Debra.

"So, it must have happened in one of the wings," Debra surmised.

"All right, this is the last round I need to see," Katherine's demanding voice echoed back to where the girls were searching. "Ava?"

Ava stepped forward and bellowed, "I need girls 1–20 and boys 20–40. Boys in the back line," she reiterated. "Come on, people; we don't have all day!"

"That's me," Francy said, tapping Debra on the shoulder.

"Okay, go. I'm going to look up stage right," Debra confirmed as the two girls split up.

Debra moved further upstage, dimming the light of her cellphone. Glancing over her shoulder, she noticed Ava glaring onto the stage, counting the number of heads in view.

Debra slipped out of Ava's line of sight and slowly swept her light along the floorboards before shifting it to the heavy, dusty velvet curtain on her right.

"I don't even know what I'm looking for," she admitted to herself. Debra walked cautiously, inspecting every crease in the floorboards, every rip in the curtains, and every mark along her route. Drew's words from the dressing room below echoed in her mind: "All of us are here for a reason, aren't we? Maybe we've been looking at this the wrong way."

Debra strode purposefully across the stage, her steps deliberate as she approached the curtain on the far wing, with her cellphone's light casting brief, measured glimmers across the darkened space. With each sweep of the light, her unease increased, and she murmured her thoughts in the silence.

"A button… someone must have lost this. And a needle… that could be dangerous…" she noted softly, her voice laced with tension in the stillness.

Then her eyes caught something—something unnervingly familiar. "A clump of dark hair?" she whispered, the realization striking her like a shock. It was the same shade and texture she'd seen in Phillip's impeccably kept bathroom. A shiver ran down her spine.

"How curious," she murmured. Without hesitation, she retrieved a delicate lace scarf from her bag and, with almost reverent care, used it to lift the hair from the floor. "You're coming with me. I believe I know who this belongs to." She folded the hair into the scarf and tucked it away, her movements careful yet swift.

As she began to pivot, something stopped her—a strange sensation beneath her feet, an inexplicable pull as if the floor itself resisted her. She froze. "What is this?" she wondered aloud, her gaze scanning the floor for the unseen force at work.

"What are you doing?" a voice broke through the silence from behind her.

"Oh my God, you startled me! Drew, look what I found. I think this is Phillip's hair. I saw the same clump in his bathroom when we searched his apartment."

"Debra, that's great detective work," Drew said while embracing her.

"And what is this?" Debra asked, looking down at the sticky residue dried onto the floor. Her light traced the perimeter of what appeared to be a small patch.

"I'm not sure," Drew replied, his gaze following her light.

"Do you hear that?" Debra asked, turning toward the front of the house.

"Hear what?"

"Exactly," she said, her heart quickening. "The music has stopped."

"We need everyone on stage, please," the choreographer's voice echoed through the theatre.

The auditionees moved to the center of the stage.

"Listen up," Ava called out. "We are hiring one girl and one boy. If we are interested, we will be calling your agent."

"Look, there's Francy and Israel," Debra pointed out through the crowd.

"That's all?" Israel responded to the stage manager's statement.

"That's it," Drew nodded. "They either like you or they don't."

"Miss Debra," a voice called from behind her. Katherine approached and tapped her on the shoulder. "May I see you at the piano?"

Surprised, Debra turned around. "Oh yes, of course, Katherine."

Debra gasped as the choreographer walked away, her excitement giving way to panic. "Drew, what if she suspects something?"

"There's one way to find out," Drew said, nodding toward the piano.

Debra took a deep breath and pulled her shoulders back. "Drew, hold my bag?"

"We will be on the street," Drew replied as he took Debra's bag, secretly wishing her luck.

"What's that about?" Israel asked, glancing over his shoulder as the three of them left the stage and emerged onto the street.

"I bet they're going to hear her sing for the part. The choreographer has been interested in her from the start," Drew said with a smile.

# Chapter 6
## Midtown

The heart of Midtown pulsed with frenetic energy. The towering sky-scrapers cast long shadows over the crowded sidewalks as a sea of pe-destrians surged forward, their steps quick and purposeful. Yellow cabs maneuvered with precision through the nearly gridlocked streets, horns blaring as they moved among a myriad of bike messengers, street vendors, and crosswalk traffic in a well-orchestrated urban symphony.

Amid the chaos, Aisha and Israel found themselves in the back of one such taxi, lurching and stopping as their driver navigated the con-gested avenue. They gripped the worn leather seats, eyes darting between the slow-moving traffic and the imposing buildings that scraped the sky. The cab driver maneuvered aggressively between lanes, muttering curses in a thick outer borough accent.

Outside, a crowd surged. Suited executives power-walked past wide-eyed tourists while food cart vendors called out their wares above the din. The acrid smell of exhaust blended with the inviting aroma of roasted nuts and sizzling street meat.

"Welcome back," Israel joked as Aisha frantically rolled up the win-dow.

"This is nauseating," she blurted, half-hoping the taxi driver had heard her. "I should have called an Uber," Aisha groaned. The taxi driver remained silent.

"It was nice of Mr. Belltone to put us up in one of his apartments on the Park."

Aisha mocked, "He's got so many properties, I bet he can't keep track of them all." She slid her large, round sunglasses down to rest on her perky little nose. "It's not the Waldorf, but it has great light."

Israel tapped the partition between the taxi driver and the back seat. "If you take Broadway, we'll avoid some of the traffic," he suggested, but received no response.

"Speaking of which, how was your Broadway audition?" Aisha asked, raising an eyebrow over her shades, clearly intrigued.

Israel leaned back, stretching his neck. "Exhausting!" he groaned dramatically. "But Debra got the part!" His expression brightened. "Now we have a foot in the door."

"Well, that's fantastic! Debra can certainly do what she does best," Aisha said with a knowing edge in her voice. "Dig deeper."

As they neared Richard Belltone's office, the streets became even more congested. Aisha and Israel exchanged a tense glance, wondering if they would make their appointment on time as they raced through the urban rush. The city's relentless tempo pulsed around them, indifferent to their small mission amid the greater bustle of Midtown.

"We're going to be late," Aisha muttered, checking her watch for the third time in as many minutes.

Israel nodded, his gaze fixed on the flashing street signs. "Richard Belltone's office isn't far now. Just a few more blocks—if this traffic ever eases."

The cab jerked forward suddenly, tires screeching as it narrowly avoided a delivery truck. The driver cursed colorfully, adding to the discord filtering through the windows. Aisha and Israel exchanged a glance, silently wondering if walking might have been faster in this midday madness.

"That's it, I'm out of here," Aisha exclaimed after the near miss. "Stop the cab—we're getting out!"

The driver glanced at them in the rearview mirror and pulled over, stopping the meter at the same moment. "Twenty-eight bucks," he slurred.

"To barely cover ten blocks? That's ridiculous," Aisha said, extracting cash from her small purse and handing it over reluctantly. "Let's go," she instructed Israel.

The Belltone Tower emerged into view, its soaring spire seemingly slicing through the sky as it rose majestically a few blocks away on the Avenue of the Americas. "There it is," Israel said, pointing urgently. "Let's go."

Aisha and Israel passed through the revolving doors into a sunlit lobby with floor-to-ceiling windows stretching nearly thirty feet high, its glass facades reflecting the chaotic motion below. A long marble desk attended by ten receptionists dominated the space.

"Hola," Aisha greeted a young, dark-haired man who had been on the phone.

The receptionist smiled, wrapping up his conversation politely, and replied, "Hello, how can I help you?"

"Hi," Israel interjected. "We are here to see Candela, Mr. Belltone's private secretary. We have an appointment."

He quickly smiled at Israel. "Yes, of course. Your name?"

Aisha cleared her throat and peered over her sunglasses.

"Ah, I mean, your names?" the receptionist corrected.

"Aisha and Israel," she enunciated slowly.

"Just one moment," he assured, picking up the phone and dialing Candela's extension.

"You can go up now. It's the penthouse. It has its own elevator—far right-hand side," the receptionist indicated as he buzzed a gate to let them through.

"If you need my number, I can give you that too," Israel flirted.

"Must you tease everyone, Isra?" Aisha chided, gently pushing him through the gate. "¡Vamos!"

The penthouse elevator whisked the pair upward fifty-five stories, their ears popping during the ascent. The doors slid open to reveal a young, well-dressed brunette with a pleasant smile. Candela, Mr. Belltone's longtime assistant who managed his daily affairs, was the ideal person to help them with their plans. Her expression shifted from friendly to shocked as she immediately recognized Aisha from her movies.

"Oh my goodness," Candela gasped. "Mr. Belltone didn't mention I'd be meeting celebrities," she said to the couple. "Aisha? You're Aisha, right? I've seen all your movies." Her gaze stayed fixed on the starlet, who smiled quietly behind her glasses.

"Hi, I'm Israel!" he said, extending his hand. "Yes, this is Spain's most cherished goddess."

"It's a pleasure to meet you both," Candela grinned. "Come this way. Can I get you something? Coffee or water?"

"Just some answers, mi amor," purred Aisha.

The office hummed with activity as Candela led the guests down a long hallway to Mr. Belltone's office. She unlocked the polished wooden doors and pushed them open.

They entered a space with panoramic south-facing windows. Beyond, the busy New York harbor lay in the distance with the World Trade Tower centered near the island's edge. To the west, the Hudson River bordered New Jersey.

"Wow, now this is a corner office," Israel marveled.

Inside Richard Belltone's office, an oppressive air filled the space. Aisha and Israel followed Candela to an imposing mahogany desk. "This is Mr. Belltone's computer." Candela reached into her sleek skirt pocket, pulled out a piece of paper, and handed it to Israel. "His username and password. He told me once, but I have to write everything down. I don't trust my memory," she added with a sheepish smile.

\Israel leaned over the computer and typed quickly. Aisha stood nearby with her arms crossed in concern, while Candela paced, watching the scene.

"Israel, are you sure you can handle this?" Aisha asked, doubt evident in her tone. "The file was deleted months ago. The system was wiped clean."

Israel smiled confidently. "You know me, Aisha. When something disappears from the system, that's just the start. I've got a few tricks up my sleeve." He continued tapping at the keyboard.

"It's not really gone—just hidden or overwritten," he explained after a pause.

"So you're acting like a digital detective now? I hope your tricks have improved since last time," Aisha smirked. "I still remember the Miami police office crashing when you tried to access the server."

Israel chuckled. "Hey, Detective Vincent gave me permission."

Aisha turned to Candela. "We were trying to analyze bank statements between criminals."

"That was only a temporary setback. And who fixed it?" Israel asked with a playful grin before returning his focus to the screen. "This is different. We're not tampering with the server now. We're after a deleted file—a completely different ballgame."

Candela squinted at the screen. "Wait, do you mean the autopsy file? The one my boss said was 'unrecoverable'? I'm not sure this is a good idea." She bit her lip and exchanged a glance with Aisha before looking back at Israel.

"Exactly that one." Israel moved to Mr. Belltone's rolling chair, pushed himself across the desk, grabbed a pen from its holder, and bit down on it. He then returned to the computer. "I have access to things most people wouldn't dream of. Deleted doesn't mean it's gone—it just takes more effort to find. With the right tools, it's simple." He spun in the chair and pressed ENTER.

Candela hesitated. "I'm not convinced, Israel. The file was erased, overwritten—the system was practically scrubbed. How will you recover something so sensitive?"

Israel raised an eyebrow. "Sensitive, you say? That's what makes it exciting. The more someone tries to cover something up, the more interesting it is. The leftover data is like a trail, and I'm pretty good at tracking it." He paused, then added, "There we go..."

Aisha stared at the screen. "You actually found it? No way..."

"Told you. A deleted file doesn't just vanish. The data lingers in fragments across sectors. I just needed the right algorithm to reconnect it. And... here it is." He pressed a few more keys. "The full autopsy report, exactly as it was."

"But now what? What do we do with it?" Aisha asked. "We need to get this to Elena and Grace…"

Israel pressed PRINT. "You're right. We can't leave it on the machine forever. For now, I've made a backup." The printer in Mr. Belltone's office whirred to life as it produced the recovered file.

"It's encrypted, so no one will know what we've uncovered. I'll transfer it to my home computer where it'll be secure."

The three stood silently, watching as the pages emerged from the printer.

Aisha took the last printed page and read it aloud, "Cause of death: Acute myocardial infarction."

"A heart attack?" Candela asked.

"Contributing factor: neurotoxin poisoning." Candela looked confused. "Wait, neurotoxin poisoning? I've never encountered that."

Israel pulled out his cellphone and dialed Drew. "Hey Drew, you're on speaker. We have the report in hand. It says the autopsy found traces of neurotoxin poisoning. What can you tell us about that?"

"Hmm…" Drew replied, searching his memory. "Look further in the report. Was the neurotoxin identified?"

Aisha quickly scanned the report. "Yes, here it is—ethylene glycol poisoning."

"Hmm… ethylene glycol. It's a chemical found in antifreeze and other industrial products," Drew observed as he brought the phone closer to his ear to speak over the traffic. "I imagine that, depending on the dose, it could trigger severe neurological and physiological effects."

"Hold on," Candela interrupted. "Are you saying that Mr. Belltone's son's heart attack wasn't simply due to a blocked artery? It was triggered by something else? This is Candela, by the way—Mr. Belltone's personal assistant."

"Exactly, Candela," Drew confirmed. "If someone is poisoned by a substance that impacts the nervous system, it can cause sudden disruptions in heart rhythm, leading to a heart attack. And it appears that's precisely what occurred."

Candela whispered into the phone, "If the report is accurate and this wasn't merely a heart attack… then it's murder, and someone out there is getting away with it."

"Yes, it seems like a sophisticated form of poisoning. It could have been inhaled or ingested," Drew paused, considering the consequences. "A heart attack triggered by such poisoning would be very difficult to detect unless you knew exactly what to look for."

Aisha quickly scrolled through the report and spoke into the phone, "It states that the autopsy revealed a buildup of lactic acid in the blood, leading to metabolic acidosis. This isn't something typically caused by food or environmental toxins—this was done on purpose."

"So, someone poisoned him…and made it appear as a natural heart attack?" Candela suddenly whispered.

"That's what it appears to be. Most doctors would simply view the heart attack as a result of genetics, diet, or stress…" Drew nodded to himself. "You know, Mr. Belltone's suspicion was correct—whoever did this knew exactly what they were doing."

Aisha stopped abruptly and read aloud, "Identification markers: a two-inch scar over the right patella and a one-inch LX tattoo beneath the right medial malleolus."

"What?" Candela asked.

"The right ankle bone—a tattoo? I didn't know Phillip had one. I never noticed it," Drew said, sounding confused. "That must be new. It would explain the initial autopsy report from the hospital."

"That's right," Aisha agreed. "The LX symbol in the initial autopsy served as an identification mark."

"The doctor who performed this autopsy also died from a heart attack?" Israel asked.

"Yes, yes," Aisha confirmed.

"Okay, Drew, we'll get this over to Elena and Grace. We'll keep you posted, amigo!" Israel's fingers hovered over the keyboard as his eyes scanned the screen. A soft click echoed through the room, followed by a sudden, bone-chilling silence. Then, with a jolt, the entire office plunged into darkness. The fluorescent lights overhead blinked once, twice, and then went out completely. Screams and shouts could be heard from beyond the office door.

"Israel! You did it again," Aisha yelled.

"I didn't do anything," Israel insisted. "It wasn't me!"

An alarm began to sound—a high-pitched screech that rattled the very foundations of the building.

Candela's heart raced in the darkness. "Israel, did you tamper with something?" she asked, beginning to panic.

Aisha's breath caught in her throat—a clear sign something was amiss. "Get ready," she murmured, barely audible over the building's growing apprehension. "Israel, what did you do?" she demanded, her voice low and tense as she moved toward the door.

Israel didn't have time to explain. "The system's been compromised. We need to move, now!" His fingers fumbled with the door lock in the dark. They heard a soft click before the door swung open.

Suddenly, a figure dressed in black—a shadow—darted past the office door. It moved quickly, almost too fast to see.

"Did you see that?" Candela whispered, her voice sharpened by a creeping dread.

Before anyone could respond, frantic footsteps echoed nearby.

Immediately, a young woman bolted past them, her swift movement catching everyone off guard. Her terrified scream echoed down the hall, and an office worker—her face pale and etched with panic—sprinted past as if chased by relentless pursuers.

"The servers are on fire!" the office worker screamed, her voice raw with fear before she vanished into the darkness.

Aisha's eyes narrowed. "Who was that person in black?"

Candela merely shrugged. "We can't let them get away," Aisha stated calmly, her voice carrying a chilling resolve that sent a shiver down Israel's spine. She then turned to Candela. "We need to follow that person."

Without waiting for a reply, Aisha moved swiftly, her heels clicking against the marble floor as she darted into the dark corridor, closely followed by Candela and Israel.

The office was in complete chaos. What was once a pristine space had become a cacophony of blaring alarms, erratically blinking lights, and frantic shouts from employees scrambling for safety. Yet, none of it mattered; their sole focus was to find the elusive figure that had just slipped away.

"Go that way," Candela directed as they ran down the hallway, their footsteps echoing off the cold, sterile walls.

Aisha's breath came in shallow gasps, her mind racing to connect the dots. "Whoever that was, they planned this. They had to know that we were coming. And now, they're slipping away."

Suddenly, Israel's hand shot out to grab Aisha's arm, stopping her abruptly. "Wait—look."

In the dim glow of the emergency lights, they could just make out a faint figure in black slipping through a door.

"What is that room? Where does it lead?" Israel insisted. It was where the shadow had disappeared.

"They are the employee locker rooms." Candela led them along the smoky hallway, moving cautiously as every instinct urged her to be careful.

There was a sudden flash, and the auxiliary lighting illuminated the office.

"That's the backup lighting," Candela reassured.

The heat from the fire down the hall was already palpable where they stood. They pushed the employee locker room door open just enough to peek inside, and something caught Aisha's eye.

"Isra, grab that," Aisha whispered, pointing to a large glass water bottle.

The air in the locker room carried a metallic scent of sweat and antiseptic mixed with a thin layer of smoke billowing in from the fire down the hall.

Aisha, Candela, and Israel moved stealthily down the narrow aisles between rows of lockers. Their footsteps echoed in the otherwise still room, but they knew they couldn't afford to slow down.

"He's somewhere ahead," Israel said, pointing down the long row of lockers.

The overhead lights stuttered intermittently, casting long, eerie shadows across the gleaming metal lockers.

"Stay sharp," Aisha hissed, her voice barely audible over the creaking of metal doors. "He's here somewhere. He's close."

"We should split up," Israel whispered.

"Are you kidding?" Candela replied, nearly in tears. With every turn and every locker they passed, tension surged through her; the hairs on the back of her neck stood on end. The feeling of being watched was almost suffocating, as if a dark presence lurked nearby, waiting to strike.

Then, a sudden noise: a soft shuffle, a metallic scrape.

Israel's head snapped toward the sound. At the far end of the room, a locker door swung open and then slammed shut with a force that sent ripples through the air. Candela reacted to the broken silence. "Oh my God."

Aisha's eyes darted to Israel, but before she could speak, he raised his hand for silence. His gaze then shifted upward, locking onto something above them—something they hadn't noticed before.

The ceiling was lined with a grid of reflective ceramic panels. The overhead light glinted off them, casting faint reflections on the shiny surfaces below.

"Look," Israel whispered. "We can see his reflection in the tiles above."

Aisha stopped in her tracks, her heart skipping a beat as she followed Israel's gaze. Slowly, she looked upward to see the shadow of a figure moving in the adjacent aisle. Though his face remained unseen, his silhouette advanced steadily—moving with a slow, deliberate twist of his head, like a predator stalking its prey.

"He is heading toward the far corner of the room," Israel whispered.

"That's where the lockers thin out and there's an exit," Candela managed to say between breaths.

"We've got to get to him," Aisha growled under her breath, her eyes fixed on the moving reflection. "We can catch him now."

Without thinking, they sprang into motion. Israel led the charge, tiptoeing quickly and closing the gap between them and their quarry. Aisha and Candela followed closely; every step synchronized in their pursuit. They could hear his feet shuffling, his breaths coming in quick bursts, his body tense with anticipation. He was so close.

But then, just as they thought they had him cornered, the figure darted to the side and slipped behind a row of lockers. His reflection vanished, and the sound of his movements was swallowed by the profound silence of the room.

They skidded to a halt, their eyes darting from side to side.

"Where did he go?" Candela whimpered, breathless, scanning the room for any sign of movement.

Israel's eyes moved upward again in search of reflections. That's when he noticed a faint glimmer of motion—a shadow gliding through the grid of lockers, advancing toward them.

"Psst, in here," Israel signaled, motioning for them to follow him into the bathroom stall.

The girls slipped into the stall next to Israel. He pressed a finger to his lips in a quiet gesture and then pointed upward.

The stranger's reflection was clear, cautiously advancing.

"Wait for it…" Israel murmured. "He placed his palms on the back of the stall's door."

The girls copied his gesture, trying to steady their labored breathing and suppress the rising panic.

Israel watched as the figure moved closer. "Ready?" he signaled.

With one swift push, the trio swung the door outward, striking the dark figure and sending him tumbling backward. They looked up at the ceiling tiles to see the assailant sprawled on the floor.

"Is he dead?" Candela nearly cried, fear evident in her voice. They paused, immobilized by the surge of adrenaline.

Israel slowly lifted his gaze toward the tiles; the reflection was gone. In the distance, a door was being pushed open.

Aisha muttered a Spanish curse. "He's got away."

They heard the door slam shut, its impact reverberating through the room. They were too late.

Israel growled as he slammed his fist against the door. The metal hinges rattled, yet the door held firm. The figure had vanished into the dark, slipping away once more.

Something caught Aisha's eye—a glimmer on the floor, half-hidden beneath an open locker. She bent down and reached for it.

A silver key lay on the floor. It was large and ornate, unlike any office key she had seen. What intrigued her most was the strange symbol engraved on it—a sleek, metallic insignia of a coiled dragon-serpent around a crown, its eyes gleaming with malice.

Aisha's pulse quickened as she examined the key, a cold realization creeping in.

"Is this a key from your office?" Aisha asked Candela.

"No, I've never seen anything like it."

"It looks antique—another symbol," Israel interjected, his face tightening as he turned back toward the door. "We've lost him. But this... could be the break we need."

Their distraction was abruptly interrupted by a voice shouting, "This is the fire department. Anyone in here? Call out!"

"Yes, in here!" Candela yelled. "Please help us!"

Three New York firemen appeared in the now smoke-laden locker room.

"Did you notice anyone else in here?" one fireman asked Aisha.

"No," Aisha gasped as they were escorted to safety by New York's bravest.

"We'll find out who he is," Israel assured, his voice low with determination. "This isn't over."

A fireman escorted the trio outside, where chaos reigned: fire trucks, police vehicles, and a gawking crowd. Another New York moment was unfolding on 6th Avenue.

Several of Candela's staff rushed over to check if she was alright and to learn what had happened.

Aisha coughed from the lingering smoke. As she reached into her small purse for a tissue, her eyes caught something else. About a hundred feet ahead, a man dressed in black with a hood appeared to search frantically through his pockets. "Isra," she called, gripping Israel's arm tightly.

"Are you alright?" Israel asked as he noticed the man Aisha was watching.

"Hey— you!" Israel yelled.

The man in black turned quickly upon realizing he was being pursued and leapt onto a light green Vespa parked nearby.

Without hesitation, Aisha bolted forward. She dashed past Israel, who was already giving chase, his heavy breathing evident. The Vespa's engine grew louder as the man in black started to pull ahead.

Israel's heart pounded with each beat, reminding him of what was at stake. He saw Aisha ahead, her long strides cutting through the crowd, yet even her speed couldn't match the motorcyclist. The city was a labyrinth of traffic and pedestrians, but the man in black was making a clean escape—darting through the intersection of 42nd Street and 6th Avenue with precise determination.

Aisha glanced over her shoulder at Israel, breathless. "We need to catch him, now!"

"That's the plan," Israel grunted, his breath coming in sharp bursts. Yet even as he spoke, it was clear the chase was turning futile. The two-wheeler was simply too fast amid the heavy traffic and crowds. The man in black was getting away.

"Aisha, look—just ahead." A delivery boy on a moped pulled to the curb, a pizza box tucked under one arm. Israel's eyes narrowed, and Aisha immediately understood.

Without a word, they sprinted toward the moped. Israel grabbed the delivery boy's shoulder. "Hey! Get off the bike!"

The boy froze, eyes wide and mouth agape. Israel swung one leg over the scooter. "We're not here to hurt you—just clear a path!"

The delivery boy hesitated a moment before scrambling backward, muttering in panic. Israel kicked the moped into gear, and with a sharp twist of the throttle, they surged forward. Aisha climbed aboard, gripping his waist. "We'll return your bike—wait here!" she yelled as the moped accelerated.

"Hold on tight!" Israel shouted as the engine roared beneath them, propelling them into the chaotic midtown traffic. The world became a blur of honking taxis, swerving bikes, and frantic pedestrians. Yet Israel focused solely on the man in black, who was now cutting through the streets ahead. He wasn't far behind.

"He's turning east on 32 street!" Aisha shouted over the roar of the engine.

Israel twisted the throttle and accelerated as they rounded a corner, cutting through the intersection just in time to see the man in black vanish down Broadway. Israel's grip tightened on the handlebars as they pursued, dodging pedestrians and idle cars waiting for the light to change. The tires screeched while sliding sideways to negotiate the sharp turn.

The man's Vespa engine growled ahead as Israel pushed the moped harder, every muscle in his body demanding more speed. They were extremely close—yet the man in black remained faster, executing dangerous, reckless turns that Israel barely managed to follow. His pulse pounded in his ears, and his focus narrowed until nothing else existed. All that mattered was catching this guy and stopping him immediately.

"He's heading toward The FDR Drive," Aisha directed. "There—he took that side street."

Israel maneuvered the moped down an alley that opened onto a broader street running parallel to the East River, with the Brooklyn Bridge looming in the distance, its shadow stretching across the pavement like a dark hand. The man in black was headed straight for it.

Israel revved the engine again, pushing the bike to its limit. But the Vespa ahead was slipping away. He could see the bridge now, just ahead—the steel giant standing like an insurmountable wall between him and his target.

"We're losing him!" Aisha cried, feeling helpless on the back of the bike, her role reduced to giving directions.

"Not yet!" Israel barked, a spark of determination crossing his face. He veered the moped into a hard right turn, aiming for a narrow under-pass that led to the industrial district along the East River.

Aisha gripped him tighter as they skidded into the underpass, the rough concrete scraping against their tires. The Vespa was barely visible now, yet Israel could still hear the distant sound of its engine diminishing as the man in black surged toward the Brooklyn Bridge.

"He's taking that auxiliary road to your right," Aisha pointed over his shoulder.

Israel slammed on the throttle one last time, pushing the moped through narrow industrial streets—the route now a maze of rusted build-ings and train tracks snaking toward the water.

"Now!" Aisha shouted, urgency filling her voice.

Israel's eyes locked onto the man in black, who was speeding toward an old train yard adjacent to the looming arches of the Brooklyn Bridge. The tracks lay desolate, overgrown with weeds, the air thick with the scent of rust and diesel.

"He's heading for that warehouse!" Aisha shouted, frustration edg-ing her voice.

"I see him," Israel replied. With a sudden burst of speed, they surged forward—directly toward the Vespa. Israel leaned into the turn, the mo-ped swerving perilously as they closed in. The man in black glanced over his shoulder, his hoodie concealing his face as he sensed the pursuit.

Israel attempted to pull alongside the Vespa, reaching out so that his fingers brushed the man's jacket. But before he could grab him, the man in black swerved violently, colliding with a stack of crates and forcing Israel into a sharp turn to avoid the falling loads.

"No!" Aisha shouted, watching as the man disappeared along the train tracks leading deep into the warehouse, swallowed by the gloom of the aging machinery.

They skidded to a halt at the edge of the train yard, the Vespa's engine sound fading into an eerie silence.

Israel clutched his head in frustration. "He got away. Twice!"

Aisha exhaled sharply, her eyes scanning the darkness. "Not for long," she said with resolve. "We'll find him. He can't stay hidden forever."

Israel nodded grimly, the bitterness of defeat lingering, yet he refused to let the chance slip away.

Aisha sighed heavily. "I can't imagine where that leads."

# Chapter 7
## Flatiron District

Drew was sprawled on the living room floor. Phillip's book was open to the final pages as he repeatedly mulled over the images and riddles in his mind. "What was Phillip trying to convey?" Drew wondered as he searched for a logical pattern or narrative.

"Why was Phillip writing things out in codes and riddles?"

"You know Phillip," Elena said, peeking out from the kitchen, "he always had a fascination with puzzles. I actually think it helped him manage life and his OCD."

"You've got a point," Drew murmured.

Elena brought a large cup of steaming coffee to Drew in the living room. He took a sip, the warmth lingering within him.

"We don't really know if the intruder who broke into Phillip's apartment was even searching for this book. Maybe it was a junkie in the neighborhood looking for cash." Elena sat on the sofa next to Drew and brushed her hair back.

"Then why be so meticulous? Whoever broke in removed their shoes before entering and wiped away any traces of dirt on the windowsill." Drew scratched his head. "Whoever it was, they were there for something specific – either they knew Phillip or had been instructed on how to treat the apartment."

"Phillip had an expensive painting hanging on his wall," Elena noted as she braided her hair on one side.

"He also kept an expensive watch on his dresser along with designer clothes and shoes in the closet, none of which were disturbed. The only item out of place was a stack of books." Drew recalled the images vividly. Glancing back at the book, he tried to interpret the symbols.

Elena listened intently as Drew explained the meanings behind each sign.

"The broken chain could represent betrayal or severed ties. It might also mean freedom," Drew began. "The key in a lock signifies access or the opening to new opportunities."

Elena examined the symbols etched on the paper.

"The eye symbol," he continued, "often stands for perception, insight, and awareness."

"That's broad symbolism," Elena interjected.

"The scale of justice," Drew added, "is a familiar emblem of our justice system. It represents weighing evidence impartially or reflecting a moral dilemma."

"The snake," he explained, "can symbolize evil, temptation, betrayal, or deceit. And the hourglass," Drew concluded, "typically represents the passage of time."

"Phillip must have been recording information he discovered, yet was too frightened to write it plainly. What could have scared him enough to resort to such caution?" Elena wondered as she finished the braid.

"We have to go, Drew."

Drew closed the book and slid it under the sofa, covering it with a blanket.

"I can't believe what happened to Aisha and Israel yesterday! I'm just glad they are alright." Elena turned the key in the lock and firmly secured the door. "The image of that key Aisha texted you is unlike any other key I have seen. A three-pronged key is truly unique."

"It seems very rare." Drew brought up the image of the key on his phone again. "It certainly appears to be centuries old. I sent the image to Mr. Belltone—perhaps he can identify its origin."

"I'd love to see what it opens. Maybe it corresponds to the key in Phillip's book?" Elena asked.

"Confirmation bias," Drew retorted.

"I know, I know," Elena shook her head. "I'm merely fitting the evidence to an uncertain theory. Well, it's a theory." She changed the subject. "It was considerate of Mr. Belltone to house us in different apartments across the city…"

"I thought it might be safer for us to be split into groups around town," Drew paused at the top of the steps. "It just seems like someone is one step ahead of us…anticipating our every move."

"Well, I'm glad we're in the East Village. It reminds me of the old days, and in times like these, any sense of familiarity is comforting. We have to figure out who is onto us," Elena confirmed. She pushed open the front door of the prewar building and jumped off the stoop. "Let's head to our favorite coffee shop; it's time for a second cup!"

For as long as they could remember, Café Vivaldi occupied the corner of Eighth St. and St. Marks Place. Housed in a small storefront on the block, the coffee shop was known for its excellent coffee and affordable prices compared to other New York coffeeshops.

Doris was a disheveled, charming, and charismatic fixture of the neighborhood and had worked at Vivaldi's for as long as Elena could remember. Her slightly rotund figure matched her cheerful persona, and her engaging eyes drew you in. Her lipstick often strayed outside the fine pencil line that defined her lips, and her wide-set eyes were highlighted by large false eyelashes. Her tousled brown, unkempt hair and layers of brightly colored clothes complemented her mismatched rouge, accentuating her warm heart.

"As I live and breathe…" Doris boomed as Elena walked in the door.

"But, do you? Really?" Elena replied with a matching smile.

"Still as charming as never!"

"I love you too." Elena hugged her friend, and Doris squeezed her tightly before stepping back to look her up and down, pushing her hair behind one ear.

"I thought you ran off with a handsome prince," Doris joked.

"No," Elena replied, "I thought he ran off with you."

"You think I'd be working in this dump if I ran off with a prince?" Doris huffed. She paused to adjust her apron, twisted halfway around her waist. "It's only been a New York minute. Where've you been? Nicaragua?"

"Miami."

"It's still a Latin country," Doris retorted, a devilish grin on her face. "And that Cuban coffee..." she laughed. "It's better than the brown water we serve here." Doris held up an empty coffee cup, turned it upside down, and shook it.

"It's good coffee here," Elena protested.

"Awww, sweetie, you've failed me," Doris frowned.

"Again?"

"More so!" she laughed.

"Between you and me," Doris whispered into Elena's ear, "the coffee from the cart across the street is much better."

Elena shook her head, smiling at her friend whose stereotypical New Yorker charm only added to her appeal.

"Okay, what'll you have?" Doris asked.

"Two coffees: one light and sweet, and one regular," Elena replied.

"How we payin'? Cash, card, ducets, Monopoly money?"

"Yes..." Elena responded.

Drew walked up to the counter alongside Elena, smiling at Doris.

"Well, well, and who is this youngish man?" Doris said, looking Drew up and down. "Oh, don't tell me—your long-lost brother!"

"Of course," Elena lied.

"You're two peas in a pod. I could tell you're related." She stepped back, placing her hands on her hips as she observed Drew and Elena together. "You see," Doris added, shaking her head slowly, "when you've been around as long as I have..." She paused, "You've been around as long as I have!"

"Makes sense," Drew replied with an even bigger grin.

"Ahhh," Elena sighed, looking to Drew, "I miss the New York banter!"

"I know I do," Drew smiled.

A large yellow checkered cab pulled up in front of Café Vivaldi. Grace stuck her head out the window and waved. "We're here!"

"Grace texted me that she was coming to pick me up. We have an appointment with the new mortician at the City Morgue."

"Mr. Belltone keeps his word," Drew confirmed.

Elena hopped into the waiting cab and headed off to the Flatiron District.

Detective Jameson sat across from Grace and Elena, his thick Brooklyn accent and signature aftershave filling the cab. "Elena… how you doing?"

"Detective Jameson, this is a surprise. I didn't expect to see you here," Elena said with a half-smile. "Grace?" she turned to her friend, raising her eyebrows at their unexpected guest.

"Ahhh," Grace smiled sheepishly. "I figured we were all on the same side, you know? We were just hanging out," she confessed.

"Oh, I see," Elena replied.

"So here's the story, ladies: we've got a problem. The coroner—the guy who was supposed to explain how your friend died—is now dead, and we can't get straight answers."

"What do you mean?" Elena asked, her brow furrowing in confusion. "I just got the autopsy report emailed to me on my phone."

"That's the point," Jameson said, shaking his head. "Drew said you'd keep me informed if you found anything."

"I'm keeping you in the loop," Elena insisted. "I just got the info. Mr. Belltone recovered the autopsy report he thought was deleted from his computer," she lied, hiding how they had really obtained it.

"The morgue replaced the dead coroner with someone else who's being tight-lipped. I tried to enter the morgue to find out more about your friend's passing, but they wouldn't let me in without a warrant, and the judge denied one."

"Why not?" Grace asked, shifting in her seat.

"The judge didn't find probable cause."

"What do you mean?"

"You know—there wasn't enough evidence for a search warrant. They ruled the cause of death as a heart attack."

"Heart attack?" Elena huffed.

"No disrespect, but it was ruled a heart attack with no proof of poison or foul play."

Grace shifted uncomfortably back in her seat once more. "We are going to talk to the new coroner now. Maybe he can clarify the situation."

"You got a warrant?" Detective Jameson laughed, his tone laced with skepticism.

"No," Grace smiled, "we just asked. Given that Mr. Belltone discovered the autopsy—performed by their original mortician, Dr. Foster—they agreed to review it."

The New York City Medical Examiners' building was not a place anyone looked forward to visiting—unless absolutely necessary. This was one of those unavoidable moments.

The harsh fluorescent lights buzzed overhead as Detective Jameson, Elena, and Grace walked down the sterile white hallway toward the mortician's office. Faint rustling and the clink of metal instruments echoed off the walls.

"I can't believe we're about to meet the new coroner. You think he'll know anything about the previous one? His predecessor?"

"I don't know, Grace," Elena sighed. "But after everything that's happened, we need someone who's thorough. We can't afford any more mistakes."

"Let's not get our hopes up." Jameson grumbled. "The last guy died from a heart attack. It's common. Most people go that way. How's that supposed to inspire confidence?"

"Okay, let's just keep an open mind." A note of defiance undercut Grace's words. "We don't know what happened yet, Jameson. We can't jump to conclusions."

"Grace is right," Elena agreed softly. "If we're going to find answers, we need to remain receptive."

Jameson offered a wry smile. "Receptive? Look, I don't trust anyone who shows up right after a coroner dies under suspicious circumstances. Maybe I'm just more cautious."

They reached the office doors. Jameson knocked twice before entering, the hinges groaning as the door opened.

Two security guards halted them. "What do you need?" one asked firmly, blocking their path.

"Hi there," Grace said with a smile. "We're visiting a friend—Dr. Stevens?"

"He's not available," the other guard interjected.

"How strange," Grace drawled. "We just got off the phone with him. We have a lunch date."

The guards exchanged glances.

Without hesitation, Grace created a distraction by untying the Hermes scarf that held her long green braids, then letting them fall along the right side of her body. "Sorry," she said, raising both hands over her head and sweeping her braids around her face to frame it perfectly.

The security guards and Detective Jameson watched, puzzled by Grace's routine. She quickly gathered her braids into a neat bundle, tossed them forward, retrieved the scarf from her forehead, tied it behind her neck, and then flipped her hair back.

"Dr. Stevens," Elena called. "Nice to see you."

The security guards turned to see Elena already standing in the open doorway of the coroner's office. Dr. Stevens was seated at a desk, looking up from a pile of papers. His pale complexion appeared almost translucent. A man in his late sixties, he was entirely grey and wore dark-rimmed reading glasses perched at the tip of his nose. His serious appearance was both blunt and honest.

"What can I do for you?" he asked, rising his eyes from the stack of white paper that nearly blended into his surroundings. He dismissed the security guards with a gesture. "They have an appointment with me," he confirmed.

"We're here about the former coroner, Dr. Foster." Jameson searched for the right words. "I've got a few questions about his death."

"Mr. Belltone called and mentioned that you have the autopsy my colleague performed?" Dr. Stevens nodded, adjusting his glasses. "Dr. Foster was well-respected, and his death was unexpected." He shook his head. "It was a difficult period for all of us. Dr. Foster had served here for years."

"We are so sorry for your loss, Dr. Stevens. We're not here to add to your troubles," Grace interjected, her high cheekbones lighting up when she smiled sincerely. "We just need to understand what happened to him—and if it might be connected to our friend Phillip's death."

"We know it must be hard, but if you could help us put the pieces together…" Elena said with determination.

Dr. Stevens paused, his expression turning serious. "I understand. But you should know, Dr. Foster's death wasn't an accident. I believe he was poisoned."

"Poisoned? How can you be so sure?" Jameson asked skeptically.

"Can I see the autopsy report on Mr. Belltone's son?" Dr. Stevens inquired, sounding uneasy.

Elena quickly retrieved the PDF on her phone and opened it.

"May I?" he asked, reaching for the phone and moving toward a projector in the corner. He connected a cable to Elena's phone, and soon a complete image of the report appeared on a white screen.

The trio watched as Dr. Stevens carefully reviewed the report prepared by his predecessor. "Dr. Foster was a forensic detective. If he sensed even a single anomaly, he pursued every lead until he uncovered the truth. He was also my mentor," Dr. Stevens stated proudly.

"That explains why you are so invested in this," Grace smiled.

Dr. Stevens walked over to a file cabinet in the far corner of the room and pulled out a folder. "I performed the autopsy on Dr. Foster. He had a heart attack as well. However, I discovered anomalies in his hair and tissue samples. I detected traces of an unidentified toxin in his system. After reviewing Phillip's report, I noticed certain similarities."

"Really?" Elena exchanged a knowing look with Grace.

"Unfortunately, I had very little time to continue the autopsy because Dr. Foster was Jewish and Jewish law requires the body to be buried within 24 hours after death," Dr. Stevens said, lowering his head. "I wish I had insisted one more time."

"Detective Jameson, are you hearing this?" Grace called to the man on the phone. "Jameson, are you paying attention?"

He simply raised one hand as he continued talking.

"I also observed chunks of hair falling from his head, but I didn't connect the dots then. I saved some hair along with tissue samples."

"On that note, Dr. Stevens, one of my colleagues, Debra, found this hair backstage at Phillip's theatre. We think it may be his, as it was collected at the spot where he had the heart attack." Elena retrieved a delicate lace scarf from her nap sack—the one Debra used to secure the sample. "She also has a hair sample from his apartment. They appear similar." She handed both samples to Dr. Stevens.

Dr. Stevens carefully unwrapped the scarf, extracted the hair, and sealed it in a labeled plastic bag. He repeated the process with the apartment sample and then returned to Phillip's autopsy report. "I noticed that Dr. Foster detected toxicity in Phillip's liver," he said gravely. "It's disturbing, but it fits. Foster's symptoms were similar to Phillip's: severe irritation of the abdominal lining, subtle burns in the esophagus, and organ failure. Initially, a heart attack was cited as the cause of death, but it was likely just the final stage of poisoning."

Grace's eyes narrowed. "Who could be behind this?"

Now off the phone, Jameson crossed his arms. "This is starting to appear as a pattern. But you're telling me that both Foster and Phillip were poisoned? That seems too much of a coincidence."

Dr. Stevens replied calmly, "It's not a coincidence, Detective. Someone intended for them to die. And now, with both cases under review, I'm determined to get answers."

"But why them? Why Foster?" Grace asked softly.

Dr. Stevens gave a solemn look. "Dr. Foster was always stirring up trouble. He may have uncovered something dangerous, and I believe someone silenced him before he could expose it. As for Phillip... he might have discovered something, perhaps too close to the truth. Dr. Foster's computer was sabotaged, which is why we didn't have a copy of Phillip's autopsy."

"So, are we talking about a cover-up, and have we been chasing shadows all along?" Jameson growled.

"Not shadows. Just pieces we need to assemble," Elena replied firmly.

Grace turned and looked directly at Dr. Stevens. "So, what happens now?"

"We return to the autopsies and investigate further. I'll review the records for both cases to see if I missed anything. If foul play is involved, we will uncover it," Dr. Stevens stated quietly.

Jameson reluctantly nodded. "Fine, but we need concrete evidence before making any accusations."

"Dr. Stevens, we need everything—whatever you have," Elena affirmed.

Dr. Stevens nodded. "You'll receive everything."

The three exchanged knowing looks and thanked Dr. Stevens as they left. "Watch your back, Doc," Jameson warned. "If someone eliminated your previous doctor, you might be next. Stay vigilant." He muttered, "Poison? Who would have thought?"

"Well, what do you think, Detective?" Elena asked as they stepped outside.

"Come on, let's walk and talk," Detective Jameson suggested, gesturing across 23rd Street.

"It seems this guy is trying to force the scenario to match the cause of death. Perhaps the doctor who died from a heart attack had an unusual substance in his system, but who's to say it was related to your friend's death?" he shrugged. "I don't know—I'm just saying."

Suddenly, Detective Jameson and Elena halted. "Hey, where's Grace?" Elena looked back to see Grace already halfway down the block.

"Why do New Yorkers walk so fast? That isn't a walk; it's nearly a sprint!" Grace arrived, catching her breath.

"Come on, my girl, you gotta keep up. It's New York," Detective Jameson called back. "Okay, I'm heading back to the office. Here's my cab. Taxi!" he shouted. The yellow cab promptly stopped ten feet ahead, and Detective Jameson jumped in.

"See you later!" Grace yelled.

"Okay, doll, what's the scoop with all that?" Elena said, looking Grace up and down.

Caught off guard, Grace smirked. "All what?"

All Elena could do was raise an eyebrow.

"Let's walk and talk," Grace replied with a smile. "I don't know—I find him attractive and he seems interested in me, too." Grace shifted uncomfortably. "We've been hanging out."

"I see that," Elena observed with a sideways glance.

"Look, you're clearly infatuated with a Miami shipping tycoon who's just as taken with you—if you recall our last case," Grace reminded quickly.

"I know, I know," Elena shot back, a mischievous glint in her eyes. "Walter is a real gentleman."

"That he is," Grace agreed.

"Well, you know what you're doing," Elena gently coaxed her friend. "There's never a dull moment with a New York detective."

★★★★

Debra exhaled slowly, settling into the window sill as warm sunlight poured through the towering windows that framed her view of Madison Square Park. Below, a group of children darted joyfully in pursuit of a dog, their laughter mingling with the soft hum of the city. Nearby, parents lounged on a blanket spread across the grass, their peaceful picnic serving as a vivid reminder of the calm just beyond the rehearsal studio. A wave of longing swept over Debra, making her desire to step outdoors undeniable. Her gaze drifted southward, drawn to the iconic silhouette of the Flatiron Building. Its striking, triangular shape had commanded attention since its inception over a century ago, showcasing early 20th-century innovation. The building's distinctive Beaux-Arts details and bold, sloping edges harmonized with the city's vibrant energy.

Choreographer Katherine Goossens clapped her hands to signal the start of the next number to be rehearsed and refined. "The cast of the show will be here in two hours, Debra, so I want to make sure you and Stuart are ready to perform together."

Stuart, the male dancer hired for the part, slowly rose from a split on the floor and walked over to Debra. "Come on, you can do it," he encouraged.

"Tell me," Debra said as she stood and stretched her arms overhead. "You were already in the cast of this show. Why did you have to re-audition?"

Stuart took a big gulp of water and tossed his towel over his neck. "The role I auditioned for was swing dancer. We had a guy hired to perform every male part in the show, but he died backstage."

Debra froze. "Oh really?" she replied, carefully masking the fact that she knew exactly whom he meant.

"Yes. Phillip had to know everyone's routines in case one of the boys called in sick, so he could fill in for their role."

"So, you had to re-audition even though you were already in the cast?" Debra asked, turning her head sideways.

"We sure did. Katherine insisted that any male dancer seeking Phillip's role had to re-audition. It's no secret I had long coveted Phillip's job. But he was as strong as an ox—never missed a show, never fell ill. I thought I'd never have a chance. It's about time," he mumbled.

"Did Katherine get along with him?"

"She clashed with Phillip constantly. Rumor had it she wanted him fired; his overbearing nature always grated on her nerves. They were like oil and water. Now, with Phillip gone, the atmosphere is even more tense."

"How about Ava, the stage manager?"

"What about her?"

"Did she get along with Phillip?"

"Ava gets along with no one. Ava is Ava—bossy, loud, degrading..." Stuart paused and looked Debra in the eyes. "What, are you writing a book or something?"

"Alright," Katherine called out. "Stuart, I want you to dance the Moonlight number with Debra as if you were Jason, and then perform it again as William. They are on opposite sides of the stage, moving in contrast, and I want to see how well you execute the routine while ensuring Debra knows all the steps." She motioned to the piano player. "From the top," she commanded.

Katherine, known for her precision and no-nonsense demeanor, began by breaking down the routines. Debra worked tirelessly to perfect each step, her movements growing sharper with every repetition. At one point, Katherine raised her hand and the music stopped. "Debra, that is a double turn, and the next phrase has an accent on the 1, 3, 5, and 7 counts."

Debra nodded, grateful for the feedback. As the rehearsals progressed, she became fully absorbed in the routines, learning the intricate steps and the emotional nuances of each dance. Stuart's assumption of the male understudy role seemed no coincidence—it was a calculated move aimed at stepping into Phillip's shoes. His ambition was unmistakable, and Debra sensed his deliberate attempts to impress Katherine. Every step he took and every glance he cast was meant to secure his place as more than just a replacement.

"Good, okay—moving on. Let's see the closing number in the first act." Katherine waved to the piano player once again. "Let's take it at the chorus—5, 6, 7, 8."

Debra and Stuart moved effortlessly across the expansive rehearsal space, their movements in perfect harmony as if they were destined to dance together. They flowed seamlessly with the rising melody, each note reinforcing their graceful connection. Debra felt completely at ease with the choreography, as if it had been designed specifically for her body. Stuart, with his broad shoulders and strong legs, complemented her every movement, his grounded presence a striking counterpoint to Debra's petite frame, which radiated powerful bursts of energy and a delicate yet fierce femininity.

"Well, I see I made the right choices with you two," Katherine said. "That was practically perfect. Alright, why don't we take a fifteen-minute break? The cast will be arriving soon."

Debra was exhausted. It had been a long time since she endured the demanding schedule of a Broadway show. Her toes were numb and her neck ached from the many head rolls in the last routine.

"Debra, keep hydrating. The day is only half over and I don't want to lose you. You're doing a great job."

Debra shook her head. "It's your choreography. It fits my body very well."

"I see that." An awkward pause followed as Debra tried to segue into a conversation about Phillip. "Stuart mentioned that your male swing dancer died backstage? That must have been terrible."

Katherine's face tightened. "Yeah, it was really sad—a heart attack. So young. Who knew?" She shrugged. "He was a great dancer." Quickly, she changed the subject. "Does anyone have any questions so far?"

"All I can do is keep rehearsing the routines in my head," Debra managed to say.

As the cast gathered in the rehearsal studio, Debra felt a mix of excitement and anxiety. She was the new girl—the fresh face among the show's experienced performers. Katherine stood at the front with her arms crossed and a serious expression.

"Alright, everyone, let's get started!" Katherine's voice cut through the chatter, demanding immediate attention. "We have a lot to cover today, and I expect nothing less than perfection. Debra and Stuart will be added to every number in the show. So, be patient."

Debra stepped forward, her heart pounding. The music began, and she lost herself in the rhythm, her body moving smoothly as she executed the choreography. She had practiced all morning, and now, under Katherine's watchful eye, she felt the burden of expectation. As she finished, she glanced at Katherine, who nodded slightly with a glimmer of approval.

Throughout the day, the cast made an effort to introduce themselves to Debra, although tension simmered around the new male understudy in Phillip's former role. The group was diverse—some were welcoming, others guarded—and everyone had an opinion.

"He must have given Phillip a heart attack to get that role," Debra overheard one cast member whisper to another.

"We went from bad to worse," remarked two male cast members as Stuart danced past them.

As the rehearsal continued, tensions flared and remarks grew more caustic. During breaks, Debra watched Stuart trying to impress Katherine by overstepping or exaggerating the choreography.

"What is it with you understudies? That's not what we covered this morning. And no, I'm not accepting opinions. There is only one artistic vision here… and it's mine. You're no different than your predecessor."

"She's never happy," Debra heard a voice say from behind her.

It wasn't until 10 p.m. that Debra finally turned the key in the door of her midtown high rise—the one she shared with Francy and Grace.

"Long day for you," Francy greeted her at the door.

"Oh, my goodness, you have no idea."

"Those are the tough rehearsals." Francy's cozy pajamas and fuzzy socks made Debra long for a shower and a bed.

Debra looked around. "Where's Grace?"

"She's out with that Detective—the Brooklynite," Francy smirked.

"Oh, I see. On a reconnaissance mission?"

Francy just threw her hands up and walked into the kitchen.

"I'm heading to the shower and bed. I have rehearsal again tomorrow at 9 a.m.," Debra called out. "I'll tell you, there is a lot of animosity and jealousy in that cast."

"The usual," Francy shouted back from the kitchen.

"Not many good words about Phillip either, I might add."

"Anything sound like a lead?" Francy said after downing a large glass of milk.

"Definitely some motives, but I'm not sure if any of them could go as far as poisoning a castmate. I'm going to keep my ear open."

"Well, I'm heading out," Francy continued, her voice cutting through the quiet of the living room as she leaned forward. "Drew's been in touch with an old friend who works at a downtown nightclub. Apparently, there's an underground art auction tonight at the club. His friend thinks it might be worth checking out."

Debra raised an eyebrow, intrigued but skeptical. "An illegal art auction? That must be common in a city like this, doesn't it?"

Francy shrugged slightly, but Debra's interest was clearly piqued. "I'm going to get ready," Francy said as she closed her bedroom door.

Debra pulled her cell phone from her dance bag and speed dialed Drew.

"Mi amor," she greeted him. "Francy mentioned you're off to some questionable art auction?"

"Phillip had a famous piece on his wall that was reported stolen years ago. Marcus Larson told us it's private collectors who snatch up most of these one-of-a-kind pieces—sometimes through less-than-legal means. You know me, Debra; I've always been intrigued by what drives people—the hidden thoughts and feelings that influence their decisions."

"I know, it's your gift," Debra agreed.

"There's something captivating about peeling back those layers, trying to understand what shapes a person's motives, how they react, and what triggers their actions," Drew confessed to Debra.

"I know," she assured him. "Do you need me to join you?"

"No, there's no need. Besides, you should rest for tomorrow's rehearsal. Francy and Israel will accompany me. How did rehearsal go? How was the cast?"

"Catty," Debra replied, her tone sharp and clipped.

"Now, there's a shocker," Drew remarked with a hint of sarcasm.

"Keep your eyes and ears open."

Debra noticed the tension in his voice. "I know," she said steadily, her voice underscored by quiet understanding. "The past few days have been a whirlwind of strange events. We learned our friend was poisoned, you and Francy were targeted by gunfire, Israel and Aisha are pursuing someone through the city center, Grace and Elena are searching morgues for answers, we've uncovered secret codes, discovered an enigmatic key, and here I am, trying to expose a killer amid the chaos of a Broadway show." She exhaled slowly. "You don't have to bear all of this alone. There's no need to maintain a façade for us."

Drew's tone shifted, his words laden with unspoken truths. "I can't fully explain it, but it feels like we're barreling toward the unknown."

Debra's voice softened as she reminded him of their shared purpose. "Remember, we're a team. We stand together. Always."

Drew allowed himself a brief moment of relief as the tension eased from his shoulders. "I appreciate that, Debra. What I do know is that our friend had a piece of stolen art hanging on his wall. There's a shadowy underworld where rare masterpieces are exchanged, slipping through the cracks of legitimate markets into the hands of the elite. Maybe that's what got him killed? Tonight's auction isn't just about watching—it's our chance to uncover the hidden factors driving the art world's black market."

"I understand," Debra said with resolute determination. "It's more than an opportunity. It's a clue we need to follow."

Drew felt the determination strengthen him. "This isn't just about curiosity; it's about grasping the pulse of a secretive world. The deeper we go, the nearer we get to the truth."

"Then you're on the right path. But tread carefully."

# Chapter 8
## Alphabet City

Fiona St James was a flamboyant and extravagant figure in New York's vibrant downtown nightlife. With his striking appearance—donning a tight black bustier, a wig reminiscent of Marilyn Monroe, flawless makeup, and a radiant smile—he effortlessly commanded attention. Although he stood tall in 4-inch heels, Fiona showcased grace and poise. Positioned at the nightclub entrance, he guarded the door like a veteran.

As Drew approached, Fiona exclaimed, "Sweeeetie!" while raising both arms high. He confidently strode over to greet Drew, bending gracefully on one knee to deliver air kisses before wrapping both arms around him in a tight, warm hug.

"I should have known you'd be in charge of this shindig," Drew declared, tightening his embrace. He then introduced his friends: "Fiona, meet Francy and Israel. Fiona and I used to dance together back in the day."

Fiona shared an expressive smile as he exclaimed, "Finally… some people with human heads! You two cuties absolutely must come dance with me!" With a high-pitched screech, he spun around and playfully tapped the shoulder of the stoic, burly bouncer who stood motionless beside the red velvet rope. "Sweetie," he cooed, "it's not going to open itself!"

Momentarily caught off guard, the bouncer looked at Fiona with an unwavering expression before realizing that he was meant to open the ropes and allow Drew and his friends inside. A look of recognition crossed the bouncer's face.

"Ahhh, there it is," Fiona said with a mischievous grin as the bouncer bent down and unhooked the rope.

"Walk this way!" Fiona called, striding down the steep staircase before them and leading Drew, Francy, and Israel through the gilded doors into a world of darkness and debauchery.

The palatial underground nightclub pulsed with dark purple light as the house music reverberated off the towering 10-foot chandeliers suspended along the center of the dance floor. The crowd parted as Fiona's admirers greeted him with waves and air kisses. He acknowledged each fan with puckered lips, calling them by name—"Sweetie, how are you? Sweetie, you look amazing! Sweetie, long time no see."

Almost instantly, DJ Rocca skillfully blended one of the club's most popular dance tracks with a familiar house favorite, prompting the crowd to erupt in recognition.

"Oooyyeee!" Fiona shouted exuberantly. "I love this song. Let's dance!" He grabbed Israel and spun him around so they faced each other, one hand running down his chest. Then, he reached for Francy's arm and pulled her close behind him. The two dancers quickly complied, enclosing Fiona as they moved passionately to the pulsing beat from the club's advanced sound system.

Drew quickly noticed a familiar face push past him in the crowd. "Mr. Larson?" he called over the deafening music. "Hey, that's Mr. Larson from the Whitney Museum." He turned to see his three friends lost in the music on the dance floor, unaware of his call.

Pushing through the dense crowd and keeping a close eye on the museum curator, Drew maneuvered past partygoers writhing in his path. Larson's stature made him an unmistakable target, drawing Drew further into the disco. "Now, where are you headed?" Drew mumbled as he found himself near the back of the club. Glancing left and right, he finally spotted Larson in the distance pushing through a door concealed behind red velvet curtains.

Drew reached the wall and pulled back the curtain just as the door clicked shut. "Damn it," he murmured, chastising himself for falling behind. Frustrated, he tugged on the door, rattled the handle, and pushed against the metal frame, but it refused to budge.

Breathing heavily, he stepped back in defeat, watching the red velvet curtains engulf the door.

"Well, sweetie...it's not going to open itself."

Drew turned to see Fiona standing tall in 4-inch stilettos, a key card elegantly held between his perfectly manicured nails. Flanked by Francy and Israel—who watched like steadfast sentinels—Fiona, the Marilyn Monroe lookalike, exuded an almost superhero-like aura.

Drew stammered, "I-I didn't think..." as he struggled for words.

"I saw you dash out of the corner of my eye," Fiona slurred in his Bronx accent, pursing his lips. "Nothing escapes me, honey. I even brought backup."

Francy and Israel exchanged proud glances.

"There is a secret auction tonight. They're selling rare art once believed lost or stolen," Fiona informed them. "Remember, this is why I called you."

Fiona drew back the velvet curtain and swiped his key card. The door clicked as Israel pulled it open, allowing his friends to descend further into the club's basement. Then, Fiona reached into his bustier, retrieved two additional plastic key cards, and handed one to each guest.

"That's only three key cards. What about yours?" Drew contested.

"Don't worry about me. Put these around your neck and don't question me," Fiona said with a smirk.

As they descended the staircase, the pulsating bass of the dance club receded into a haunting echo, giving way to a refined, classical atmosphere. The dark blue lighting was complemented by the vibrant strains of violins performing a soft sonata that welcomed guests into the exclusive realm of underground art.

Two security guards blocked their path. "Let me handle these two bricks," Fiona whispered. "Sweeties," he exclaimed, opening both arms towards the security guards as if he were greeting old friends.

"IDs," one guard barked rudely.

Fiona signaled Drew and his friends to move ahead; their badges briefly caught the light as they slipped through the large black door behind the men. "I'll be right with you," Fiona offered a wide, reassuring smile.

"Come on, guys, let's go." Drew herded Francy and Israel into the next room.

"Mr. Larson," Drew exclaimed.

The curator stood in the center of a round, carpeted foyer, eyeing the two choices before him—a red door on his left guarded by a beautifully dressed Asian woman, or a green door on his right watched over by an equally attractive Scandinavian woman.

"Ahhh, hello," Mr. Larson greeted, clearly surprised to see Drew. "Are you buying art for Mr. Belltone?" he asked, his tone laced with astonishment.

"Mr. Larson, what a pleasant surprise," Drew replied with a smile. "Are you buying art for the museum?"

Almost taken aback by the question, Mr. Larson quickly responded, "Oh no, no, heavens no." He twitched nervously, glancing around as if searching for someone.

"These are my associates, Francy and Israel."

"How do you do?" Mr. Larson asked politely. "Are you both art buyers as well?"

"Enthusiasts!" Israel answered, adjusting his dark-rimmed glasses.

Several people entered the foyer. Meanwhile, the group of classical musicians positioned between the red and green doors continued playing a soothing melody that encouraged the buyers forward.

Mr. Larson scanned the room as if expecting to recognize someone, then leaned in and whispered, "What did Matisse, Picasso, and Renu have in common?" He paused as if to let Drew answer, then continued, "They all hid clues in their paintings."

"I've heard such things could be true," Drew echoed.

"Leonardo da Vinci hid secrets in his paintings," Mr. Larson boasted.

"For example, the letters 'L' and 'V' are concealed behind the right pupil of the Mona Lisa, and the letters 'B', 'S', and 'E' are hidden behind her left pupil."

"How intriguing," Francy chimed in, nudging Israel playfully. Her eyes shone with curiosity, mirroring the excitement in the room.

"An art historian in Spain claims to have discovered the number '72'—or perhaps 'L2'—etched beneath the bridge behind the Mona Lisa!" Mr. Larson's voice grew louder with each word as his passion for art history sparked interest in everyone.

Drew, ever the pragmatist, raised an eyebrow and interjected, "So, what treasures are you hoping to uncover tonight?" His attempt to steer the conversation back was met with a knowing smile from Francy, who appreciated Drew's grounded approach.

Clearing his throat and tempering his excitement, Mr. Larson explained, "Well, it's rumored that the number '72' could be the key to a hidden cache of Renaissance artworks—possibly even lost sketches by da Vinci himself. Imagine works lost to time, waiting to be rediscovered!" His eyes gleamed as he added, "And 'L2'? Some speculate it might refer to a location, perhaps a secret chamber or a forgotten gallery that holds the very essence of the Renaissance."

Francy leaned closer, her voice barely above a whisper. "But why hide such treasures? What could be so valuable that it needed to be concealed?"

Mr. Larson shrugged, undeterred. "Ah, that's the mystery, isn't it? Some believe it was to protect the works from destruction during the turmoil of the French Revolution. Others think it was simply to keep them safe from art thieves roaming the streets of Paris. Whatever the reason, the thrill of the hunt drives us, doesn't it?"

Drew nodded, his skepticism softening. "So, what do we do? How do we begin to search for these treasures?"

"Well," Mr. Larson said in a conspiratorial tone, "tonight we gather clues. There are whispers of an old map hidden in La Croix's painting, called Hidden Places, that might lead us to New York's greatest antiquities. If we can find it, we might just uncover the truth behind his identity and the secrets it holds."

Israel's eyes widened with excitement. "A treasure hunt! Count me in! But where do we start?"

Mr. Larson grinned, his enthusiasm infectious. "It is being auctioned off tonight—along with the Cadenza Wheel by Rene and a 16th-century astrological globe said to have belonged to Nostradamus himself!"

"These are exciting times," Israel echoed Mr. Larson's excitement.

"Yes, but which door do we choose?" Francy asked.

"Why the green door, of course," Mr. Larson replied as he glanced at their key cards. "Except you," he pointed to Drew. "You have the red door! You must really know someone in the organization."

In surprise, everyone checked their key cards to confirm Mr. Larson's claim. "Yeah, I really know someone…" Drew murmured.

"Fiona!" Drew exclaimed as his iconic downtown friend entered accompanied by two security guards.

"Oh, there you are! I'd like you to meet… ah, what are your names again?" Fiona didn't wait for an answer. "My boys," he drawled. They were just showing me around. He quickly flirted with one and then the other.

One of the security guards held up two fingers in signal to the women waiting at the door.

"Please, we are starting soon," the Asian woman announced.

"We need everyone inside," the Scandinavian woman said to the remaining crowd in the foyer.

"Thanks, boys," Fiona said, motioning to the security guards. "We'll see you inside." Then Fiona quickly gathered Drew and waved to Francy, Israel, and Mr. Larson as they dispersed into their respective rooms.

"I don't even want to know how you managed all that," Drew whispered in Fiona's ear as they flashed their key cards and walked in.

"Will your friends be all right?" Fiona cooed.

"They will manage. And how did you ever get your hands on these key cards?" Drew offered a tentative smile as he watched his two friends vanish through the green door.

"Red's my favorite color, anyway," Fiona boasted as they disappeared into a world they had not yet imagined.

The green auction room was dimly lit yet lavish. The walls were draped with deep emerald velvet curtains that cascaded to the floor, casting soft shadows over the polished marble.

"What are we doing, hidden away in a nightclub basement in Alphabet City on the outskirts of Manhattan?" Francy asked, grabbing Israel's arm. "I don't understand how Phillip got involved in all this."

"Don't worry, mama. It's all going to work out. You'll see," Israel assured her, pushing his glasses further up his nose.

"I hope you're recording all of this," Francy said, squeezing Israel's arm.

"These glasses are amazing!" Israel remarked.

They both looked up to see a low-hanging chandelier, its soft golden light shimmering gently, just enough to bathe the polished mahogany furniture scattered throughout the room. A sleek black lacquer podium served as the focal point, its sharp edges glistening under the spotlight.

Marcus Larson nodded in the opposite direction, signaling that he was awaiting someone.

Francy nudged Israel. "Look who it is."

"Who is that?" Israel asked, his curiosity evident.

"Jonathon Mathews, Mr. Belltone's art curator," Francy whispered.

"Mr. Belltone has both rooms covered," Marcus Larson explained to Francy. "I guess that's one way to get access to art… having a broker in every room."

"A broker?" Israel inquired.

"Yes, you know—someone who negotiates on your behalf," Marcus stated matter-of-factly.

"Francy, how are you?" Jonathon said as he stepped behind her, speaking close to her ear.

"Jonathon, how are you? Looking for rare art?" Francy managed nervously, uncertain of what to say.

"What brings you here?" Jonathon asked, a curious expression on his face as he turned to Marcus for an explanation.

"She's here with me," Israel interjected. "I need something for my bathroom wall," he blurted out before softening his tone with a warm smile.

"Well, it's nice to see you again." Jonathon scanned her briefly. "I must confess, I'm searching for art for a client with questionable tastes," he admitted, biting his lower lip.

"I guess we're all in the same boat," Israel remarked. "I won't tell if you won't…" he added with a nervous laugh.

Jonathon then turned and walked away.

"He's rather intense," Israel commented to Francy.

"Artist. Temperamental," she replied.

The auctioneer, dressed in a smartly cut suit, stepped confidently to the podium. The fact that he was about to present stolen art did not faze him at all. He introduced the first piece: "Look here. This is the Seax of Beagnoth, a 10th-century Anglo-Saxon knife found in the Thames estuary in 1857. The knife is decorated with copper, brass, and silver patterns. One side of the blade features the complete 28-letter Anglo-Saxon runic alphabet, along with the name 'Beagnoth' in runes." He paused for the crowd's reaction. "The runes likely had a magical purpose, and Beagnoth could be the name of either the owner or the blacksmith. This is one of the rare pieces with runes directly on the blade. We will start bidding at five hundred thousand."

"Looks like a kitchen knife to me," Israel whispered.

"The piece up for auction was taken from the British Museum," Mr. Larson confided to Israel. "I must have this Viking knife," he insisted as he raised his key card.

"Five hundred thousand," the auctioneer acknowledged. "Do we have six?"

Another key card was raised at the front of the room.

"I see you… six hundred thousand! Can we go to seven?"

Mr. Larson's key card shot up swiftly and precisely.

"Seven hundred thousand! Do we have eight? Eight hundred thousand?"

A few cards were raised, but Mr. Larson's kept appearing with a firm snap.

"Eight hundred thousand! Nine hundred thousand!"

The bids surged. Additional key cards were lifted, yet Mr. Larson's card remained ever-present and unfazed.

"He's relentless," Francy remarked in disbelief.

"One million! I have one million. Do I have one point two million?"

The tension mounted as the room grew tense, and eyes darted to see who might falter first. The auctioneer's voice cut through the quiet alongside the soft rustling of the crowd as the bid escalated.

"One point five million!" someone called out while raising their key card.

More cards were raised, and Mr. Larson's appeared again, fueling the bidding war.

"Two million!" the auctioneer declared.

A hush fell as all eyes turned toward Mr. Larson. Without hesitation, his card shot upward once more.

"Two point five million!" the auctioneer challenged.

The atmosphere buzzed with energy. The stakes had never been higher, yet Mr. Larson's card remained steady and confident.

"Three million!"

A brief silence ensued. No one else raised their card, and the crowd held its breath.

"Going once! Going twice!" Mr. Larson's card was the only one still raised, his grip unwavering.

"Sold! For three million dollars!" The auctioneer's mallet struck the lacquered podium with finality.

The room erupted in subdued murmurs. Mr. Larson's calm smile barely changed as he nodded, his prize secured. "A worthy acquisition," he murmured.

"Impressive," Francy commented.

★★★

In another part of the basement, the red auction room felt even more secret. Drew's eyes scanned the room, noting the stone walls—worn from years of concealment—and adorned with intricate hangings whose colors ran deep and muted. The subtle glow of sconces softened the dark shadows with ambient light. Drew also sensed the aroma of expensive cigars mixed with a hint of whiskey.

"You always know where the shady places are," Drew whispered to Fiona.

"I know. I almost felt a little guilty," Fiona joked. "You said Phillip was involved in something dubious…what could be more questionable than this?"

The auctioneer stepped forward with practiced grace, surveying the crowd before announcing the piece on offer. "Good evening. Our first item, a long-lost painting by elusive artist La Croix, titled Hidden Places, acquired from the Prague Museum in 2017…"

"Acquired…huh," Fiona commented. Eyes shifted his way.

"…we now have it here for you. Bidding starts at one million dollars."

"That's a painting I was just looking at in the La Croix catalog at the Whitney." Drew was in shock.

"Since when are you into modern art?" Fiona looked at Drew with equal shock.

"Phillip had the other painting—stolen from the Prague Museum and displayed on the wall in his apartment!"

"Surely he didn't steal it," Fiona shook his head in disbelief.

"Of course not. But how did he acquire it?"

The auction room vibrated with tension. Shadows of eager faces moved across the walls as the stolen painting, its vibrant colors still defiant against its tainted past, was slowly revealed under the spotlight. The room fell silent for a heartbeat, and then the bidding began.

"Ladies and gentlemen, the piece you've all been waiting for—an original painting, long lost and now resurfacing with a history as rich as its brushstrokes. Let the bidding commence at one million dollars!"

A single bidder raised his key card, and a ripple of excitement spread through the crowd.

"I see you. Do I have one million five?"

A few more key cards went up, the bids escalating faster than anyone could track. Phones began to ring as brokers scrambled to answer.

"Two million. Bid two million," one broker announced.

"Two, I have two. Do I have two million five?" the auctioneer shouted.

"Three million. Yes, three million," responded another broker on a cell phone.

The room pulsed with the speed of the escalating bids, the sound of desperation rising with each new offer. Drew and Fiona stood close to the front, their eyes locked on the painting, still trying to grasp the chaos unfolding before them. The price soared with every passing second.

"I have five million!" The auctioneer pointed to a man in the far corner, his face shrouded in shadow.

The room fell silent. Five million—an astonishing sum for a stolen piece of art—yet the desire for it was unmistakable. Drew's gaze met Fiona's; both exchanged silent shock.

"Five million. Going once... going twice...!"

A murmur of disbelief passed through the room as all eyes fixed on the raised key card. The crowd waited, and frantic phone calls filled the background as brokers whispered to their anonymous clients.

"Sold for five million dollars!"

A wave of tension broke over the room, and voices buzzed in confusion.

"Who in the world would pay that much for it?" Fiona whispered to Drew.

Drew scanned the room, his instincts alerting him to something amiss. "We need to find out who that was."

They both turned toward the bidder on the phone. They watched him hang up and slip away toward the back of the room. Drew moved forward, trying to catch a glimpse of him—a man clad in a brim hat and pinstriped suit. But it was too late; the bidder had already melted into the shadows of the underground space.

"Where does that door lead?" Drew asked Fiona as they maneuvered through the crowd.

"It's the employee locker room, I think," Fiona replied as they pushed through the throng already immersed in the next bidding. The auction noise persisted as they burst through the door, their footsteps echoing in the cavernous hallway. Ahead of them was a grand staircase with an ornate banister gleaming under the dim light.

Without hesitation, they ran up the stairs, their breaths quick and shallow.

"They have to be here to claim their prize, don't they?" Drew gasped, now out of breath. Reaching the top, he glanced over his shoulder, heart pounding. Fiona was already dashing down a narrow corridor to the left. He followed, his mind frantically seeking a plan.

"No one leaves with their winnings," Fiona whispered. "They do that to secure the art." Fiona paused abruptly, his hand on the doorknob of the first room. Turning to Drew, his eyes wide with urgency, he said, "In here." They slipped into the room, closing the door quietly behind them. Fiona switched on the lights, revealing lockers and benches arranged before them. He wiped his forehead and sank onto a locker room bench. "Damn it," he cursed, "I got a run in my stockings! These were brand new!"

"Where could he have gone?" Drew panted.

"There must be doors that lead to the parking alley behind the building," Fiona said, gesturing behind him.

Suddenly, they heard a door spring closed—a heavy thud echoing in the distance.

Drew raced to the back of the locker room. He spotted a rusty exit sign pointing down a narrow hallway. "It's here," he called out. Fiona met him at the doorway. "Come on, let's go," Drew instructed.

The door opened into an alley. A band of early morning light was just touching a row of garbage cans at the end of the narrow street. "He's gone," Fiona exhaled.

"Hold the door," Drew said as he stepped into the alley. He paced from one end of the street to the other, but there was no sign of the man.

★★★

The green auction room buzzed with excitement as art mongers fixated on a notorious object. Their eyes shone with an almost predatory delight as they surveyed the stolen treasure.

"Showing here, the Red Trinket Box, once owned by the fourth emperor of the Qing dynasty, Qianlong, whose reign was one of the longest in Chinese history. This is made of cinnabar and red ochre. It is a locked box containing mysterious contents."

The guests maintained a cool, controlled demeanor, but their eyes betrayed their involvement in something far from ordinary as they focused intently on the ancient treasure.

"Everyone looks starstruck," Israel whispered to Marcus Larson.

"This piece has made the rounds. It's rumored to have been owned by kings who stole it from emperors and passed through the hands of infamous art thieves who smuggled it across continents. Legends say it was once hidden in the catacombs beneath the Louvre, only to reappear decades later in the private collection of a notorious underground dealer in Rome." Marcus was sweating—he too was affected by the ancient box. "Its history is as shadowed as the dark corners where secrets like these are kept, and no one truly knows how many lives it has either upended or enriched."

"Bidding starts at two million." The auctioneer signaled the start, and bids began pouring in. Francy noticed Jonathon Matthews raising his key card repeatedly while talking on the phone.

"Four million five," the auctioneer announced, pointing to a woman dressed entirely in black. A veil draped over her head added an element of mystery while obscuring her identity.

"Five million," Marcus Larson responded, catching Francy and Israel by surprise.

"Got a big bidder on the phone?" Israel asked, glancing at Marcus.

There was no response from Larson.

The woman in black raised her key card. "Six million!"

"Seven million," Jonathon Matthews called over the din of the crowd, raising his key card frantically.

"Seven million," the auctioneer confirmed as he pointed to Jonathon. "How about seven million five?"

The crowd murmured in disbelief. Marcus Larson remained on the phone.

The woman in black raised her key card again.

Silence fell over the room as the auctioneer took control. "Seven million, five hundred thousand. Going once, going twice…" He paused before declaring, "Sold to the lady in black," his gavel striking the lacquered podium to signal the final bid.

Francy looked across the room. Jonathon Matthews, still on the phone, shook his head in disappointment—angry. She glanced at Marcus Larson, who appeared distraught as the surrounding crowd expressed their disbelief.

"Well, you win some, you lose some," Israel said, turning toward Marcus Larson with advice.

All Marcus could do was smirk.

"You still have your expensive knife," Israel added, attempting to console him.

"Well, there's always tomorrow's auction," Francy smiled.

# Chapter 9
## Rockefeller Plaza

Veronica Belltone stood at the entrance to the opulent Rainbow Room, a vision of grace and poise. Her jeweled crimson gown and matching shoes sparkled in the light, announcing her as a force to be reckoned with. On her arm was New York's leviathan, her husband Richard Belltone, clad in a black tuxedo that exuded understated elegance. His presence was commanding, though his eyes revealed a subtle unease as he surveyed the gathering.

As they entered, the room fell silent, and the three hundred guests instinctively parted to create a path for the couple toward the revolving central dance floor. The floor rotated gracefully, lending a dynamic focal point to the space. Tiered seating encircled it, providing unobstructed views of both the floor and the panoramic cityscape seen through the floor-to-ceiling windows.

Veronica's smile was warm, yet her gaze seemed distant, as though her thoughts wandered far beyond the festivities. Richard, ever attentive, rested a reassuring hand on her back.

Perched on the 65th floor of 30 Rockefeller Plaza, the iconic Rainbow Room symbolized New York City's timeless elegance and architectural grandeur. It was also the space the Belltones would convert into a distinguished venue where art met finance, music met dance, gourmet cuisine mingled with philanthropy each year.

The couple approached Francy and Drew. Francy greeted them with a knowing smile, her eyes briefly meeting Richard's in a silent understanding. Drew offered a polite nod, his curiosity piqued by the subtle tension in the air.

Veronica turned to Richard, her voice a soft murmur. "I hope everything is in order for tonight," she said, her concern evident.

Richard nodded, his expression unreadable. "Of course," he replied, though his tone lacked conviction.

Veronica Belltone loved such social events. They made her feel like the belle of the ball once again, even as she carried the quiet sorrow of a lost son and the marks of time on her mind. That sadness shone in her eyes, reflecting the heavy burden she still bore. Yet tonight was about celebration.

As she extended her hand to Francy, her lips parted in a delicate smile. "Francy, it's important that you, Drew, and your friends are here to enjoy the evening."

Francy smiled warmly.

"It's been far too long since we celebrated anything," Veronica said. Turning to Drew, she added, "You should know that Richard and I truly appreciate you considering helping us find clarity following our son's passing."

"It's our pleasure, Mrs. Belltone," Drew responded, and he couldn't help but note the genuine joy in her voice.

Veronica turned to her right and took the hand of the woman standing just behind her. "I want you to meet my dear friend, Jeanne Lois Van Italie."

Francy quickly smiled and extended her hand. "How do you do?" she asked as she leaned over. Jeanne Lois replied, smiling, "I am truly enjoying the art and festive atmosphere tonight."

"Are you a painter?" Francy inquired.

"Oh no, I dabble—just a bit. But I appreciate modern art," Jeanne Lois responded with a smile aimed at Mrs. Belltone, as if seeking her approval.

"She's a connoisseur of art, my dear," Veronica added, prompting Mrs. Belltone and Jeanne Lois to exchange a knowing glance.

Jeanne Lois Van Italie appeared to be in her early 40s and exuded an air of sophistication beyond her years. "An old soul in a young body," Francy recalled Phillip always saying about young women who appeared worldly. She was of average height with a slender and graceful build that carried the poise often associated with athletic discipline. Her heart-shaped face featured high cheekbones and a delicate jawline, and her fair skin had a natural, healthy glow.

Realizing who Francy was, Jeanne Lois reacted swiftly. "Oh, you're one of those detectives," she gasped, turning to Mrs. Belltone for confirmation.

"Go on, dear, we are all friends here," Mrs. Belltone encouraged. Drew exchanged a look with Francy, his eyes conveying that their presence was not meant to be hidden. Leaning close, he whispered, "So much discretion."

"And you are Drew, correct?" Jeanne Lois addressed him.

"Hi, yes, I'm Drew," he replied, taking her hand and gently kissing it.

Jeanne Lois blushed at his gesture. "A detective and a gentleman," she remarked. Her deep hazel eyes, framed by long lashes, radiated warmth and introspection as she flirted with Drew. She swept her long chestnut hair away from her face, accentuating her playful charm.

Veronica's eyes wandered slowly across the expansive space, smiling at the display of artworks by emerging artists. The 23-piece dance orchestra played her favorite tunes from the 1930s in the background. She moved toward a large sofa, where Jonathon Matthews appeared unexpectedly and assisted her in taking a seat.

"Lovely, Jonathon. I appreciate the choice of artists you have selected for this event. Thank you." She addressed him with respect as she and her friend observed the new installations.

"Francy, it's always nice to see you," Jonathon extended an arm as Francy followed the women to the chaise.

The tension within the group was unspoken, yet Drew sensed an undercurrent of uncertainty. "Where did you find these unique artists?" Drew asked Jonathon.

After a brief pause, he replied, "In the streets and nightclubs of New York," accompanied by a playful wink.

Jeanne Lois gave a nervous laugh.

Francy observed the interaction. Jeanne Lois's gaze lingered on Jonathon a moment longer than necessary, a glimmer of something unreadable passing between them. She then turned her attention back to Veronica, her smile unwavering.

Jonathon, ever the art enthusiast, quickly turned to engage in another conversation with a guest, his animated gestures standing in contrast to the subdued atmosphere.

Mr. Belltone tapped Drew on the shoulder. "I know it's not the time or place…"

"It's always the time and place," Drew interrupted. "What's going on? How are you doing?"

"About the picture of the key you sent me— that key was in my office. Whoever torched the servers tried to steal it from a display case."

"'What is the key for?'" Drew inquired.

"It was the key to a box once owned by my father, Damon. According to him, he acquired the antique at a market in Beijing in the late sixties."

"This box has an intriguing history. How do you think it fits into our investigation?" Drew asked.

"I honestly can't say. The box was stolen from my father during a home invasion in the early eighties. It was empty, and the key was stored separately in a secure location. After his passing, I displayed the key in my office as a tribute. The box was useless without it."

"So, the person who set your servers on fire was also stealing the key. That is odd," Drew remarked. "Aisha and Israel followed this individual downtown to a warehouse near the Brooklyn Bridge. Does this mean anything to you?"

"It does not," Mr. Belltone considered. "I also have some news. The police recovered several 22-caliber bullets from the buildings on Park Avenue where you were chased by that black Mercedes."

"I was wondering about that," Drew nodded.

"Police traced them to a gun stolen from a shop in New Jersey about three years ago."

"Did you get anything on your camera footage from the Waldorf lobby?"

Richard retrieved his cellphone and brought up two photos from the security camera. "Do you recognize these two men?"

Drew leaned toward Mr. Belltone, grimacing at the photographs of the two men suspected of assaulting three staff members at the Waldorf Astoria. The first man, in his early 40s with short, dark hair and a medium build, wore a black leather jacket with rolled-up sleeves and sported a noticeable tattoo of a dragon on his left forearm. The second man, appearing to be in his early 50s with graying hair and a stockier frame, wore a blue denim jacket and bore a pronounced scar along his right cheek.

"Detective Jameson reported that nothing surfaced in the criminal database; he will conduct a deeper investigation."

"Is Liam, your building manager, going to be alright?"

"Yes, he will recover, and my security guard and doorman are expected to be fine." Mr. Belltone shook his head as he contemplated the consequences.

"Can you send me the images of these suspects?" Drew asked. "I want my team to have these photos. Speaking of which…"

"Mr. and Mrs. Belltone, allow me to introduce Grace, Elena, Israel, Debra, and Aisha," Drew said, his voice warm with pride.

Grace offered a firm handshake, her admiration evident.

"Such beautiful braids, my dear," Mrs. Belltone complimented.

Elena nodded with a welcoming smile.

"Our Phillip was a big fan of your music," Mr. Belltone added with a smile.

Israel adjusted his glasses and gave a courteous nod. "Pleased to meet you both," he said.

Debra extended a friendly hand, her enthusiasm evident.

Mrs. Belltone complimented Debra on her matching dress choice. "We look great in this color," she said with a smile.

Aisha smiled warmly, exuding confidence.

"My dear, you are even more beautiful in person than you appear in your films," Mr. Belltone remarked enthusiastically.

Veronica Belltone observed each team member with keen interest. "It's a pleasure to meet all of you," she remarked warmly. "I feel as though I've known you for some time." Her comment, though subtle, hinted at her deep familiarity with Drew's team and the high expectations she held.

"Well, tonight is your event," Drew announced.

"And we hope you have a beautiful evening," Francy encouraged.

"Enjoy your dinner," Mr. Belltone added as he escorted his wife to their table.

"That was sweet," Aisha smiled as she watched the couple make their way to the front of the room, eager to reach their seats before being surrounded by guests offering their congratulations. The couple's journey was a delicate dance, winding through clusters of well-wishers, each eager to share their joy.

The team moved toward their table, located at the foot of the dance floor. The table faced outward, with the Empire State Building illuminated in red and blue lights behind the spectacular glass panes. The crystal "curtains" on the windows and the glass balustrades transformed the exterior light into dancing rainbows, adding a touch of whimsy to the sophisticated setting.

As the orchestra's harmonious strains from a bygone era filled the air, the waitstaff emerged gracefully to attend each table. They adorned the settings with an array of exquisite appetizers and placed decanters of fine wine, setting the stage for an unforgettable dining experience.

The main course arrived with a flourish: a perfectly seared, tender steak accompanied by a succulent lobster tail, embodying the classic surf and turf combination. The steak, cooked to perfection, boasted a rich, smoky flavor and a melt-in-your-mouth texture. The lobster, with delicate meat that was sweet and buttery, reflected the ocean's bounty.

The feast was complemented by an abundance of side dishes—each more delectable than the last—and an ample selection of wines, their complex notes enhancing the flavors of the meal. The evening unfolded like a symphony of taste and elegance, leaving an indelible impression on the Belltone guests.

"Alright, everyone, now that we are staying in different parts of the city, we might be safer, but we are less likely to get our facts together," Drew said, moving closer so all could hear him over the music. "Let's try to piece this together. Aisha, you found an odd-looking key that our arsonist dropped in Belltone's office."

"He must have had it on his person, because I heard something metallic drop when he hit the floor. That's when I found it," Aisha explained.

"I just confirmed with Mr. Belltone that the key was in a display case in his office. It belonged to an old box his father picked up years ago in China. The box was stolen from the Belltone home during a previous home invasion."

"This could be a long shot," Francy wondered, "but we saw a very old and mysterious Asian box bought at an auction by a woman dressed in black. She seemed confident in her bid. She outbid Jonathon Matthews and the museum curator, Marcus Larson, by a million dollars. They both appeared very interested in it."

"Yeah, but so did the whole room," Israel reminded her.

Drew could only shake his head. "The good thing is, Israel was able to retrieve the autopsy from Mr. Belltone's computer before the arsonist set Belltone's servers on fire." Drew patted Israel on the back.

"And thanks to Aisha and Israel, we got the autopsy report into Dr. Stevens' hands. He was the protégé of Dr. Foster, who did the original autopsy," Grace confirmed.

"He definitely believes that both Dr. Foster and our dear Phillip were poisoned. He is reviewing tissue and hair samples to confirm the type of poison used, its indications, and how it could have been administered," Elena stated, finishing the glass of wine in front of her.

"Speaking of which," Drew continued, "have we considered the connection between Phillip and the theatre? Debra, what are you hearing from the cast?"

"You know theatre folks," Debra said, leaning in. "There's always some gossip. If you give someone a lead, they'll run with it. Katherine the choreographer, Ava the stage manager, and Stuart the understudy all had negative things to say about Phillip. I even heard some cast members make unkind remarks about him." Frustrated, Debra swept her blond hair from her chignon and rewrapped it. "We start rehearsals in the theatre tomorrow. I'll have a better opportunity to look into it."

"What about the mystery man who dropped the key Aisha found? He tried to burn down the Belltone office and destroy their servers. That's a significant escalation—a sign of desperation," Drew suggested. "The killer knows we're getting closer, and they're frightened."

"They?" Grace asked.

"There are multiple people involved here. Mr. Belltone confirmed that he has two suspects who attacked his staff at the Waldorf. I've just texted everyone their photos."

"So, we have a series of events: a mysterious key, a stolen painting, a book of secrets, a home invasion, Drew and I being shot at, a fire at Belltone's office, and two deaths by poison. All seemingly connected." Francy shook her head in disbelief.

"But how? What's the link between all these incidents?"

"The personal attack on the Belltone son appears to have triggered this chain of events. The fire, the key theft, and the server destruction suggest a personal vendetta."

"We need to investigate these connections. Phillip was poisoned to silence him or prevent further incidents," Drew said, overwhelmed by his thoughts.

"I'll review the data on Belltone's servers. I also secured backup copies of some suspicious files," Israel said quietly.

"We begin rehearsal in the theatre tomorrow. I'll try to gather more details from the cast," Debra confirmed.

"I'll examine the link between Phillip and Dr. Fosters' death and check for further updates from Dr. Stevens," Elena noted.

"I'll check if Detective Jameson has uncovered more leads on our two suspects," Grace said with a smile.

"Francy, Aisha, and I will follow up with Marcus Larson at the museum tomorrow to gather more information about last night's auction," Drew added.

"Be mindful of your surroundings and choose your conversations carefully. Someone seems to be one step ahead of us, anticipating our moves," Drew warned, his expression stern. "Just be careful."

The group nodded in agreement, each determined to uncover the truth behind the mysterious events.

"That's too much wine," Drew said as he stood up from the table. "I'm heading to the men's room."

Drew moved past couples dancing to the orchestra's rendition of Blue Danube. He walked along the wall of windows toward a back bar, illuminated by concentric circles of light from the ceiling.

In a shadowed back hallway, Drew recognized Mr. Belltone's voice engaged in a heated, tense confrontation with another man. Barely audible, Drew halted and listened intently, remaining unnoticed.

"Weston, the situation has escalated. The blackmailer demands more—they're relentless," Belltone voiced.

"I understand your concern, but meeting their demands will only empower them. We cannot negotiate with extortionists," the other voice replied calmly.

"You don't grasp the seriousness of this," Belltone said aggressively. "If we don't comply, the consequences could be catastrophic."

"We don't even know if Phillip was one of their victims. Complying would set a dangerous precedent, potentially spiraling out of control."

"I don't have time to waste, Weston," Belltone pleaded. "The clock is ticking." "Then we must find another way. Perhaps we can turn the tables on them."

"How? We don't even know who they are. They use anonymous channels—encrypted emails, untraceable phone calls, and burner accounts," Belltone said as he paced. "And how are we paying them?"

"They demand payments in cryptocurrency, sent to various accounts in the Cayman Islands."

"That only complicates efforts to trace the funds," Belltone smirked.

"We could collect information on them and expose their vulnerabilities. Discrediting them would strip away their leverage," a calm voice explained.

"And what if they catch on and start to retaliate?"

"We'll take precautions and cover our tracks," the voice whispered.

"It's risky," Belltone snapped.

"But constantly paying them off is risky too. At least this way, we regain control."

"Just pay them what they want. I can't afford any risks," Belltone said as he slammed his hand against the wall and walked away.

Startled, Drew quickly retraced his steps and found himself back at the bar, his head spinning.

"Drew, you look like you've seen a ghost!" Debra said as she approached, a nervous expression on her face, with Israel by her side.

"Listen, I just overheard a conversation between Mr. Belltone and another man. He's being blackmailed!"

"By the other man?" Israel asked.

"No, by an anonymous person. He must have a compromising secret he's willing to pay huge sums to hide," Drew explained.

"So, who was Belltone talking to?" Debra asked, glancing in both directions.

"I don't know. I only heard the name 'Weston.' Perhaps he's a business manager or an accountant?" Drew wondered.

"Israel, you and Aisha met with Belltone's executive assistant. Perhaps Candy knows that name," Debra suggested.

"I'll ask her," Israel said. "I believe I saw her at the party."

"You should have a one-on-one talk with Belltone. Being black-mailed is crucial information he omitted," Debra advised, looking at Drew, who agreed silently.

Francy placed her hands on Debra's shoulders. Startled, Debra jumped. "Oh, you scared me!" she gasped.

"I thought you were headed for the ladies' room?" Francy laughed.

"I got sidetracked," Debra replied.

"It seems they need their own room!" Francy remarked, nodding toward a dark corner of the bar.

"Isn't that Belltone's curator?" Debra winced.

"Yes, Jonathon Matthews," Drew confirmed.

"And who's the woman he's pursuing?" Debra asked.

"Her name is Jeanne Lois Van Italie," Francy added. "She's a good friend of Veronica Belltone and seems like a willing participant."

"Well, Francy," Drew said seriously, "we have a new development—Belltone is being blackmailed."

"Guys, there you are," Elena said as she approached Francy at the bar. "Dr. Stevens just texted me."

Drew looked over to Elena. "What did he say?'"

"He received a death threat."

"What?" Drew couldn't believe what he had heard.

"He called Detective Jameson to inform him about it. Jameson visited him earlier today to discuss the findings in the case involving Dr. Fisher and Phillip. His response was underwhelming. He appeared dismissive and suggested he examine further for additional proof."

"Did Jameson offer him any protection?"

"Jameson said he would send a squad car to monitor the place."

"Not very promising," Drew nodded.

Elen read the remaining text aloud. "Given Mr. Belltone's commitment to uncovering the truth about Phillip and Dr. Fisher, I believe it's essential we continue our investigation. I would like to meet with you both on the rooftop lounge of the Knickerbocker Hotel in Time Square at noon."

"Now that's promising." Drew smiled.

"Wait, there's more," Elena continued. "To avoid detection, there is a secret door at the Knickerbocker Hotel. Go to the Times Square subway stop. Look for a white door with a faded metal sign that says 'Knickerbocker.' You will find it at the eastern end of Track 1 on the shuttle platform."

"That's not too ominous," Debra blurted. "Are you sure this is not a trap?"

"I told him we would meet at the rooftop at noon," Elena confirmed.

"Ladies and gentlemen, we would like to begin the presentation, please." An announcement resonated through the speaker system as the orchestra launched into a familiar Glenn Miller tune. The room buzzed with excitement as everyone hurried back to their seats for the exhibit.

"Good evening, dear friends and patrons," Marcus Larson announced over the microphone. "We are proud to introduce the museum's newest collection of fine artists, each distinct and deserving of recognition." Dressed in black tie and patent leather shoes, the tall art curator had his hair slicked back, exuding an air of sophistication. Unruffled by the din of voices in the restaurant, he explained which color ribbons corresponded to each prize category. "Every artist's work is available for purchase this evening, and we truly appreciate your patronage."

"So, this is how museums generate interest in new artists and exhibitions?" Debra asked, looking at Drew.

"It seems to be working," Drew remarked, as a rush of guests moved toward their favorite paintings.

"It appears to be a silent auction," Elena suggested.

"This is where the major revenue comes from," a gentle voice announced from behind them. Jeanne Lois stood nearby, her silver sequin dress shimmering under the lights.

"Jeanne Lois," Francy responded. "What do you mean?"

"Your friend is right," Jeanne Lois said, nodding toward Elena. "This is a silent auction. Guests approach the items they favor and place bids on the artwork. They write a number on their colored paper and drop it into the bowl accompanying each piece. Each person is identified by a specific color, so the auctioneer can associate the bid accordingly."

"Very clever," Debra added as she introduced herself to Jeanne Lois. "I imagine everyone tries to outbid each other."

"Yes, they have only one bid, so they often write down an extravagant amount to win. It's all a game of ego." Jeanne Lois rolled her eyes.

"People and their money," Grace interjected, introducing herself as well.

"Rich people will do almost anything to impress their friends and neighbors," Jeanne Lois said, biting her lower lip. "They strive to keep up with their peers' lifestyles and possessions, often engaging in competitive displays of wealth and status."

"Like peacocks!" Israel interjected, bowing his head slightly in acknowledgement of Jeanne Lois.

"Another attractive detective?" Jeanne Lois flirted.

"We're here to help," Israel smiled.

"Have you solved the case yet?" Jeanne Lois turned directly to Drew for an answer.

Drew paused, glancing at his colleagues. "It's still an active investigation. We really can't discuss it."

Jeanne Lois blushed. "Oh, I understand. I was just curious. You are all whom Veronica speaks about."

"Is that Jonathon fellow your boyfriend?" Aisha interjected.

Jeanne Lois quickly recoiled in her response. "My dear, you are very lovely. You seem familiar to me."

"I get that a lot," Aisha smiled. "He's quite handsome."

"It's complicated," Jeanne Lois whispered.

"Handsome?" Aisha asked with an uncomfortable giggle. "No, I mean our relationship."

"Well, the ring is lovely," Aisha noted, observing everything closely.

Jeanne Lois simply replied, "Thank you. I'd better place my bid before my favorite painting is taken," she said with a polite smile. "It was nice meeting the Sexy Seven." Then she turned on her heels and headed toward the bar.

"Now, where did she get that nickname?" Debra inquired.

"Doll, you're famous whether you like it or not," Elena laughed.

Israel suddenly noticed Richard Belltone's executive assistant. "Look, there's Candela on the dance floor."

Aisha grabbed Israel and led him to the dance floor. "Let's see if she knows who this Weston guy is."

The music in the room changed as the orchestra shifted from the sweet swing of Benny Goodman to Glenn Miller's "Moonlight Serenade."

Candela glided across the dance floor in her mauve sequin dress, which moved in harmony with her graceful steps, every move reflecting the poise of a true professional.

"The girl's got moves," Israel announced as they met at the edge of the revolving dance floor.

Candela kissed her two newfound friends on the cheek. "I haven't seen you two since we escaped the fire," she said, a concerned look crossing her face. "The last time I saw you, you were chasing that thief down the sidewalk. Does that happen often?"

"More than we'd like to admit," Israel replied with a nervous laugh.

"Candy, darling, do you know someone named Weston who works for your boss?" Aisha asked directly.

"Weston? Yes," Candela confirmed. "He's Mr. Belltone's head of accounting and has been with him for ten years."

"Must be a loyal employee?" Israel inquired.

"Oh, absolutely," Candela responded. "He's Mr. Belltone's right-hand man and consults with my boss on everything."

"Does he work in the office where we met you?" Aisha probed further.

"He does. Their offices are on opposite sides of the floor." Candela noticed Richard Belltone gesturing at her from across the room. "Mr. Belltone needs my assistance," she said politely with a warm smile. "These silent auctions never run smoothly. Would you excuse me?" With that, she made her way through the crowded restaurant.

"So, Weston is the money guy." Israel scratched his head.

"Yes, the first person you turn to when things go wrong," Aisha agreed.

"They both know someone is blackmailing the company, but they don't know who." Israel mused aloud, "Maybe I'll find something in those files I downloaded."

# Chapter 10
## Time Square

Debra arrived at the theatre rehearsal early enough to warm up and discovered the theatre staff ready for her arrival.

Stage door attendant "Johnny" met her at the backstage entrance. "A big welcome to our newest star," he said, handing her a pass and a time card for checking in and out.

Her costumer greeted her on stage with a rack of costumes. "I sized this just perfectly for you," the tall, slender woman confirmed as she helped Debra with her show outfits. "This is your policewoman outfit for act one," she explained. "I didn't think this hat would fit," she grumbled. "I'll make some adjustments," she added, focusing on every detail.

Her vocal coach waved at her from across the stage. "Hi Debra! Can we go over the finale number when you're done with costumes?" he asked politely.

"You can have her," the costumer said with a wave, her wrist pin cushion looking more like a weapon than a handy tool.

The vocal coach moved energetically around the musical score, correcting notes and runs that Debra struggled with. "If you have your lyrics memorized, that's half the battle," he confided.

"Debra? Debra!" A familiar voice echoed from the stage right wings.

"I'm here… onstage," Debra called back.

Ava emerged from the wings. "Oh, I thought you were finished," she said, gesturing with her right hand while adjusting her headset with her left.

"We're finished," the vocal coach stated dryly.

"Oh good," Ava replied with a half-smile. "Let me show you your dressing room."

Debra gathered her dance bag and sheet music and followed Ava as she briskly navigated the backstage area and descended a flight of steps. Debra immediately recognized the route.

Ava led her down a long hallway to a familiar door on the right.

Debra slowly looked up at the initials on the door. "Oh, my initials are DA. Debra Arditi, not PW."

Ava slowly turned the key and pushed the door open, pausing in front of Debra to offer a remark. "PW. Policewoman. Your character in the show," she said dryly. As the door creaked under pressure, she swung it fully open. Switching on the light, she was startled by the dusty message scrolling across the mirror. Catching Debra's horrified expression reflected, Ava nodded. "This girl hated me," she murmured, pulling a cloth from her back pocket and wiping the mirror clean.

"Which girl?" Debra quickly asked.

"The girl you're replacing. She was with the show for only six months," Ava remarked.

Debra's unease was apparent.

"Don't worry," Ava confided. "I'm not a toxic person. I know I can be a bit gruff and bossy..." her voice trailed off.

Debra sensed Ava lowering her guard, if only for a moment. Her need to unburden herself was evident. "Go on. I understand what you're saying."

"You do?" Ava asked, clearly surprised.

"Yes, of course," Debra replied with a gesture. "I've been accused of being bossy, arrogant, detached."

"As a stage manager, it's essential to lead effectively by setting the tone and ensuring that the cast and crew are in the right place at the right time. This role demands assertiveness and clear direction." Ava seemed to rationalize her approach more for herself than for Debra.

"Listen, just keep being yourself," Debra advised. Seizing an opportunity, she added, "I rehearsed with the new understudy, Stuart. Do you know him? He took someone else's place, right?"

"Stuart was in the chorus. He auditioned for the understudy role after we lost Phillip."

"Phillip had a heart attack backstage, correct?"

Ava grimaced. "Yes, it wasn't good. Some thought he was drunk or high—he wasn't himself. He looked either doped up or hung over," Ava recalled. "It was completely out of character for him. He always loved the show and was exceptionally professional," she added.

"Drunk or high?" That didn't sound like him. Debra struggled to understand his behavior. "Did you notice anything else unusual?"

"Oh, did you know him?" Ava asked, surprised.

"Yes," Debra replied solemnly. "We worked together. We were friends."

"He seemed off. Rumor had it he was distraught over a girl."

"Really?" Debra nearly sang her response.

Ava sensed she was revealing too much and pulled back. "I'm sorry; I'm not one to gossip."

"No, I'm not either. But Phillip was my friend, and I was curious about him. We hadn't connected in a long time, so his sudden death was a shock. I had no idea he was struggling with alcohol or relationship issues. I'm really surprised to hear that." Debra dusted the chair in front of her makeup table, spun it around, and sat down.

"Phillip was always professional. It all happened over two nights, and then—suddenly—he was gone!"

"Did people think that was strange?"

"You know, half the cast was oblivious while the other half dealt with his obsessive-compulsive behavior and his arguments with Katherine. The swing dancers are the most neglected people in any show."

"I know—they hang around the theatre every night, waiting for someone to call in sick or fall ill on stage. It's a thankless job. What would he have argued with Katherine about?" Debra pressed on.

"Choreography, timing, hours, work efficiency… you name it. They were like oil and water." Ava shook her head, trying not to dwell on it.

"When the cops arrived after his death, Katherine told us simply to state our whereabouts and that we all got along as a cast. Some Irish flat foot was in charge—and he didn't seem to care."

A surge of questions exploded in Debra's mind, but she decided her information was sufficient to move on. "So…" she paused, "is Stuart's dressing room upstairs? I assume he took Phillip's old dressing room, right?"

"Oh, no way. It's bad luck."

"What's bad luck?"

Ava stopped and looked at Debra. "You know, you're in the theatre."

"Yes, that's right," Debra replied promptly. "It's considered bad luck to assign a dressing room to a new cast member who is replacing someone who has passed away."

"Stuart's dressing room is upstairs—but in the room next door. Look, I have a laundry list of tasks to complete before rehearsal begins, so…"

"Of course," Debra smiled. "I'll leave you to it. And by the way," she added with a gesture, "it was nice talking to you!"

★★★

Elena and Grace made their way to the Times Square subway station, slipping into the 42nd Street entrance tucked between 7th and 8th Avenue.

"This place is massive!" Grace clung to Elena's shoulder as they passed through the turnstile.

"Welcome to the 'Crossroads of the World.' About fifteen subway lines converge here."

"I don't know how anyone finds their way," Grace said, glancing at the mural on the east wall as she followed Elena down the steps. Commuters darted past them in every direction, moving with the rhythm of a well-rehearsed performance. "How do you not crash into people?"

"A little secret," Elena raised her voice above the commotion, "always bear right! It's an unspoken rule." She guided Grace through the thick crowd straight to Track 1 of the S train. "This is the shuttle to Grand Central."

"Look," Grace squealed, her eyes lighting up. "There it is. The white door with the metal sign—Knickerbocker."

Elena glanced over her shoulder before turning the knob. It stuck slightly, and the two of them had to push together to get it open.

Inside, they were met with black-and-white parquet floors and polished wood-paneled walls. A dim hallway stretched before them, ending in a heavy red curtain. Elena moved forward, gently parting the curtain.

"It's the hotel bar!" Grace said, stunned.

"Come on," Elena urged. "Let's find the elevator to the rooftop lounge."

Dr. Stevens arrived right on time, dressed in a tweed three-piece suit and freshly shined shoes. His pale complexion seemed even more pronounced against the textured fabric and the sharp midday light.

"Thank you for meeting me. I apologize for the secrecy, but I'm honestly a bit scared right now."

"We understand. That's been our reality lately too," Elena replied gently.

They took their seats as Dr. Stevens opened his leather briefcase and pulled out a thick file.

"Both of our friends were poisoned. It was the same toxin in both cases." His expression was grave.

Grace's face tightened. "What kind of poison are we talking about?"

"I tested the hair sample your friend Debra found at the theater, as well as the samples I collected from Dr. Foster. It was ethylene glycol. It's absorbed or ingested—either way, it's deadly."

Elena's brows furrowed. "What is it exactly?"

"It's a toxic chemical found in antifreeze, de-icing solutions, and other industrial products. It has a sweet taste, but it's extremely dangerous. It attacks the kidneys, brain, and heart."

"That's terrifying," Grace said, wincing.

"Here's the key," Dr. Stevens continued. "This particular batch had a unique marker. When used in antifreeze, ethylene glycol is often mixed with a bright yellow dye to help detect leaks. The one I found? It had a yellow-green signature—not common. That made it stand out."

"If it's fluorescent, would it glow under UV light?" Elena asked.

"Like a black light?" Grace added.

"Exactly," Dr. Stevens nodded. "I'd use a Wood's lamp, but yes, a black light would work."

"So, you think they drank it?" Elena asked.

"There were no puncture wounds on Dr. Foster. The evidence points to ingestion. This poison dissolves easily in liquids—something as simple as a drink of water could deliver it without raising suspicion."

"You're saying it's that easy to poison someone?" Grace looked stunned.

"Yes. And the symptoms develop in stages. It depends on how much is consumed and how much time has passed," Dr. Stevens said, flipping to a page of test results.

"What do the symptoms look like?" Elena asked.

"Within the first twelve hours, it can mimic alcohol intoxication—euphoria, clumsiness, even slurred speech."

"How odd," Grace commented.

"In twenty-four to seventy-two hours, symptoms such as difficulty breathing, dehydration, and a rapid heartbeat would appear. Depending on the dosage, this could lead to kidney failure or cardiac arrest."

"Let's reconstruct the poison's path. We have two similar cases that we must connect to determine their relationship." Dr. Stevens spoke with determination and directness.

"First, we need to consider the delivery method. Could the poison have been administered in a glass of water, coffee, or even a smoothie?" Elena shifted in her chair.

"We must examine Phillip's last few days—who was around him? Who had access to his food or drink? Is it possible the poison was administered during an event or meeting?" Dr. Stevens inquired.

"If we are to track down the culprit, we must investigate further—and quickly, before the perpetrator realizes we are onto them." Grace's eyes betrayed her anxiety. "This is scary."

"We must also determine the poison's origin by investigating any unusual purchases or activities. Pinpointing who had access to the toxin will bring us closer to finding the culprit." Dr. Stevens returned to his leather briefcase, retrieved another file, and quickly located his colleague's information. "Dr. Foster received a high dose of ethylene glycol that caused his system to fail within twelve hours. I found traces of the toxin in the coffee spilled on his white coat and hands."

"Coffee?" Elena asked.

"Initially, I dismissed the coffee stain, but upon retesting his clothing, I detected traces of the toxin in the stain. Its chemical composition was more degraded than that found in Phillip's sample, making it more caustic.

"More dangerous?" Grace queried.

"Yes—it is harmful to the touch. Although not inherently corrosive, when the toxin ages, mixes with other chemicals, or is exposed to heat or oxygen, it can become dangerous and leave marks on the skin." Dr. Stevens spread his hands.

"So, Dr. Foster had poison in his coffee? Is coffee readily available in the morgue?"

"Yes, in our break room."

"But then, wouldn't everyone be affected—or worse, dead?" Grace swallowed hard, feeling beads of sweat form on her forehead.

"Someone likely served him a cup of tainted coffee, knowing his habitual love for the beverage." Dr. Stevens switched back to Phillip's file. "Grace, Elena, notice something on Phillip's initial autopsy report from the hospital—a symbol marked 'LX' on the back page." He pointed to the image in the photocopies.

"Yes," Elena confirmed. "This was the autopsy conducted by the hospital where Phillip was taken after his death."

"Now, here is the report your friend retrieved from Richard Belltone's computer—the one conducted by Dr. Foster at the City Morgue. He noted that the same symbol appeared as a tattoo on the inside of the victim's right ankle."

"As a tattoo?" mused Grace. "Drew mentioned that."

"I never recall Phillip having any tattoos," Elena recalled. "He was always against them, considering them a vulgar affront to his body."

"So what changed?" Grace wondered, glancing at Elena.

"We do know that this is the signature of the street artist La Croix," Elena confirmed.

Dr. Stevens tilted his head. "You mean a street artist like Banksy or Keith Haring?"

"Yes," Elena explained. "La Croix is a painter, sculptor, and street artist."

"The tattoo likely signified a personal commitment or connection. While tattoos often hold significant personal meaning, in this context it might simply serve as an important detail for identification."

"Alternatively, it could provide a clue to Phillip's emotional or psychological state, particularly if the death was suspicious."

Dr. Stevens paused, considering Elena's observation. "If the death was related in any way to the tattoo or the relationship it represented, this detail could be crucial." His forensic mind raced: perhaps the tattoo was linked to foul play or tied to a dispute or emotional crisis.

"See, doc," Grace smiled, "you're thinking like a detective now."

"But there is no way to confirm this with the victim deceased."

"However, someone who knew Phillip better might provide proof." Elena had an idea and quickly texted Debra.

"If you're at the theatre, ask Phillip's cast mates about an LX tattoo on his inner right ankle."

Moments later, Debra texted back, "On it."

"We also know that Phillip was a fan of the artist's work; he even had one of his paintings in his apartment," Elena recalled, referencing information Drew had shared.

"So, clearly Phillip admired the artist's work—there's the connection. He likely found the work impressive," Grace mused. "So why not have his signature tattooed on your ankle?"

"It doesn't fit Phillip's profile," Elena insisted.

Dr. Stevens continued. "Ethylene glycol is found in paint and related products. Paints, solvents, and industrial chemicals often contain volatile organic compounds that can affect the nervous system when inhaled or absorbed through the skin."

Grace's eyes widened. "Wait, so you're saying the killer could have used paint to poison him?"

"It's possible. Consider this: Phillip could have been exposed indirectly. The toxin may have been mixed into a paint can or added to a cleaning solvent. When he came in contact with the paint—whether by inhaling fumes or through skin contact—the toxin would enter his system, either immediately or gradually with prolonged exposure." Dr. Stevens contemplated the chain of events.

Elena paused. "So the killer could have poisoned him without direct physical contact—just by contaminating his environment with toxin-laced paint?"

"Right," Dr. Stevens nodded. And the frightening part is that it might not be obvious to anyone. The paint may have been used in an ordinary renovation—something that appeared completely innocent. But if someone tampered with the paint or solvent, it would be like setting a time bomb. The longer the exposure, the higher the risk. By the time Phillip suffered a heart attack, no one would associate it with the paint; it would look like a natural occurrence. "We need to examine the painting in his apartment. If the toxin was present there, we might find a clue," he added as he made notes in his files.

"I'm sure we can get our hands on the painting in his apartment," Elena suggested.

"However, I lean toward the idea that both our colleagues were poisoned via ingestion—they both experienced severe abdominal irritation, minor esophageal burns, and organ failure."

"We need to find the source of this, right?" Grace asked.

"Identifying the source would indeed provide more conclusive evidence." Dr. Stevens shifted in his seat, his eyes darting nervously.

"Detective Jameson mentioned he placed a patrol car in front of your office," Grace inquired.

"Aha, yes," he replied.

"Well, we'll protect you," Elena offered. "How were you threatened?"

"It was a phone call from an automated system—you know, those pre-recorded messages."

"Scare tactic," Grace responded, trying to ease Dr. Stevens' fear.

"It happens when I'm alone, when I truly fear for my life," he said. A long, uneasy silence fell among them. "There's one more thing."

Elena studied his expression. "Okay, this doesn't sound good."

"The Belltone family is among the oldest in New York. Alongside the Rockefellers, Stuyvesants, Vanderbilts, and Roosevelts, their lineage has been meticulously recorded and examined for centuries. I ran a DNA analysis on a hair root sample that Debra provided. Phillip's DNA signature doesn't match."

The girls exchanged puzzled glances.

"Phillip's grandfather, Damon Belltone, has his DNA on file in a database. Apparently, when he was young, he had a conflict with the mob over constructing his theater in the Theatre District. It was alleged that he killed a mobster—so his DNA was collected as evidence. Although he was eventually acquitted, the sample remains." Dr. Stevens pulled a handkerchief from his back pocket and wiped his forehead.

The girls were riveted by his words.

"I compared the DNA from Phillip's hair sample with his grandfather's, and they do not match."

"Wouldn't there be variations between the DNA of Phillip's grandfather and his father?" Grace asked, seeking clarification.

"Yes, minor variations can occur. However, both Phillip's father and grandfather share the same Y chromosome—passed down with minimal changes. Thus, Phillip's Y chromosome should be nearly identical to theirs. Clearly, it is not."

"So, Phillip was adopted?" Elena asked, furrowing her eyebrows.

"It appears so." Dr. Stevens leaned back in his chair, looking almost relieved to have disclosed this information.

"This is getting too deep," Grace remarked, taking a sip of her white wine.

"I suggest keeping this confidential until we obtain substantial evidence."

Elena stood up, determined to unravel the web of deceit.

"Start at the New York Public Library. New York's famous families have well-documented histories there."

"We will assemble the team. We'll uncover the truth and report back," Elena confirmed. "Thank you, Doctor."

# Chapter 11
## Fifth Avenue

The New York Public Library stood as a titan amidst the busy traffic of Fifth Avenue. Its imposing stone columns and towering, Roman-inspired façade had clearly withstood the test of time.

Drew, Israel, Aisha, Debra, Grace, Francy, and Elena stood before the iconic building, each struck with awe as they admired its impressive features. Twin lions guarded the entrance like steadfast sentinels. Carved from the finest granite, their muscular forms exuded strength as their powerful paws rested elegantly on the steps. Their stoic presence spoke of wisdom, ancient power, and an unyielding commitment to protect the knowledge stored within the marble halls.

"What a work of art," Debra said sincerely.

The library was more than a repository of books; it was a sanctuary of history, its walls concealing stories of the past. Today, it was rumored to hold the secret they had pursued for weeks.

Upon entering, they discovered a main reading room with soaring ceilings painted in vibrant hues. Murals recounted tales of learning and discovery.

"I've lived here all my life yet rarely stepped inside," Drew admitted.

"I still have my library card," Elena said proudly.

Massive chandeliers hung above, their light passing through tall, arched windows and bathing the space in a soft afternoon glow.

"This way," Elena pointed.

The marble floors echoed beneath their feet as they made their way toward the genealogy department, passing statues of ancient scholars and towering shelves filled with books older than any of them could fathom.

The Rose Room, the centerpiece of the library, was an expansive, open space spanning two city blocks. Its ceiling featured three large murals of ethereal skies, while rows of reference books lined the walls. Natural light streaming through eighteen archways bathed the room. Wooden tables paired with brass lamps and comfortable chairs provided an ideal setting for study.

Grace marveled at the library's Roman architecture. "It's as if we have stepped into an ancient temple of knowledge," she whispered, her voice filled with wonder as she traced the cold, smooth columns framing the entrance.

"What beautiful columns," Debra remarked as she moved toward the marble pillars at the room's corners, admiring their craftsmanship.

Drew suddenly froze, caught in a moment of deep thought. "That's it," he stammered. "Rome. Julius. Julius Caesar. It's a Caesar cipher—the code in Phillip's book."

Drew quickly retrieved the mysterious book, opening it on the spacious table to the bookmarked page.

"Of course. It is a type of letter substitution where each character in the plaintext is shifted by a fixed number of positions in the alphabet."

"A hidden message?" Grace asked as a sudden realization crossed her face.

"Caesar used it in his private correspondence so that only someone with the key could decipher his messages," explained Drew, his mind racing.

"A key?" Debra asked.

"Yes, the key is the specific shift in letters that will reveal the answer," Israel explained, mentally working through a sequence of letters.

"So, how do we determine the key?" Francy inquired as she examined the sequence of letters.

"It's in his riddle," Drew replied.

In ancient times, a ruler, wise,
Used letters as secrets, hidden from eyes.
A number was chosen, neither high nor low,
A shift in positions, a code to bestow.
Three steps forward, the answer is near,
Just solve the riddle, a solution appears.
What's the key, a clue you must see,
To unlock the message that will be set free.

"I don't get it," Grace said.

"Before computer coding, we had Caesar's cypher—one of the earliest and simplest encryption techniques," Drew explained. He retrieved a pad and a pen from his backpack and quickly began jotting letters.

"Yes, I see it now!" Israel exclaimed. He moved the book to the center of the table so everyone could see it. "Three steps forward, the answer is near," he repeated.

Drew rushed to the large whiteboard in the corner. "Let's write out the key." Taking a marker, he wrote the alphabet; Israel followed.

"Start at A in the alphabet and shift three letters forward," Israel illustrated.

"A, B, C," Debra calculated aloud.

"Nope," Drew pointed out. "Shift three letters over starting from A."

"Ahhh, B, C, D," Elena suggested. "Let's try this."

"So, the key starts with the letter D, not A. If we replace each letter with its corresponding letter in the key," Israel hesitated, "we should be able to decrypt the message."

"I see the pattern," Francy said. "D equals A, E equals B, F equals C…"

"Everyone, take a sheet of paper and a pen. Let's decode this." Israel tore pages from his pad and retrieved some pens from his side pocket.

The group gathered around the conference table and began writing out the key by listing the alphabet and aligning the shifted letters underneath.

PB

JUDQGIDWKHUV

RWKHU

VRQ

A heavy silence enveloped the room, broken only by the occasional groan or carefully chosen curse word. Seven minds worked in silent unison, each deciphering their next clue with methodical precision.

Francy's voice broke the silence—sharp and insistent. "We don't have time to second-guess. We need to decipher this sign now, or we're wasting our time. Everything depends on it." Her words resonated with undeniable truth, and the urgency increased as everyone grasped what was at stake.

Elena was two steps ahead. She spelled out the answer on her piece of paper.

## MY GRANDFATHERS OTHER SON

The other six exchanged glances, uncertain of the meaning as they contemplated the results. Drew spoke up. "Phillip's grandfather had another son besides Richard Belltone?"

"A son who died?" Francy asked.

"In childbirth?" Debra added.

"No. If Phillip used a code, he wanted to keep it secure for a reason," Drew surmised.

"An illegitimate son!" Israel muttered, piecing things together. "It makes sense now."

"That would have been a scandal of the highest order, especially back then," Debra said, her face registering shock. "In a time when family lineage was everything and any deviation from the norm was not only frowned upon but often erased from history."

"Exactly," Elena agreed, her eyes narrowing in thought. "Phillip's grandfather having an illegitimate child would have shaken the family to its core. They were wealthy and influential—people whose reputation could not bear such a stain."

"In that era, social propriety was paramount. It wasn't just about saving face—it could cost you everything," Drew observed. "The family must have gone to great lengths to suppress this secret. And the child... that's where the trouble begins."

"Yes, the illegitimate child. Consider this," Aisha said as she moved to the front of the room. "Someone born into scandal yet carrying the blood of a powerful family wouldn't simply vanish. The question is—was this child completely erased from history, or did they grow up under a different name and a new identity?"

Francy turned to Drew, a confused look on her face. "Richard never mentioned that when we met."

"Maybe he didn't think it was relevant," Drew suggested.

"Or perhaps he doesn't even know," Debra countered. "It might be a secret that no one in the family truly understands."

"Did Phillip know he was adopted?" Aisha stated firmly. "Let's not forget why we're here."

"You're suggesting Damon Belltone had an illegitimate son and Richard Belltone had an adopted one?" Debra sat down in the plush chair behind her. "How does anyone sleep at night with so many secrets?"

"And who benefits from keeping this hidden?" Grace interjected. "Someone who stands to lose everything if the truth emerged. If the illegitimate child were ever recognized, they could claim a share of the wealth and challenge the established inheritance."

Drew flipped through Phillip's book. "A fortune tied to legacy. The stakes couldn't be higher. They'd be a direct threat to the family's power, especially if recognized as a rightful heir. It makes sense now—there is a lot at stake: the family's history, the wealth, and the reputation they fought to protect. This could be the basis of the blackmail."

"So, we're looking for someone motivated to conceal a past that could undermine the future," Elena said uncertainly. "Are we reading too much into this? Could this be why Phillip was killed?"

"We need to find out who was excluded from the family's history," Drew deduced. "They've been deliberately left out—and that omission is key to solving this mystery."

"Maybe this will help," Francy said, holding up Phillip's mysterious book. "We have another riddle to solve." She thumbed through the pages. "Drew, here it is," she read aloud.

Signifier:

Behind the curtains, secrets hide,
Where actors wait and plot their stride.
A guardian stands, its mouth held tight,
Unveiling magic, out of sight.
Turn the knob a click will sound,
A box of mysteries to be found.
What place am I, where stories begin,
With hidden spaces and tales within?

Signified:

JV
YXZHPQXDB
TXOAOLYB

Drew looked closer at the page. "Ok, let's see where this takes us."

Grace frowned at the line, "A guardian stands, its mouth held tight? That doesn't make sense to me."

Francy read the next line aloud, "Turn the knob, a click will sound." Clearly frustrated, she repeated, "A guardian stands, its mouth held tight? That still puzzles me."

"What kind of guard keeps its mouth shut? Could it be a statue—some figure meant to stand guard? Yet, why would it have its mouth so firmly closed?"

Debra flipped through the pages of the book, trying to connect the clues. "What if the guardian isn't a statue, but something more practical?" She traced her finger along the riddle. "The phrase 'mouth held tight' might refer to a lock—a lock that doesn't open until activated. And the guardian could be the mechanism keeping something secure. But what about the knob?"

"Where actors wait…" Drew reiterated.

Israel leaned back, hands steepled in thought. "The knob might be a turning mechanism, perhaps part of a door or a vault. Here, the 'guardian' could be the lock or even the door itself, something that protects what lies beyond. 'Mouth held tight' might describe a sealed opening, like a door that shuts securely when locked. And the click? Perhaps that sound is from the lock engaging."

"Maybe the click is the sound made when the lock is engaged—a door, a vault, something with a turnable knob that makes a noise when secured."

Grace looked up, a brief moment of understanding crossing her face. "So, we're considering a locked entryway of some sort—a safe, perhaps? Something with a mechanism that, when unlocked, produces that click? It must be something significant…"

Debra nodded thoughtfully. "Precisely. A door, a safe, or even a secret compartment. The click signals that it's been opened, like gaining access to something concealed. The riddle isn't only about the guardian—it's also about the locking mechanism. The knob is essentially the trigger."

Israel's eyes brightened. "It might be a hidden door in plain sight, so well-disguised that it isn't noticed until the mechanism is activated by the click." He paused, tapping his fingers on the table. "We should look for a knob that doesn't appear to be a knob at all—possibly disguised as part of the wall or an ornamental feature."

Drew added, "If we solve the signified with the key, we will have the answer. We can discuss its meaning later."

Before Drew could finish, Aisha shouted, "I've got it!" She began spelling out the message.

## MY BACKSTAGE WARDROBE

Grace's expression changed. "So, the guardian is a closet door or entrance, but we need to find the knob that doesn't look like one—hidden in plain sight? It's starting to make sense, yet we must narrow it down. Where would someone hide something meant to protect what's important?"

"Maybe a free-standing dresser or drawer in Phillip's dressing room backstage at the theatre."

"Turn the knob and you'll hear a click," Aisha recited. "He must be indicating where he hid something—maybe evidence."

"But we were in Phillip's dressing room and found nothing," Israel said, frustration edging his tone.

Debra sighed. "I can explain it now. The dressing room we discovered during the audition belonged to the girl whose spot I took. The initials above each dressing room door represent the character. Mine is Police Woman, PW—not Phillip Wright." A flush of embarrassment crossed her face as she realized they had all jumped to conclusions.

Israel's face turned red. "That was my assumption."

"It was a logical assumption, Israel," Drew confided. "We all jumped to that conclusion."

"Well," Debra said with a half-smile, "the other assumption we made was that Phillip wrote that cryptic message on the mirror about Ava. That isn't true—the dancer I replaced wrote it. She and Ava didn't get along, and it was her parting message to Ava."

Silence fell among them.

After a beat, Drew broke the quiet. "This is the essence of detective work," he explained. "It doesn't mean we doubt our judgments; rather, it reminds us that appearances can be deceiving—what we see or hear isn't always the whole truth."

"Ava offered intriguing insight into Phillip's behavior 48 hours before his death," Debra said as she smoothed out her jeans and sat at the table. "Some thought he was drunk or high, but Ava insisted he wasn't himself. He looked either doped up or hungover," she recalled. "She mentioned it was completely out of character—Phillip always loved the show and was astute and professional."

"Drunk or high? That aligns with the symptoms Dr. Stevens described when someone is poisoned with ethylene glycol," Elena explained.

Grace interjected, "Dr. Stevens also mentioned that the poison—which killed both Phillip and Dr. Foster—exhibits a distinctive fluorescent yellow-green signature."

Elena's voice rose in excitement. "Since it's fluorescent, it will glow under UV light!"

"Like a black light?" Grace added.

"That's incredible news, girls!" Drew said, while several patrons glanced over with troubled expressions.

"Debra, did Ava mention anything unusual?"

"She said there were rumors that Phillip was distraught over a girl."

"Wow, really?" Drew mused, recalling a few girls Phillip had been seen with over the years. He exchanged a glance with Elena and Francy, who both shrugged. "Let's note that and use it if necessary."

"Why don't we head upstairs?" Elena suggested. "Maybe we can learn more about Phillip's true story."

They moved through the grand marble lobby back toward the Fifth Avenue entrance.

"Look—the gift shop!" Debra exclaimed, clearly eager to go in.

"Great idea," Elena mused. She entered the elegant shop and scanned shelves filled with classic novels and memorabilia that captured the spirit of New York City. Among the items, a small black light caught her eye—a compact device roughly the size of a key fob with a sleek, unassuming casing. Its purpose became clear when she noticed nearby postcards and trinkets displaying hidden fluorescent designs under its beam, adding a hint of mystery to the shop's vibrant selection. Sensing her interest, the shopkeeper explained that these miniature black lights were popular among theatergoers and tourists. Elena purchased the device, eager to put it to an unexpected use.

Drew and Grace immediately understood. "It's always good to be prepared," he said with a smile.

"Good thinking, girl," Grace added.

The group arrived at the genealogy desk, where an elderly librarian greeted them. Her silver hair was pulled back in a neat bun, and her eyes shone with the insight that only many years of experience can provide.

"We're looking for records on a very specific family," Drew said, his voice calm yet edged with urgency. "Billionaire Damon Belltone?"

The librarian gave a discreet nod. "Ah, yes, the Belltone family. I can help with that." She led them into a back room lined with filing cabinets that guarded secrets of the past. The air carried the faint scent of old paper and leather.

Aisha's eyes widened with anticipation. "This is incredible. I never imagined we'd find something this extensive." Her fingers began flipping through the files as they gathered around a long wooden table.

Israel removed his black Ray Ban glasses from his bag. "I'm going to record everything," he grinned. "Here we go," he said as he pulled out a weathered document. The group leaned in, scanning the text.

"Damon Belltone was ninety-five when he passed," Aisha read.

"He was married to Marie Belltone. She died at eighty-five," Israel continued.

"This article claims he was acquitted of murdering a mobster!" Aisha exclaimed, her voice rising sharply.

"That's how Dr. Stevens obtained a DNA sample," Grace added.

"Here is Richard and Veronica Belltone's file," Aisha announced. Quickly flipping through the pages, she stopped at a copy of a birth certificate that did not match their expectations. Instead of the usual "Belltone" surname, Phillip's certificate displayed an alternate name—one that had been crossed out and replaced with Richard's own.

"Here it is," Aisha confirmed. "There's also a paper here stating that Phillip legally changed his name to Wright."

"Mr. Belltone told Francy and me this information when we met him, as we all knew Phillip by his stage name," Drew murmured, studying the document.

Elena leaned forward. "But there's nothing here about Damon's illegitimate son—no birth record or public announcement."

The group exchanged glances as the significance of the discovery settled in. The quiet library suddenly felt charged with hidden stories waiting to be uncovered.

"Let's get everything we can," Drew said, determination clear in his tone. "If Damon Belltone went to such lengths to bury the truth, there must be more to the story."

As the group examined the records further, they uncovered additional documents: court files, sealed records, and old newspaper clippings hinting at long-hidden family scandals. Each file revealed a family that had consistently guarded its reputation with extreme care.

"Tomorrow is opening night," Debra reminded everyone.

"After the show, we'll go backstage to congratulate our 'petit ballerina'," Drew smiled. "That way we'll have a chance to see what secrets might be hiding in Phillip's dressing room."

# Chapter 12
## Broadway

Debra hadn't experienced an opening night in quite some time. The fact that it was on Broadway made it even more special. Her dressing room was adorned with flowers from friends, and a gift basket filled with treats—chocolates, water, a hand towel emblazoned with the show's name, and assorted snacks—awaited her.

All her colleagues stopped by to wish her well. "Break a leg," Stuart said as he poked his head through her door. "You're going to be fantastic."

Debra blushed at the compliment. "It was kind of one of the cast members to sit out tonight so you could perform their part," she replied with a smile. "So, it's really both our opening night."

He bowed as he backed out. "Heads up," he whispered, "the boss is coming."

Katherine knocked on the door.

"Katherine, come in," Debra gestured for her to sit.

Wearing a subtle smile, Katherine settled into Debra's chair by the makeup mirror. "I have a few notes," she began. "Watch your hand positioning in the finale—they tend to rise above your head when they should be held at an angled side position by your waist."

"Thank you for your advice," Debra said, listening intently.

"Also, exit stage left from the upstage wing at the end of Act One—not the middle wing. There's too much…" Katherine paused. "What's the word in English?" she murmured. "Traffic," she recalled.

"I certainly will," Debra replied. "Where is your accent from?"

"I'm originally from Belgium," Katherine answered softly.

"I was thinking Swiss or French. I was even going to say Luxembourg because of your fair skin and light eyes," Debra said warmly.

"I even get mistaken for someone from the Midwest," Katherine shrugged.

"I must say, your choreography fits me perfectly; I really appreciate your dance technique. And I have to tell you—that ring is stunning," Debra remarked, captivated by how the mirror's lighting enhanced its brilliance.

"My fiancé gave it to me this year," Katherine blushed as she held the ring up for Debra to admire.

"I was engaged once," Debra recalled, her eyes lingering on the delicate band around Katherine's finger, its subtle gleam concealing a secret she chose not to reveal.

Katherine stood, kissed Debra on both cheeks, and wished her luck. "Merde!"

Debra's opening stage performance took place in a theater reminiscent of the grandeur of the 1920s. The Grand Theatre—a masterpiece of Art Deco architecture—boasted a lavish interior with geometric patterns, polished metal fixtures, and intricate detailing that transported the audience back to an era of opulence. The stage was framed by ornate proscenium arches, and the backdrop burst with rich, vibrant colors, setting the tone for the evening's performance.

When the final curtain fell, the theater erupted in applause, its appreciation echoing through the splendid halls. Drew, Grace, Aisha, Elena, Israel, and Francy awaited Debra backstage.

"Congratulations, beautiful!" Drew exclaimed as Debra emerged from her dressing room.

Debra curtsied as her close friends marveled at her performance, their faces aglow with pride and admiration. Backstage buzzed with excitement as cast and crew exchanged stories and laughter in celebration. Debra pointed to the initials above the door.

"Okay, okay, I get it," Israel said with a smile.

The air was filled with the fragrance of fresh flowers and the lingering echoes of laughter, which spoke to the unforgettable evening. Several cast members stopped by Debra's dressing room to offer their congratulations.

"Let's wait until the backstage excitement subsides; then I'll show you Phillip's dressing room."

"It's vacant?" Grace observed.

"The room isn't in use. I forgot that it's tradition not to assign a departed cast member's dressing room to a newcomer," Debra explained, pointing up the stairs. "Phillip's dressing room is on the main floor."

After greeting several more well-wishers, Debra changed into her street clothes. "It's the perfect time to explore," she suggested.

With the backstage commotion subsiding, Drew proposed, "Let's go now so we have time to look around."

Debra led the way upstairs to the main stage level. Backstage appeared calm, and from the wings she spotted a lone "ghost light" standing in the darkness.

"Why do they call it a ghost light, anyway?" Grace asked.

"It's a single, bare light bulb left on stage when the theatre is empty, primarily as a safety measure to help people find their way in the dark," Debra explained.

"Yet there's also a superstition that it keeps the theater's resident ghosts content by offering them a light to perform by," Drew remarked, pausing to watch the glow on its stand.

Elena added gently, "It symbolizes respect for the theater's history and its possible spirits. Phillip must be pleased."

Israel confirmed to the crew, "He'll be even more pleased when we complete what he started!"

"Here it is," Debra murmured. She pointed above the door, where the initials 'US' were prominently displayed. "Understudy."

"Where did they put the new understudy?" Drew asked.

Debra gestured toward the dressing room next door.

"It's locked," Francy whispered. "Israel?"

Before he could speak, Debra extracted a bobby pin from her hair. Israel knelt and manipulated the pin through the keyhole. A sudden click signaled them to turn the knob and push the door open.

The dressing room was small but immaculate; the walls were pristine white and glowed faintly in the weak light filtering through the single window from the nearby streetlamp. A full-length mirror hung on one wall with an ornate frame reflecting the room's sparse decor. A picture hung on the opposite wall. The only other furniture included a tiny chair, a makeup mirror, a rolling rack for costumes, and a lumbering antique wooden wardrobe whose polished surface echoed the glow of the walls.

They entered cautiously, scanning for clues that might explain what had happened to Phillip. Every detail felt eerily familiar yet cold, as though something significant had been lost. They had to be swift—staying too long risked being caught.

Francy guarded the door outside while Debra and Israel searched the room, listening intently for any signs of approaching footsteps. The ticking of the clock on the wall sounded unnervingly loud in the silence.

"Don't turn the light on," Elena urged in a hushed tone. She retrieved the black light souvenir she had bought at the New York Public Library's gift shop. "It isn't a wood lamp, but it works on the same principle."

"Now, what can you tell us?" Drew murmured as he and Elena meticulously scanned the dark dressing room.

Elena slowly swept the black light over every surface until, suddenly, it revealed a yellow-green glow on Phillip's makeup table.

Debra gasped in the darkness as the glow illuminated their faces, reflecting a lemon-lime aura in the mirror. "He was poisoned here," she exclaimed, a tear welling at the corner of her eye.

Drew flipped the light switch, which was located on the wall beside the entrance.

"Oh, my goodness," Debra stuttered. "It's another La Croix painting."

The group saw that the painting depicted two black cats facing each other.

Debra identified the painting as "Seeing Double." "I saw this in Marcus Larson's office in the Whitney's digital catalog of La Croix's works."

Elena stared at the signature. "Yes, this is definitely the symbol tattooed on Phillip's ankle, according to Dr. Stevens."

"Phillip really liked this artist," commented Grace as she walked over to the wardrobe in the corner.

As Drew moved forward, the aging floorboards creaked under his steps. He caught his reflection in the mirror and noticed the rusted air vents weakly blowing cool air behind him.

"Phillip spent almost two years doing this show," Francy suggested from the doorway. "There must be something he left behind."

"The problem is," Debra confided, "they cleaned out his dressing room six months ago."

Drew immediately noticed the ornate wardrobe. Though not particularly large, it dominated the room. "This must be the wardrobe Phillip referred to in his limerick." His heart began to race as he sought to confirm the connection.

He approached, running his hands over the cool wood. The door was solid and heavy, yet it swung smoothly on well-oiled hinges when he pushed it open.

Inside, the wardrobe was surprisingly spacious, with rows of neatly arranged hangers suspended from three long bars.

"Hangers," Drew reported to Francy.

"That's it?" Debra hissed, peering around the corner as she watched Drew stare blankly into the wardrobe.

Drew shook his head, agreeing sarcastically with her implied disappointment.

The air inside was musty yet not unpleasant, carrying a faint aroma of old cedar mixed with a hint of faded perfume.

"How did the rhyme go in Phillip's book?" Drew called out.

Elena mentally recited the words.

"A guardian stands, its mouth held tight,
Unveiling magic, out of sight. Turn the knob a click will sound,
A box of mysteries to be found."

As he admired the craftsmanship, he noticed three small, inconspicuous projections on the bottom shelf. They were oddly placed, seemingly designed to be overlooked or to serve as mere decoration. Drew knelt and attempted to turn the first knob, but it didn't budge. Instead, he reached for the one farthest from him.

With a soft click, the wardrobe's bottom dropped, revealing a large hidden compartment. Israel and Debra turned at the sound of Drew's discovery.

The compartment, both deep and wide, was ample enough to hold a small trunk. Its walls were lined with plush velvet, lending it a regal appearance.

"There's something here," Drew called out from behind the wardrobe, ensuring Francy could hear him.

She peeked into the room. "What is it? What did you find?" Her excitement resonated throughout the space.

He reached in and explored. "It's a plain wooden box with no markings."

"It looks like one of those large tie boxes from the '30s," Elena remarked as she turned to examine it more closely.

The box's top hinged upward to reveal a compartment filled with an assortment of intriguing objects: ornate jewelry boxes, dusty esoteric books with faded titles, and a small, finely carved wooden statue.

"There! What is that?" Debra exclaimed, unable to hide her excitement.

As Drew pulled out a mirrored box, his heart pounded. His reflection in the glass revealed his anticipation. He opened the box with trembling hands, revealing a stack of old photographs.

Disappointment washed over him.

"Pictures," Israel said to Francy.

Although the photographs were interesting, they did not seem like the clue he had hoped to uncover. However, upon closer inspection, he realized these were not ordinary photos—they were beautifully preserved, with many containing handwritten notes and captions.

One photograph, in particular, caught his eye: an old black-and-white image of a young woman with an intense, haunting expression. Drew turned it over to reveal a handwritten note.

"This is Mother. She had the most beautiful eyes, but they saw too much," Drew read from the back. The woman's dark brown complexion glistened like the sand in the background of the photograph.

As he continued flipping through the photos, he felt a profound connection to the person who had left them behind. These were not mere mementos but a glimpse into a life, a story waiting to be told.

"Why would Phillip have these old photos in his dressing room?" Debra asked.

"Maybe they aren't his. Perhaps they were here before he arrived," Israel suggested. "They were hidden."

Suddenly, Drew paused at a photograph of an older man on the same beach, his arm around a young man. The black-and-white image was damaged, with a corner torn away. "Francy," Drew called, "you have to see this!"

Francy scanned the hall to ensure no one was approaching, then joined Drew at the wardrobe. "What is it?" she asked, peering over Drew's shoulder at the boy's image. "Is that…?"

"A young Jonathan Matthews," Drew confirmed.

"Jonathan Matthews?" Debra asked, glancing at Drew.

Drew removed his dance bag and produced a small plastic bag containing a torn corner of a photograph that had fallen from Phillip's book of symbols.

"No?" Francy inquired.

"Is that the piece of paper we found in Phillip's symbol book?" Debra observed, anticipating Drew's next move.

Drew aligned the torn corner with the photograph, and the images fit together perfectly. He pressed the two pieces together and slowly turned the picture over. "Dad and me." The reconstructed image revealed Jonathan Matthews with his father.

"Oh my God," Israel exclaimed, suddenly grasping the implications.

"So, why are these photos of Jonathan Matthews in Phillip's dressing room?" Francy asked, rising as she heard a noise in the hall.

"There's a manila envelope under that ledge," Francy noted, pointing to the drawer's corner.

Drew handed the photo of Jonathan Matthews and his father to Francy. He examined the wardrobe and carefully retrieved the sealed envelope from under the ledge. With precision, he pried open the seal. "More photos," he whispered. As he extracted the 8 x 10 prints from their protective sleeves, Debra gasped.

"That's Richard Belltone with…"

"Jeanne Lois Van Italie," Francy replied, her voice laced with anger. "Mrs. Belltone's friend."

"Well, I wonder if Mrs. Belltone knows how friendly Jeanne Lois and her husband are," Israel remarked, his eyes wide with surprise.

"Phillip has pictures of his father having an affair with his wife's friend." Drew instinctively felt the pain Phillip must have endured and quickly returned the photos to the envelope.

"She seemed quite friendly with Jonathan at the Rainbow Room on the night of the fundraiser," Debra asserted.

"That girl is climbing the social ladder," Francy commented, her tone laced with disgust.

"This must be the leverage they are using against Mr. Belltone as blackmail," Drew speculated as he pieced together the puzzle. "So, Phillip discovered the indiscretion… and?" he paused.

"Was he going to confront his father?" Francy added.

"Why would Phillip be withholding this information?" Debra asked, her expression mirroring the group's bewilderment. Her confusion was palpable, as if grappling with an unsolvable puzzle. The room fell into heavy silence, each person contemplating the gravity of the situation.

Reacting quickly to a subtle sound in the hallway, Francy approached the dressing room door, only to be blocked by a formidable figure.

The group gasped in surprise.

Standing firmly in the doorway, the stage manager's commanding presence was unmistakable.

"What are you doing in here?" she demanded, her voice resonating with authority.

# Chapter 13
## Midtown East

"What are you doing here?" the stage manager repeated, pushing her way through the group. She stood in the center of the small room and looked around, trying to understand what they were up to.

Drew rose from the wardrobe, holding a small corner of the photo in his hand as he switched places with Francy. Debra quickly grabbed the handful of photos and papers from behind Drew's back and handed them to Israel, who tucked them into his shirt.

The stage manager's face flushed with tension. She stared at each of them, her eyes moving between Drew and his crew with fierce determination.

"Well?" she demanded, her voice sharp and firm. "What exactly are you doing?" She expected an answer.

The silence stretched, each second feeling like an eternity. Drew stepped forward to confront the angry woman, who was now using her headset to contact security.

"Alright. It's all okay," Drew tried to reassure her. "I'm sorry I didn't catch your name," he said calmly.

She suddenly paused. "Ava," she replied curtly.

"Ava, these are my friends," Debra announced. "They came backstage to see me after the show ended." She moved slowly toward Ava.

"Debra, there is no reason for you to be here. I'm going to have security escort your friends out."

"Ava, there's no need to call security," Drew said, motioning for her to lower her headset.

"What is your reason for being here?" she repeated.

"Ava, we were all friends with Phillip. We worked and spent time together. I just wanted to remember him one more time," Drew confessed.

Debra showed genuine empathy. "I really wanted to show my friends his former dressing room. There's nothing suspicious happening here," she insisted, turning and leaving the room.

The stage manager was taken aback. "Well, you shouldn't be in here," she huffed. After one last glance around the empty room, she stormed out. "We're closing the theatre in thirty minutes," she announced as she left.

"Are we really going to leave this rare La Croix painting here to decay?" Grace whispered. "Elena, quick, help me get it off the wall."

Elena peeked out of the dressing room and slipped back in to help Grace remove it. "Man, it's heavy," Elena said as she removed the framed artwork from the wall.

"You're right!" Grace exclaimed, surprised by its heaviness. "Let's take it to Debra's dressing room for now," she instructed.

Drew looked back when he heard Israel click the dressing room door shut, then realized what Elena and Grace had done. "Oh my God," Drew said, shocked, tapping Debra on the shoulder.

"For goodness' sake..." Debra began, unable to finish her sentence.

"Quick, let's move it to your dressing room for now," Elena urged. "Hurry, hurry—we can't risk being caught. Israel, do you have your pocket knife on you?" she whispered.

"You know me. I never go anywhere without my gadgets," Israel replied, searching his pockets and producing the knife from his dress coat.

Elena examined the painting for a strip of canvas she could remove so she'd have enough paint for analysis by Dr. Stevens.

"There. Right there," Grace pointed out as she reached down to lift a portion of the canvas stapled to the back of the frame.

"That's perfect." Elena knelt and cut a strip from the artwork. "Israel, thank you." She quickly folded the knife and tossed it to him.

"Good job, Elena," Drew said as he re-tucked his dress shirt into his pants and closed his dress jacket. A sudden flash overwhelmed him. "Debra, can you take us backstage to the spot where you found Phillip's hair?"

Debra looked up. "Yes, I think so. Come on." She hurried everyone out of her dressing room and led them back upstairs. "It was somewhere back here, behind the last backstage crossing." She led the way, walking slowly.

"Debra, remember the sticky substance you discovered near where you found Phillip's hair? The spot where he passed?"

She immediately felt resistance beneath her shoes. "Here. It's here," she exclaimed. "Elena, use your black light in this area."

She quickly pulled the light from her purse and turned it on. Splashes of yellow-green glowed beneath the beam, and the group gasped.

"If Phillip died here, he must have held the liquid in his hands," Drew deduced.

"Maybe it was in a glass of water?"

The group quickly spread out, surveying the area. Elena slowly walked along the boards, back and forth searching for any further signs.

"There are some cups and bottles here," Aisha called out.

Elena ran over to her and directed her light toward the vessels stuck behind the proscenium. The water bottle immediately glowed. Shock passed between them. Drew pulled a silk handkerchief from his front jacket pocket and carefully freed the bottle from the backstage wall.

"Dr. Stevens has some evidence to analyze." Drew's voice brimmed with excitement. "If Philip had this water bottle in his hands when he suffered his heart attack, he would have dropped it. This is too far from the scene of his crime." He stared at the gap between the spot where Philip collapsed and the proscenium. "It's possible that the murderer found him on the floor and, in a panic, tossed the bottle further backstage."

"Why wouldn't they take it with them?" Aisha asked.

"Perhaps others witnessed his collapse, leaving the murderer no time to conceal the bottle without drawing attention. Tossing it into the proscenium was probably their immediate reaction," Drew speculated.

"Maybe the paramedics threw it aside to clear the area, not realizing it was the murder weapon," Israel volunteered.

"The fingerprints on the bottle will provide a clearer story," Drew confirmed.

"We need to involve Detective Jameson in this news, don't we?" Grace leaned toward him.

"We've discovered some sensitive information over the past twenty-four hours, Grace. I'd prefer to speak with Richard Belltone first, out of respect for his privacy. Don't you agree?"

"Yes, yes. Oh yes," Grace confirmed.

"In the meantime, let's deliver this evidence to Dr. Stevens tomorrow morning. He can provide a better forensic analysis of what we're dealing with."

★★★

The following morning, Drew sat on the apartment floor once again, staring into Phillip's book. Although Adele Nozedar's book teemed with symbols and signs, Drew focused on the notes and limericks Phillip had handwritten on its pages.

"I guess you're expecting it to talk to you," Elena called from the kitchen.

Drew mumbled an affirmative response, soon losing himself in its further interpretations. "Maybe the symbols are telling a story," he called back.

"Or maybe they are just random marks capturing moments in Phillip's timeline—instances when he noticed something unusual and marked it."

Drew changed the subject. "Did you text Dr. Stevens?"

"Yes," Elena answered shortly.

"What did he say?" Drew asked, half-listening.

Elena entered the living room with a cup of coffee for Drew. "He hasn't gotten back to me."

Drew paused his work, giving Elena a puzzled look and a silent thank you for the coffee. "I hope he's alright. Should I call him?"

"Let's give him the benefit of the doubt," Elena suggested. She returned to the kitchen and soon came back with a bag of items from the previous night. "We have one swatch of painted material from the back of a La Croix painting, a bottle with fingerprints, and a box full of pictures and documents."

Drew examined the items they had discovered at the theater. "There must be some answers here. I'd like Dr. Stevens to see Phillip's book as well."

★★★

The Morgan Library, once the private library of banker J.P. Morgan, was now his legacy museum and research library, housing over 350,000 objects including illuminated manuscripts, music, photographs, and paintings. Dr. Stevens would love spending hours in its inspiring atmosphere.

He made his way to the outdoor garden, moving through the crowd, his tension heightened by the fear of a death threat looming over him. As he scanned the gathering, he noticed Elena and Grace, accompanied by Drew and Francy, making their way through the glass lobby bathed in warm summer light. He signaled them and watched as they stepped out into the garden, parting the crowd before them.

"Dr. Stevens, it's great to finally meet you," Drew said as he extended his hand. "This is Francy, and, of course, Elena and Grace have been your liaisons."

"Hi Dr. Stevens, we have several pieces of evidence for you to examine," Elena said with a smile.

They were soon joined by Aisha, Debra, and Israel, who also greeted the doctor. Always well-dressed, his white linen suit complemented his alabaster skin. Only his powdered blue shirt provided the contrast that made his grey hair and dark-rimmed reading glasses stand out. His sharp eyes reflected both intrigue and caution.

"What a beautiful location," Aisha remarked, taking in the scent of freshly cut grass mingled with a hint of lavender and the rustle of roses along the trellis, which provided a calm backdrop to the conversation.

"We also thought it might be valuable to show you this symbol book that was a favorite of our friend Phillip. He recorded several significant symbols, signs, and limericks on the back, all pertaining to this case," Drew explained.

Dr. Stevens' eyes lit up. The words "secrets and symbols" seemed to catch his attention. "That's what this library and museum are filled with," he said with a smile, looking around. "May I take a look at the book?"

Drew opened the publication to the back pages, where he had been studying it with Elena, and handed it over. Dr. Stevens studied the symbols that Phillip had recorded. "The broken chain, a key in a lock," he said aloud. "The eye, the scales of justice," he paused, then added while tilting his head in response to the next two images, "The snake and an hourglass."

"It looks like hieroglyphics," Grace observed aloud.

Dr. Stevens closed his eyes. "I don't think so. Egyptian hieroglyphics combine symbols for entire words with symbols for individual sounds."

"A pictogram, maybe?" Elena suggested as she stared at the pages.

"Perhaps," Dr. Stevens said, pursing his lips. He paused again before continuing, "I believe this is a pictograph—a more mathematical chart designed to represent data. In this case, I suspect your friend was indicating either his passage through a certain period or someone he was concerned about."

"A girlfriend, perhaps?" Aisha inquired.

"Together these symbols outline a journey from liberation—the broken chain represents freedom, the key signifies the discovery of opportunities, the eye stands for the pursuit of knowledge, and the scales embody the quest for justice." Dr. Stevens paused briefly before continuing, "In this context, the snake signifies the confrontation with moral challenges, and the hourglass marks time's fleeting nature."

The group was spellbound.

"This progression reflects the balance between freedom, knowledge, morality, and temptation, all set against the relentless flow of time," Dr.

Stevens remarked, smiling as though he had just solved the New York Times crossword puzzle.

"So, you think Phillip was recording someone's journey or their life path?" Drew asked, dumbfounded.

"Yes. It wasn't his own path—it was an observation of someone he was watching."

Dr. Stevens' interpretation proved insightful.

"Phillip was a keen observer of his surroundings. I believe his recording served as a coping mechanism for his obsessive-compulsive nature. It was cathartic," Drew realized. He discreetly slid a bag containing their gathered evidence to Dr. Stevens.

"I'll take care of this," the doctor reassured Drew.

Dr. Stevens closed the book and carefully slipped Drew's bag of evidence into his satchel.

"It sounds like you've uncovered something significant," Drew agreed. "That's fascinating."

"That's why I love coming here," Dr. Stevens said while admiring the surroundings. "Art has its own story to tell, and it helps me break free of my analytical mindset."

"Well, this calls for a cocktail!" Elena exclaimed. "Israel, let's order a round of champagne for our good doctor."

"Doctor, clearly your pastime gives you immense pleasure," Debra observed.

"Then I must share my passion for Tiffany lamps," he smiled at Debra. "There's a garden exhibit of Art Nouveau lamps. Would you ladies like to see them?"

Aisha blushed. "Of course we would," she said, linking arms with Debra as they moved further into the garden.

Suddenly, a bone-chilling scream shattered the calm afternoon air. Drew tensed, instinctively turning toward the sound. Near the garden's wrought-iron gates, a man in a dark coat and hoodie was sprinting away, his footfalls echoing on the cobblestones.

Aisha's eyes narrowed in alarm as panic surged through her. "The book!" she shouted, her voice a mix of disbelief and urgency. "The book is gone!"

The group spun around, their gaze fixed on the empty space where Phillip's book had just been—snatched from sight. Aisha clenched her fists as the gravity of their mission crashed down on them.

Drew's heart pounded as he turned to her, his voice firm with resolve. "We're not letting him get away. Let's move!"

Without a second thought, the crew took off in hot pursuit as the nearby crowd parted for them at the garden's entrance. Drew's mind raced with questions—who would dare steal from them in broad daylight? And, more importantly, who was this?

"Dr. Stevens, get somewhere safe!" Drew yelled as he dashed through the iron gates onto Madison Avenue. Close behind him ran Aisha, Debra, Francy, and Grace. Dr. Stevens called out to Elena and Israel, who immediately sprinted after them.

Ahead, the thief darted toward the subway entrance, the gap between him and the crew narrowing with every desperate stride. Adrenaline surged in Drew's veins, propelling him forward as his team blurred in pursuit.

"He's heading for the 6 train," Elena called out.

The subway entrance loomed ahead, its dark opening beckoning like a tunnel to escape. But Drew's pulse quickened—he couldn't let the thief slip away into the underworld of the city. Not with their treasure. Not after everything they'd fought for.

The man glanced over his shoulder, his face hidden beneath his hood. "Stop!" Drew shouted, his voice slicing through the chaos.

But the thief ignored him, quickening his pace; the grim determination in his actions only fueling Drew's drive.

Aisha, now at Drew's side and breathing heavily, kept her focus sharp. "We have to catch him before he gets on the train."

Drew could hear the thief gasping for breath. "You're not going to get away with this!" he yelled.

# Chapter 14
## Under New York

They sprinted to the subway entrance. They could hear a hurling train below them rip by on the express track. A blast of scorching heat burst over the top of the subway steps, as if the doors of hell had swung open.

"He's headed downtown!" Elena yelled breathlessly. It turned into a frantic sprint down the crowded staircase to catch the thief.

"I just saw him jump the turnstile!" Israel called, pointing to the figure in a dark hoodie and camouflage pants. "Aisha, it looks like the same guy we chased through midtown!"

Moving through the bustling crowd during rush hour felt like swimming against a relentless current. Upon reaching the platform, they quickly surveyed the dimly lit station, straining to spot the black hoodie amid the surging throng as the next downtown train thundered into the station. The motion kicked up debris on the tracks, and the faint scent of wheel grease filled the air.

"There he is!" Debra shouted above the clamor.

Drew caught his breath and signaled to Francy and Grace. "Ladies, hustle. The doors are closing!"

"Where's Aisha?" Grace gasped. "Oh my, I'm definitely not used to sprinting through subways, Drew."

"She's in the adjacent train car," Elena replied. "Come on, girl— show us your cardio skills!"

"There he is!" Grace clutched her purse tightly at her waist as she sprinted after him. "I'm not sure what I'll do if I catch him, but I'll think of something," she panted.

"Attention, passengers: this train is running express. Next stop, Brooklyn Bridge," an almost indistinct voice announced over the claustrophobic car. The subway doors closed, and the train jerked forward.

The thief forced his way through the crowd, leaving behind a trail of irritated and profanity-ladened New Yorkers in his wake. He gripped the book as if it were his final lifeline to a vanishing world.

"He's got nowhere to go!" Drew yelled.

Inside the packed subway car, there was no place to hide. The thief's only option was to force his way through the crowd until the next stop. "Let's corner him at the far end!"

The train raced through the tunnel, its interior filled with tired, curious, and reluctant passengers pushing one another aside to clear a path for the maniac in the black hoodie, who was shouting for them to move.

"He's gone through the door to the next car," Francy announced over the disgruntled crowd. She had caught up with Drew as they simultaneously dodged the startled passengers trailing behind their assailant.

"I see him," Drew confirmed as he squeezed past each person, apologizing with every step. The subway train zoomed through the tunnel—a blur of darkness punctuated by fleeting glimpses of blinking lights that created an unsettling atmosphere, further hindering movement among the aggravated passengers. Alternating between harsh fluorescent glare and momentary darkness, this shifting light caused shadows to dance across the worn interior.

"Yo, you need to chill, bro," a hulking man blocked Drew's path as he hurried through the subway car.

"Yo, that guy in the hoodie nicked something very valuable of mine," Drew retorted quickly, glancing up at his detractor.

Without missing a beat, the man turned and pulled the emergency brake positioned just to his right.

The train slid freely and screeched across the tracks. The deafening sound reverberated throughout the subway car. Passengers had to choose between shielding their ears from the high-pitched, ear-splitting squeal or clinging on for dear life as the train bucked back and forth like an accordion in a futile attempt to slow down.

Passengers gripped the handrails as the car surged forward and then jerked backward to a stop. The sudden jolt sent some sliding off their seats while others released their grip, reaching for anyone who could help them or at least break their fall.

Israel grabbed the overhead bar and swung from side to side, while Francy and Drew reached for each other. Drew had no choice but to cling to the burly man who had pulled the emergency brake. "We're going down!" Drew shouted to Francy and the instigator of this chaotic chain of events. The trio bounced off the doors and moved across the train to two passengers who braced themselves against the doors.

The train slid forward a few feet before coming to a complete stop. The man who had pulled the emergency brake slowly rose from the floor. Drew noticed that he was clearly stoned. "Yo," the man smirked at Drew, "I always wanted to do that." Passengers began yelling and screaming at the top of their lungs.

"What's going on?"

"What's the deal?"

"I need to get home!"

Elena stood and watched as the suspect, caught between two cars, struggled to pull himself up from the train couplers. A bloody handprint smeared the glass.

A woman screamed when she saw the mark, watching it fade away before her eyes. In an instant, he vanished.

Elena ran to Drew and Francy. "You good?" she asked. Without waiting for an answer, she pointed to the door. "I think he jumped off the train into the tunnel."

"Let's go!" Drew commanded. "If we lose that book, we lose everything."

Amid the throng of frustrated travelers packed like sardines, Elena spun, her eyes searching desperately for any sign of Grace.

Drew reached for the door handle and slid it open, noticing the bloody handprint smeared across the glass. There stood Aisha, straddling the opposite doorway, a book in one hand and a can of mace in the other.

"He met his match," she stated matter-of-factly. "Then the train stopped, and I landed backwards in the opposite car. The guy in the hoodie crashed into the train and slid down between the cars." Aisha pointed to where a trail of blood marked his descent over the metal step. "He has mace in his eyes and was injured, so he can't be far!"

Francy, Elena, and Israel burst in from behind, all crowding into the doorway. Their surprised expressions caught Aisha off guard.

"What? Where were you guys?" she asked, brushing her long blond hair to one side while gripping the book in the other as if it were gold.

"Oh my God, you got the book!" Israel yelled as he wiped the sweat from his forehead.

Drew peered over the edge of the car and followed the blood trail. He jumped off the train and onto the tracks.

Grace and Debra reached the group at the door. "Where is he going? He's like a bloodhound," Debra blurted.

Drew looked into the darkness of the subway tunnel. The dank odor of axle grease and the oppressive humidity stifled him immediately. His heart raced as he crouched to search for more blood droplets. "Hey," he yelled back to the group, "we're about a hundred yards from the next station. We should make a break for it!"

Without a word, Aisha scrambled down between the two subway cars. "Come on," she yelled, "this train could sit here for an hour!"

Francy quickly followed Aisha over the edge and down onto the tracks. Elena grabbed Debra as they helped each other to safety, and Grace and Israel followed suit.

They instantly heard footsteps echoing through the tunnel and then a thud as the suspect struggled to recover from his encounter with Aisha.

Debra looked up from her dismount onto the tracks to see the guy in the hoodie trying to stand, wiping the mace from his eyes. "There he goes," she pointed, "he's running."

"Isn't there a third rail here somewhere? All I need now is to be electrocuted," Grace cried out as she tiptoed across the dirt floor.

"Just stay to your right," Drew called back.

The group raced ahead, sprinting toward their suspect, who was nearly fifty yards away. Aggressive and agile, he defied pursuit by picking up rocks along the track and hurling them at his pursuers. He veered sharply, crossing the exposed tracks beneath the yawning opening of the tunnel, and moved away from the station platform directly ahead of them.

"Where is he going?" Francy yelled as she dug her heels into the dirt and sprinted after him. "He's running away from the station platform!"

The group moved carefully, hopping over the tracks and staying wary of the dangerous third rail.

The tunnel suddenly burst into blinding light as an oncoming train's headlights cut through the darkness, its unstoppable mass hurtling toward them with terrifying speed. The deafening screech of metal on metal filled the air as sparks erupted from the wheels, sending a shower of fiery embers dancing along the tracks.

"Move! Now!" Drew's voice rang out amid the chaos, raw panic evident in every syllable. "We have to cross before it's too late!"

Aisha had already reached safety when the train's horn blasted a bone-chilling wail that echoed off the tunnel walls. The conductor's desperate warning came too late—there was no stopping the iron behemoth now.

Debra's heart pounded as she leaped between the vibrating ties, each step a gamble between life and death. The very ground beneath her trembled with the looming threat.

Drew's blood ran cold as a chill shot up his back. Grace and Israel stood frozen, struggling with Elena, who had fallen. Time seemed to slow as he watched the scene unfold, aware they were seconds away from obliteration.

"I'm good!" Elena gasped, her voice barely audible over the approaching thunder.

"God, no!" Drew's scream tore from his throat as he raced back, seizing Grace's arm. Israel hauled Elena up, desperation lending them strength beyond measure. They cleared the tracks just as the train roared past, so close they could feel the searing heat singeing their skin.

185

The world became nothing but noise, wind, and terror as the train barreled by—an eternity compressed into a few heartbeats. The group fled deeper into the tunnel, which seemed to constrict around them, threatening to crush them in its stony grip.

Francy's voice cut through the fading echo. "There! He's just ahead!" Her words carried both relief and urgency as she glanced back, silently counting heads and praying they had all cheated death.

The group rounded the bend and stopped. Francy was nowhere to be seen. Neither was their suspect.

"Where are we?" Debra asked Aisha, coming to a halt. "Are we still in New York? I've never seen this station."

Drew, Elena, Israel, and Grace ran into the abandoned station behind them, their eyes wide in awe at the hidden architectural gem before them. They paused at the entrance to a breathtaking space that seemed frozen in time.

Suddenly, Francy appeared at the top of a stone and glass staircase. Out of breath, she bent over, grasping her knees as she tried to catch her breath. "That guy was fast! Even injured, and with mace in his eyes." She stood and faced the group.

"There you are," Debra exclaimed. "We thought you took a detour."

"I followed his blood trail up over the platform and up the stairs. But he got away," she huffed, annoyed that she couldn't catch him. "But we can get out upstairs," Francy pointed toward the staircase.

"Well, at least we got the book back," Aisha reminded everyone softly. She turned, fascinated by the ticket booths and turnstiles—still in place as if waiting for long-gone commuters. "This place is stunning. The details are top-notch."

The friends gathered in the center of the platform to recover from their ordeal. The space was particularly peaceful. From their resting spots in the vast underground room, they were struck by the station's impressive state of preservation.

"Wow, this must be the abandoned City Hall Station. I've never seen this before." Drew, still out of breath, was immediately captivated by the graceful curve of the platform following the natural bend of the track.

The Art Deco vaulted ceilings soared overhead, their elegant lines drawing the eye upward. As he slowly stood, Drew marveled at how the arching design created an expansive feel in what would otherwise be an enclosed space.

Elena's attention was caught by the intricate tilework on the walls. "This station is a masterpiece," she breathed, starstruck. The geometric patterns and bold colors were typical of that era. She traced her fingers along the glazed tiles of blue, green, and gold, admiring their pristine condition despite decades of disuse.

"Will you look at that." Israel's eyes were drawn to the ornate brass chandeliers hanging from the ceiling. Though no longer lit, he could imagine how they once bathed the station in a warm, golden glow. "This metalwork is impressive," he mumbled, absorbing the elaborate floral motifs that complemented the overall design.

"This place would give anyone hope." Grace's gaze shot upward to the stained-glass skylights. Rays of sunlight filtered through the colorful panes, casting a kaleidoscope of hues across the platform. The effect was almost otherworldly, transforming the underground space into something truly magical.

"Why can't every subway station be like this?" Israel wondered.

"Huh," Debra huffed. "Money. That's why."

"We've stumbled upon a piece of living history," Drew confirmed.

"And to think, this secret architectural wonder sits beneath the crazy streets of Manhattan. What a shame," Francy shook her head.

"Which way do we go?" Aisha asked, ready to see daylight again.

Francy looked back and forth along the huge platform, trying to determine which staircase she had come from that would lead to their escape. "This way," she said, pointing.

Israel guided the girls to a metal ladder. Drew reached for each of their hands, helping them move toward daylight.

"Why would that guy avoid the closer subway platform and run this way?" Drew mused aloud.

They reached the top of the stairs. "I think we went the wrong way," Debra said, looking around to get her bearings.

"I'm sure he came this way," Francy said as she looked left and right at what appeared to be a dead end. The metal platform was suspended above the tracks with only a tiled wall in front of them.

"There," Aisha pointed to the floor. "More blood."

The group spun around to face the wall.

"Look around for more blood. He must have come this way," Francy insisted.

Debra and Aisha walked back and forth along the platform, trying to make sense of the blood trail.

"Drew, look," Israel observed as he stared at cracks in the tile. He stepped up to the wall and traced a perfect rectangle with his finger amid the tile pattern.

"The blood goes right up to the wall," Francy confirmed, her determination unyielding. "He may have eluded me, but I will track him down."

"That's our Francy!" Israel cheered.

"It's a door," Drew exclaimed. "There has to be a door opener or trip that releases it. Look around, everyone!"

Grace examined the floor beneath the wall while Francy and Israel began pushing on the tiles.

"How clever. They built this into the design over a hundred years ago?" Debra commented as she watched everyone scurry along the wall's edge.

A click echoed, and everyone froze. Elena, admiring the tile work in the station below, noticed one detail. "This pattern is completely different from the others around it." She pressed a shimmering gold tile that stood out from the rest.

"You did it, girl!" Israel exclaimed, more excited than she was. The tile wall opened about an inch to reveal an inner handle that activated a trap door.

Francy quickly pulled her phone from her pocket and switched on its bright light. "More blood!"

"Do we have to go in there?" Grace asked, stepping back.

"Come on. We'll go together," Drew coaxed. "Follow Francy."

Drew, Debra, and Israel soon turned on their phone lights as well. The seven slowly ascended the stone staircase further upward.

"More blood," Francy added. The dark, dank stairwell smelled of dampness as traces of calcium and dirt dripped along the ancient walls.

As they reached the top of the stairs, a wooden door in front of them was slightly ajar. "Okay, who's going through?" Before Grace could finish her sentence, Francy and Israel were through the entrance.

Grace spun around and looked back at Drew and Elena. "Well, I don't want to go back the way we came," she said as she pushed through the door and found herself in a foyer facing another door. "Another room?"

The small space barely accommodated the seven of them. The walls were made of cement blocks. The wooden door in front of them had no handle. "Another trapped door. No handle this time," Aisha observed.

"All right, everyone take a section of the room," Drew announced as he moved to his right and began inspecting the floor.

"On it. I'll cover the left wall," Francy called out.

"Right wall for me."

"I'll check out the ceiling. Anyone got a flashlight? My phone died," Elena said, shaking her phone as if to jump-start it.

"Here, catch," Israel tossed his phone to her.

"I've got the floor," Grace added, shining her light along the dirt floor and across the borders of the room they were crammed into.

"Hold on—the floor feels different here. It's… springy?" Israel remarked, pushing his toe along the border between the floor and the door. Grace quickly shone her light in his direction.

"Let me see." Francy felt along the wall. "You're right. It's subtle, but there's definitely some give."

"I don't see any shadows or reflections that would indicate a hidden switch," Debra observed as she drew closer to the wall.

"The door frame seems ordinary, but… wait. There's a tiny groove here, almost invisible." Elena ran her finger up and down the side of the frame.

"You might be onto something. What if they're connected?" Grace suggested, moving her light between the floor and the frame where Elena was investigating.

"A pressure plate on the floor that activates something in the door frame?" Drew quickly surmised.

"Worth a try." Israel pressed down on the flexible spot on the floor. "Elena, keep your fingers in that groove."

As Israel applied pressure, a faint click echoed through the room. Debra gasped.

"The groove widened! There's a small lever inside." Elena peered closer at the exposed portion of the door. "Ah… guys… a bloody fingerprint." She was so distracted by what she saw…

"Pull it!" Aisha reacted, excited at the possibility of an exit.

Elena pulled the lever, and the door swung open with a soft hiss.

"Excellent work, everyone. Teamwork at its finest. Now, let's see what's beyond this door…" Drew stepped into the center of the wooden entrance as it gently opened into a marble hallway.

"This can't be," Debra gasped, looking left and right down the corridor.

"It's the same style as the subway station we just came through," Israel observed as he spun around, noting similar details.

"Yes, it was Guastavino," Debra confirmed. "He influenced both designs."

"We must be in City Hall." Elena turned and spotted a door bearing the title "New York City Council."

"Do you think this guy is associated with the City Council?" A look of shock crossed Debra's face.

"Or the Mayor," Drew added.

Everyone stopped and stared at Drew.

"What? They are the only two offices in here," he said, looking around as several city employees passed by.

"Now what?" Aisha asked, scanning the area stealthily.

"Follow the blood," Drew responded. "We've come this far."

They advanced about thirty feet down the elegant marble hall, keeping their eyes peeled for further clues.

"I don't see anything," Grace whispered. "What do we do if we get caught?"

"Don't get caught," Israel replied immediately.

"Act like you work here," Elena added.

In these clothes?" Grace asked, glancing around nervously.

"Look," Francy whispered, "this door handle has blood on it."

"That's where we're going." Drew quickly opened the door and ushered his friends inside.

"Quick, shut the door before someone sees us," Debra urged.

They closed the door quickly and looked around. "A conference room?"

At the center, a massive wooden table dominated the space, its surface scarred and lackluster. The rich mahogany gleamed dully in the light filtering through tall, grimy windows.

"Now that's a lot of books," Grace exclaimed upon noticing a floor-to-ceiling bookcase spanning the far wall. Its shelves sagged under numerous leather-bound tomes and dusty legal volumes. The large expanse showed signs of faded grandeur—a relic of City Hall's illustrious past.

"Mmmm, I love the scent of aged paper and musty leather," Debra admitted, running her fingers across the bound publications.

"Wait," Aisha murmured in a low, tense voice. "Someone's coming."

Instantly, the group stilled, holding their breath. Every noise and slight shift amplified in the heavy silence as they hoped their presence remained undetected.

The conference room door swung open with a sharp, unsettling creak. A young woman with bright red hair stepped inside, her eyes widening as she took in the unexpected sight of several people gathered in the room. She froze, clearly surprised. "I'm terribly sorry," she said, her voice mixing confusion with mild embarrassment. "I thought this room was unoccupied."

Aisha responded swiftly, her tone firm yet polite as she concealed her tension. "No, I'm afraid it isn't available," she replied in clipped, composed tones.

The woman's expression faltered, and her cheeks flushed with embarrassment. Without another word, she dipped her head in apology and hurriedly exited the room, closing the door behind her with a soft click. The air grew tense, as if time had slowed in the wake of the encounter.

Grace exhaled sharply, clearly rattled. "That was far too close," she said, rising from the table and adjusting her braids as if to steady herself. "What do we do now? Wait for her to come back, or… do we move now?"

Israel's gaze shifted to the door, and his body was already in motion. Without a second thought, he rushed over and fumbled with the lock. After a brief hesitation, the mechanism clicked into place. He paused, listening for any sound on the other side—the uncertainty was unnerving.

The group remained silent and tense, each of them acutely aware of how fleeting their time was.

Debra's heart raced, panic tightening her chest. "What if she saw more than she let on?" Her voice trembled, barely above a whisper. "What if she realizes we don't belong here?" The possibility of discovery loomed like a shadow just beyond the door.

Drew's gaze hardened; his posture remained steady as he stepped away from the table. "We can't afford to get lost in what ifs," he said, his voice steady yet edged with urgency. "We've got a job to finish. Stick to the task."

Without a moment's hesitation, he moved to the door and tested the handle, ensuring it was securely locked. The sound of it moving back and forth was the only noise in the otherwise still room—and it did little to reassure them.

"Guys, you have to see this." Francy interrupted as she knelt beside the corner of the bookcase.

Grace and Elena moved closer. Francy switched on the light on her phone, the beam trembling across the dusty floorboards until it reached a stain. "Do you see that?"

Drew followed the light, his breath catching. "Is that… blood?"

"A perfect half-moon," Francy muttered, crouching to examine the dark stain. "Right along the edge of the bookcase."

"That's a lot of blood! What an odd pattern," Debra said, looking at Drew. Then her eyes traced the half-moon shape from the floor to the border of the bookcase's edging. "It looks like the blood is coming from the bookcase!" The floorboards creaked around them, as if listening to their discovery.

Drew ran his fingers along the ornate woodwork of the bookcase. "This thing looks embedded into the wall, but…" He paused before removing three books from the shelf. Pressing his ear against the back of the case, he tapped it. "There's a hollow sound behind this."

Elena slowly stood, her eyes widening. "A hidden door?"

Debra shook her head in exasperation. "What is it with this place?"

"Only one way to find out," Drew said, gripping the edge of the bookcase. "Help me pull."

He tugged on the border of the case, straining against the heavy wood; his muscles tensed. Israel hurried over and wrapped his fingers around one of the shelves, pulling along with Drew. Nothing moved.

"There has got to be a trigger, like the last two walls we came through," Elena observed as she began moving books aside.

"Alright," Aisha recalled, "the first trigger was a tile that clicked open. The second door was a pressure plate on the floor…"

"These are all law books," Debra noted, running her finger over each title.

Israel grabbed a chair and pulled it over to the shelves. He climbed onto the chair and read the titles on the top shelves. "Municipal archive books up here…."

"Architecture books…" Elena observed, her eyes scanning the bottom shelf.

"David Copperfield?" Debra scoffed. "I think not. This doesn't belong here." She reached for one of the top books, and it swung outward.

For a moment, nothing happened. Then, with a groan from protesting hinges, a portion of the bookcase lumbered outward like an old door. Debra gasped. "Oh my God."

"You did it, girl!" Israel cheered as he jumped off the chair and ran to help. He slowly pulled the door open wider.

Behind the bookcase, a yawning darkness stretched before them. The beam of their flashlights barely penetrated the inky black.

"Look," Francy said, stepping back. She shone her phone's light on the floor, revealing the other half of the blood pool. "This blood is fresh. There's barely any coagulation."

"Something sinister just happened here," Elena murmured as she peered into the void. "This isn't from an injury."

They slowly shone their lights down the narrow hallway.

"We've got drag marks," Drew alerted the team. "In blood."

"There are stairs at the end of the corridor," Israel whispered, his voice tight. "They lead down."

A cold draft whispered up from below, carrying the scent of damp earth and something else—something metallic and sickly sweet.

Francy's hand found Israel's in the dark, squeezing it tight. "Whatever happened here—whoever left that blood... I think we're about to find out."

"I think we know who this is from," Israel assured.

Drew nodded, taking a deep breath, and placed his foot on the first step. The wood creaked ominously beneath him. "Stay close," he murmured, and together they descended into the unknown darkness as the secret door to the bookcase slowly closed behind them with a final, chilling click.

# Chapter 15
## River to River

The strange odor hung heavily in the air; an unsettling presence clashed with the staid surroundings. The faint yet persistent smell led them further down the staircase into a cavernous room.

"It's unbelievable," Debra whispered, grabbing Drew's arm as they reached the bottom of the stairs. "More blood," she emphasized. Then… something caught her eye. She tugged on Drew's arm harder. "What's that?" In the shadows, Debra noticed a small set of metal keys at the bottom of the staircase. She pulled another handkerchief from her dance bag and handed it to Drew. He quickly pocketed the keys.

The high ceilings were adorned with ornate plasterwork, now cracked and discolored with age. Heavy drapes, once vibrant but now faded and worn, framed the tiled walls. Ancient photographs of New York stared back at them, barely stirring in the stagnant air that seemed to trap history and secrets within its confines.

"I bet this isn't on the tour," Elena commented.

"What is this place?" Aisha whispered as she shone her flashlight into the opposite corners of the space.

"A place to store kilos of cocaine!" Drew responded as he caught sight of wrapped bricks stacked high in the glow of Aisha's light.

Israel and Drew quickly switched on their flashlights to reveal what appeared to be forty to fifty bricks, bound in brown plastic and stacked against one wall.

"Or some other drug of choice," Israel remarked. "A perfect hiding spot, under City Hall."

He darted over to the wall and lifted one of the heavy packages.

Grace was staring at a series of numbers scratched into the bricks. "Israel, can I borrow your glasses?" she asked. She snapped a few photos using Israel's Ray Bans.

"Good thinking, girl!" Israel said as he pierced the outer packaging, letting powder trickle out onto the floor. He retrieved his eyeglass case and managed to collect some of the substance.

"Israel, what are you doing?" Debra asked, panic clear in her voice.

"Evidence, mi amor… Evidence!"

He opened the backpack he carried and slid another package inside.

Francy and Elena appeared in the far doorway. "The blood trail goes right down this corridor," Francy announced, shining her light ahead.

"We've found the way out," Elena added.

Drew and Aisha surveyed the rest of the room as the others followed Francy and Elena through the doorway.

"This must be a waiting room or meeting room, somehow connected with the City Hall Station we just came from," Aisha surmised.

"Every corner of this city seems to harbor a secret," Drew whispered to himself.

"Someone is a La Croix fan." Aisha pulled back another tattered curtain to reveal a dusty painting, almost six feet tall.

"Hidden Spaces," Drew mumbled. "This was the other painting stolen from the Prague Museum a few years ago."

Aisha shot him a look. "How do you know that? I didn't peg you as a fan of modern art."

"I saw this painting being sold at the underground auction. A mysterious man outbid everyone for it. We followed him through the club, but we lost him. Now, it ends up here."

"An appropriate title." Aisha observed the signature LX in a circle at the bottom right of the painting. "Why would it be here?" She snapped several pictures of the artwork from different angles. "We better catch up with the others."

"The blood trail goes right up to these tracks," Francy announced as she led the group through a large archway, following the trail that ran to the edge of a pair of train tracks.

"Maybe they put him in one of those flatbed cars," Debra suggested, pointing to their left.

The underground tunnel stretched out like a labyrinth beneath the city, silent and dimly lit. In a secluded section of track, a series of flatbed cars sat motionless, their rusted metal frames barely visible in the gloom.

Drew and Aisha caught up to their friends. "These aren't ordinary subway cars; they're industrial-grade flatbeds, designed for transporting heavy equipment and materials through the tunnels."

As the team approached, they noticed the cars were arranged in a precise line, as if awaiting a designated operation. The lead car, slightly larger than the others, bore faint markings that had long since faded. It's cool surface carried the chill of the underground.

"Are we sure this is the way out?" Debra asked, skepticism clear in her voice.

"Our movements are making it harder to backtrack," Francy confirmed. They stepped into the front flatbed, and a soft creak announced their embarkation.

"There's no obvious control panel—just a single lever protruding from the floor."

"Pull it," shouted Aisha.

The car shifted and then lurched forward with surprising smoothness, the only sounds the soft hum of hidden machinery and the whisper of wheels on rails.

The journey was surreal. The flatbed glided through a tunnel that grew increasingly unfamiliar, branching off from any known subway map. Ancient brickwork gave way to rough-hewn stone, hinting at passages that predated the city.

The crew traveled in silence, awed by the vast space hidden beneath Manhattan's crowded surface. They couldn't shake the feeling that they had stumbled upon something never meant to be found.

Finally, the car slowed as it entered a vast, shadowy space. As the team's eyes adjusted, they found themselves in an enormous warehouse with a high ceiling swallowed by darkness. Dusty shafts of light filtered through high windows, illuminating floating motes and the faint outline of long-abandoned machinery.

"Last stop!" Elena exclaimed.

"Now where are we?" Grace screeched.

The team dismounted their unexpected escape pod and made their way to an opening in the side of the cement structure.

"We are close to the Brooklyn Bridge," Drew answered. "I saw its shadow through the skylight."

The warehouse floor was littered with enigmatic crates and equipment of mysterious purpose. In the distance, the muffled sound of flowing water and traffic reminded them of their proximity to the East River and the FDR Drive.

"So, we're under the highway?" Debra enquired.

"Yes, look—that's the East River," Drew pointed to the body of water in front of them.

"This is complete déjà vu! Israel, we've been here before!" Aisha shouted, recognizing the tracks and the scent of diesel fuel.

Israel's eyes widened. "Of course. The warehouse we followed the man in black to."

"It was here?" Drew asked, glancing at Israel.

"Yes, this is the place. Aisha, look—there's the spot where we tipped the bike over. The boxes are still on the ground."

"There's a big crowd over there," Grace observed, pointing toward a group of kids yelling and pointing at the water.

"We need to cross the highway," Debra said with trepidation. She surveyed the road in both directions as they made their way through traffic, which had slowed as drivers craned their necks to see a body floating face down in the river.

They reached the crowd. Staring at the surreal sight before them, reality washed over them like a murky wave. The thief they chased through the subway and followed into City Hall now lay as a victim of foul play in the East River.

"Did anyone call 911?" Drew asked the group of kids, who were fascinated by what looked like a mix of unreal events and a movie set.

"Oye, alguien llamó al 911," Israel repeated in Spanish.

There was no response.

"I'm calling Detective Jameson," Grace declared.

The team gathered along the riverbank. The commotion grew; traffic nearly came to a standstill, and horns blared to clear the blockade.

"Okay, Drew, what are we thinking?" Debra asked, one eye on the traffic and the other on his reaction.

"Our thief fled the scene via his secret route through the City Hall Station and into City Hall," Drew explained.

"He didn't return with what he was supposed to steal," Aisha interjected, clutching the book close to her chest.

"So, the person he was stealing for was clearly unhappy," Drew surmised. "They killed him in the conference room and moved the body through the tunnels beneath City Hall."

"That seems to track," Elena agreed.

"He's on his way," Grace informed the team about Detective Jameson.

"A direct line to the Detective?" Debra smirked, meeting Grace's eyes.

"Who killed this guy?" Grace then asked, shifting nervously as chaos swirled around them.

"It's broad daylight. This happened within the hour. Someone must have seen something," Drew observed, scanning the crowd frantically.

"Are there no surveillance cameras around here?" Elena noted, tracking the victim's apparent route from the warehouse to the water.

Red and blue lights splashed across the concrete embankment of the East River, while the afternoon heat rose from the overbaked asphalt below. Three NYPD patrol cars pulled up in a choreographed formation—the first parked parallel to the water, the second angled at 45 degrees, and the third blocking the pedestrian walkway.

Officer Martinez silenced her siren but left the light bar running. "Dispatch, 32-Charlie on scene at East River near FDR Drive and the Brooklyn Bridge promenade. Two additional units present."

"Copy 32-Charlie. Harbor Unit en route. ETA six minutes."

Detective Jameson stepped out of his unmarked car, coffee in hand.

"Who called it in?" Martinez asked, approaching Jameson.

"See that group right there?" Jameson asked, spotting Grace and Drew staring out into the East River. "They say they spotted it about fifteen minutes ago. I'll go chat with them."

"Leave it to me," the detective said, stopping Officer Martinez in her tracks. "Grace!" Detective Jameson called out as he pushed through the crowd of onlookers trying to catch a glimpse of the body.

"Officer Martinez, get this crowd under control," Jameson shouted back.

The body bobbed gently in the current—face down, dark clothes billowing around it like a grotesque jellyfish. Another officer was already stringing up yellow tape, wrangling the onlookers while his partner photographed the scene.

"Harbor Unit's coming in hot," Martinez called, gesturing toward the sound of an approaching police boat. Its spotlight cut through the murky water, creating a bright corridor on the East River.

Two Harbor officers guided their vessel alongside the body. The first, secured by a safety line, leaned over with a pole. "Look, he's caught in that eddy by the pilings."

"Move in closer," the second officer called.

"Ready for recovery," the first officer announced. "Get your end."

"Got it. Easy... easy..." came the reply.

Grace and Drew clung to each other while Debra and Israel hugged close by. Francy and Elena watched as the Harbor patrol officers respectfully removed the floater from the water and secured it on the boat. They maneuvered the body into a recovery bag, careful to preserve any evidence. The boat then docked at a nearby emergency slip, where the Medical Examiner's team waited with a gurney.

Behind the police tape, Drew observed an even larger group of on-lookers gathered, despite traffic now halted on the FDR Drive and dozens more officers on scene. Debra pressed against the barrier, her heart pounding as the body bag was wheeled past.

The ME unzipped the bag just enough to photograph the face. Debra's knees nearly buckled. "Oh God," she whispered.

Drew and Israel grabbed her arms to steady her. "Debra? What is it?"

"That's… that's Isandro—the security guard from the museum." Her voice cracked.

"Wait a minute," Grace said, her eyes locking onto Elena's with sudden realization. Her voice dropped. "He was the security guard on duty at the morgue. He was one of the guys who tried to stop us."

Elena's pulse spiked, the connection crashing into her like a wave. "Grace, you're right."

Detective Jameson's head snapped up, his eyes narrowing as if the air had suddenly thickened. "You know this man?"

Grace's hands shook at her sides. "He's one of the security guards at the morgue on the day we went." Grace shot Detective Jameson a look that could've burned through steel. "You don't remember?"

"I don't know. I don't remember every security guard, waiter, or newspaper guy I pass by in a day," Jameson muttered, trying to regain his composure as he pulled out his notebook as if it could change anything.

Drew's face drained of color as he leaned forward, his voice trembling. "Wait… Isandro? He's the one who—" He swallowed hard as Debra finished his sentence.

"He's the one who introduced us to Marcus Larson the day we went to the Whitney," she said, shaking her head.

The ME was about to zip up the bag when Jameson stepped forward. "Wait a minute, wait a minute," he called, motioning to the ME. "Don't go anywhere." He lifted the police tape and let Drew and Debra, Grace and Israel, and Francy and Elena pass underneath. "These guys have some information that might be helpful. Unzip the bag." He then turned back to the ME. "Were there any notable findings?"

"His throat was cut and he sustained a deep stab wound to the abdomen," the ME explained. "There are also signs of a struggle—bruising on the face and body. His eyes are red and bloodshot. One more thing… there is an unusual burn on the right thumb and index finger. He was cut, bled out, then tossed in the river."

Grace was just about to reveal their experience when Drew squeezed her hand firmly. She stopped mid-word and gave Drew a sidelong glance. The group fell silent. Drew detected a faint smell of axle grease on his shirt. After a pause, he asked, "Can I see his boots?"

The ME unzipped the body bag completely to reveal the shoes. Drew pulled Francy aside.

Francy examined the bottom of the boots and squeezed Drew's hand in confirmation. She quickly took out her phone and snapped a picture.

"What's that about?" Jameson asked, looking in her direction. "What do you have?"

"Just covering my bases," Francy mumbled dismissively.

Then Detective Jameson's expression changed as he suddenly made a connection. "Belltone sent me a partial photo of a boot print you found outside his son's window."

Francy exchanged a curious look with Drew, wondering where Jameson was headed with this.

"I had forensics run the print," he continued. "It's a standard-issue boot that military men wear. The superintendent of that building is ex-military, and he may have been on the fire escape handling maintenance issues."

"What about the partial fingerprint image?" Francy asked, squinting in disbelief.

"Inconclusive," Jameson grumbled.

Drew then confirmed with Debra, Elena, and Grace, "That is definitely Isandro—from the Whitney and from the morgue. That's a lead you should follow."

Jameson leaned in, brow furrowed, his voice dropping low with an unmistakable edge. His Brooklyn accent was thick as molasses, every word dripping with suspicion and authority. "I'll double back on that. In the meantime, you better be sure you're telling me everything. I don't care if you think you've been keeping things close to the vest. If there's a single thing you've been holding back, now's the time to let it out. Got it?"

He closed his notebook and stuffed it in his pocket, his voice rising. "You think I'm here to play nice? Think again. I'm not some rookie cop, and I sure as hell ain't gonna let you treat me like a fool. I need everything—right down to the last detail. And don't you dare think I won't know if you're lying. I've seen it all before."

Jameson took a step closer, his tone lowering into a menacing threat. "So I'm gonna ask you one more time—are you absolutely sure you've told me everything? 'Cause if there's even a sliver of info you're holding back, we'll be having a whole different conversation. And trust me, you won't like where it goes."

He stared each one of them down, his eyes icy and unyielding, daring anyone to test him. "You tell me everything, or you're gonna regret it."

Instantly weighing the situation, Drew decided to speak up. "Well, don't you find it interesting that we all happened to be here at the location where a body turned up?"

"And?" Jameson snarled.

"This man stole something that was ours. We followed him through the subway and into City Hall," Drew confessed.

"What did he steal?" Detective Jameson interrupted.

"A book of ours," Grace replied.

"We lost him inside the building— all we did was follow the blood trail."

"He was apparently injured," Grace quickly added.

"We discovered a secret passage in City Hall. It is there, where we believe Isandro was murdered."

Detective Jameson contained his anger, though his expression said it all. "And?"

Following the trail of the victim's drag marks, we navigated a narrow passage beneath City Hall that led into a warehouse where the elevated train tracks were visible. Drew gestured across the highway, indicating the direction they had come from.

"A book, huh? A passage under City Hall?" he questioned sarcastically.

"You heard what I said, didn't you, officer Martinez?" Drew said, confident in his next move.

"Yes, yes, I did hear that," she replied as she approached closer to the group. "I can take a few officers, and we can check it out, detective," Martinez suggested.

Detective Jameson wore a perplexed expression. He slowly turned his head, half-focused in the direction of the warehouse, then looked back at the body being zipped up in its bag. "Let's go, Martinez. Take two of your men," he commanded.

"I'm going with you," Grace insisted. "I got this, Drew." Grace pulled her pant legs over her boots and gathered her green braids into a neat bun. "Let's go."

"Elena, go with her," Drew said with a wink.

"Wait a minute… I can't have civilians wandering around a crime scene," Jameson chided.

"You will never find those secret passages without us," Elena retorted.

"Alright, you go with Martinez," he conceded, gesturing toward Elena. "Grace, you're with me. Let's go." Jameson then motioned for Martinez and two additional officers to head to the scene.

Grace and Elena waved to their friends and followed behind.

"Don't forget who's in charge here," Jameson whistled. He glanced over his shoulder, and the girls instantly knew the remark was aimed at them. The words hung in the air as he slowly turned and got back into his car with Grace. Elena jumped into Officer Martinez's car. They squealed their tires and peeled off down FDR Drive.

"You think he was angry?" Aisha smirked. "That security guard was the guy we chased through the subway. When I pulled the book from his hands, I saw his face. That was the guy," she confirmed.

"The security guard was connected to both the museum and the morgue. We need to find out how, why, and who his known associates are." Drew couldn't help but feel a chill run down his spine.

"Aisha, Debra, we're heading to the museum. We should inform Marcus Larson about his employee."

"Got it!" Israel confirmed. "Francy and I are going to the apartment. I've got a bunch of data I want to download and organize into a neat file for Mr. Belltone."

Officer Martinez turned to Elena and smiled. "You and your friends are really working for Mr. Belltone?"

Elena pulled her pigtails back and wiped the beads of sweat from her forehead. "Yes. He hired us as private investigators. We knew his son, Phillip, very well."

"That was a tragic day for the city," Martinez responded, shaking her head. "It's hard to hear when a young person's life is cut short, but when it's a high-profile case like his, the city casts a glaring spotlight on the situation." She removed her hat and placed it on the seat between them. "I sense a slight twang in your 'i' when you speak. Are you from Texas?"

Elena cracked a smile. "I sure am," she replied with a twang. "But I've lived in New York for years."

"No doubt about that. I see that moxie! I grew up in Texas, too—Mexican-American," Martinez said with a smile. "Arepas and hot dogs. The best of both worlds."

"I hear that," Elena laughed.

Martinez reached into her glove compartment and pulled out a bag of De La Rosa Mazapan candies, offering one to Elena.

Elena's eyes lit up. "I don't believe it. These were my favorite candies as a kid!"

"Up top!" Martinez high-fived her new partner. "Let's go dig around. I've always found secret passages and hidden spaces fascinating."

"Well, you're going to love this place. It's under City Hall."

Martinez turned on her siren, made a U-turn on FDR Drive, and headed for their destination.

★★★

"Why do you always resist help? When someone like Dr. Stevens offers you information, why do you dismiss it? I just don't get it, Jameson!" Grace said from the front seat as he sped down the FDR Drive.

"You see, it's like this: I've been around these blocks a million times," he said, pushing his sunglasses further up his nose. "You know what I mean? I've seen these scenarios play out countless times. I remain unconvinced until the facts truly persuade me."

"If the evidence is right there, why don't you believe it?" Grace asked, struggling to grasp his logic.

"It's not that I doubt you, Grace. It's just that some of this doesn't add up."

"This guy—the one we just pulled from the water—stole Phillip's book from us. We chased him through the subway and down a hidden corridor to City Hall. Later, we discovered that he had been killed in another secret passage inside a conference room at City Hall."

"I'm not dismissing the evidence, Grace. I just believe that without proper context, it remains incomplete." Detective Jameson kept his eyes on the road.

"So, what? Do we just ignore the facts until we can read his mind?" Grace snapped, now infuriated.

"Well, it's too late for that." Jameson replied, reaching behind the passenger's seat. "Here, Grace—have some water. You look dehydrated."

★★★

The taxi pulled up in front of the Whitney Museum. Aisha, Debra, and Drew walked through the glass doors into the spacious, modern building located along the West Side Highway. The sunlight reflected off the Hudson River, its shimmer accentuating the late-afternoon glow.

"What are we going to say to him?" Debra asked, fidgeting nervously.

"The truth," Aisha replied bluntly.

"I have a feeling he'll be very concerned," Drew remarked as he looked up at the light filtering through the tall glass windows, which cast a wide arc of color across the pristine white space.

"We're here to see Marcus Larson," Debra told a young girl at the museum desk.

"Who should I say is calling?" the girl asked with a smile.

"Drew," Debra answered matter-of-factly.

The girl nodded and picked up the phone. The trio stood silently as they watched her wait patiently for someone to answer. "He doesn't seem to be in his office," she observed. "Let me try the Gallery."

"He doesn't seem to be responding. I know he is here," she continued. "Do you know where his office is?"

"Yes, of course," Debra replied curtly. She felt beads of sweat forming on her neck.

"Please pass," the girl offered. "You can take the elevator in mid-gallery."

Debra smiled and ushered her friends inside.

"This is my first time here," Aisha commented as she admired the works on the Gallery walls. "It's not my favorite style—I prefer the classics."

Drew froze. "Look straight ahead," he whispered urgently while scanning his phone to locate the two images of the suspects that Robert Belltone had sent him. "It's the guys from the Waldorf," he managed to say.

The girls watched as a shorter man with dark hair—his left forearm decorated with a dragon tattoo—pressed the elevator button. His stockier partner, visibly nervous with a scar running down his right cheek, glanced around.

"Are those the men?" Aisha asked, leaning in.

"They share the same markings," Debra observed, squinting.

"Okay, what do we do?" Aisha hesitated.

"Let's see where they go," Drew replied, pausing. "If they see us, they may recognize us."

Debra noted, "They're getting in the elevator."

They watched as the elevator slowly closed. "They're going down?" Debra remarked as they reached the steel doors and monitored the digital display descending. "How deep does that go?"

Drew quickly scanned the area for stairs.

"I know what you're thinking," Debra said, "but remember, we took the stairs last time—they ended on this ground floor."

"You're right, Debra," Drew admitted with a tone of resignation.

Aisha pressed the elevator button. "Could this be any slower?" she grumbled, pacing back and forth.

The elevator doors creaked open with a screech, and they quickly squeezed through as the doors continued to part.

Debra noticed the last button labeled "L4" and pressed it. When no response came and the button remained unlit, she pressed it again. Frustration mounting, she exclaimed, "Come on!"

Drew paused. "What are we doing?" he muttered before an idea struck him. "Keys." He continued, "Girls, if these are Isandro's keys—the ones we found at City Hall…" but he left his sentence unfinished. He reached into his bag and produced the keys wrapped in the handkerchief Debra had given him.

"He must have had access to the basement," Drew said aloud as he inspected the key chain, the white fob dangling freely.

"The fob," Aisha murmured. "He's a security guard…"

"Was!" Debra interjected.

Drew held the white plastic key up to the elevator's panel. Instantly, the last button lit up, reactivating the elevator.

"Brilliant thinking!" Debra cheered.

As the doors closed, a faint hum filled the air, accompanied by the soft jolt of movement and the gentle creak of the cables. The descent was a slow, deliberate journey into the museum's mysterious sub-basement.

With every floor that passed, the air grew cooler. "Is that to prevent the artwork from molding?" Debra wondered, shivering slightly.

When the elevator finally halted, the doors lurched open to reveal a vast, cavernous space. The sub-basement seemed endless, its high ceilings disappearing into darkness. The floor was arranged in a patchwork of cracked tiles, some displaying intricate patterns now blurred by time. Dust swirled in beams of light from an unseen source, casting an otherworldly glow. A sudden distant rumble made the trio look up.

"It must be the A train," Drew surmised.

The trio stepped out, their footsteps echoing in the heavy silence. The stillness was broken only by the occasional drip of water from an unseen leak. Rows of old lockers lined the walls, their contents hidden in mystery—some partially visible under layers of covering, others concealed behind heavy curtains or locked behind rusted gates.

"Where did these rats disappear to?" Aisha whispered as she struggled to dim her phone's light.

In this hidden realm beneath the museum, time seemed to stand still. "This is beyond creepy," Debra muttered as the chill deepened. She struggled to bring light into the space. Suddenly, her phone's light came on—and she noticed, "Footprints!"

"That's blood," Aisha confirmed.

Drew, Debra, and Aisha crouched in the dim light. They followed the phone's glow along a path ahead. Debra adjusted her grip on her phone, casting long shadows on the cracked stone as she exchanged a glance with Aisha. Aisha's hand rested near her side, her fingers lightly brushing her phone, ready to use it as a weapon if necessary. Drew, ever the quiet strategist, signaled them to stay low and pointed to a door about a hundred yards away. Their quiet breathing blended with soft footsteps coming from the room.

Debra switched off her light as the trio approached the door. They peered through a narrow crack in the basement door while the suspects, oblivious to being watched, hurriedly removed their clothing. One man tossed his blood-stained shirt into a corner, his face contorted with panic and disgust. "Look at this mess," he squeaked.

The other man followed suit, discarding his ruined overall pants, sniffing them briefly before adding them to the pile. "Larson better get our cash tonight. I even snagged a brick of cocaine as a bonus," he said, his deep voice dripping with disdain.

"I should have done the same, but I was busy knifing that incompetent idiot." He grabbed a canvas cloth from a nearby table and began wiping himself down.

"Here, put on these overalls." The man with the dragon tattoo reached for two workman's overalls from a cabinet. "I told you we should've left the knife," he hissed in a low, urgent whisper. He wiped his hands nervously, as if trying to scrub away the memory of the crime. "This is a disaster. And that's Larson's high-value knife." He avoided touching it, fearful of staining his hands with blood. He made a face, raised his nose, and tapped it with one finger.

"We could have tossed the knife into the East River with the security guard," the dark-haired man snapped, his tone sharp. He paced in a circle, his bare feet shuffling on the cold concrete.

"Then Larson would have killed us."

The man paused, glancing at the bloodied blade on the table. "Larson doesn't have the guts! Why do you think he uses us for his dirty work? We've got to get rid of it. It's the only link tying us to the crime. If we leave it here, it's over."

He turned his eyes from the knife to the door, clearly weighing his options. "What do we do, then? It's not like we can simply walk out and act as if nothing happened. And we can't just dump it anywhere—it'll be found."

A cold, calculating silence stretched between them. Drew's pulse quickened as he caught Debra's eye. She nodded ever so slightly, urging him to continue observing. Aisha recorded the entire conversation on her phone.

"Why don't we just melt it?" one man suggested, his high-pitched voice softening to near reason. "We've got acid in the lab next door. We can dissolve the metal completely. We'll tell Larson we lost it along the way." He hesitated. "What's he gonna do?"

The other man grimaced. "That's risky. What if we get caught? There are cameras in the lab." He rubbed his temple, the burden of his choices pressing on him. "We can't afford any mistakes—not now. They're getting too close."

Aisha leaned closer and whispered to Drew, "We can't let them get away with this. We need to move now, before they realize we're here."

Debra nodded and motioned for Drew to text Detective Jameson. He slowly reached into his pocket for his phone when a low-pitched voice cut through the tension.

"Let's just burn it. We'll destroy the clothes, too. There's a furnace in the back—no trace, nothing left behind," the man declared, his decision resolute.

"Alright, then," he muttered, his resolve hardening. "We burn it all."

Drew felt a surge of adrenaline. There was no time to waste—the suspects were about to eliminate the last piece of evidence linking them to the crime. He glanced at Debra and signaled for her to move in. "You secure the knife," he ordered. "Aisha and I can handle these two."

"Are you crazy?" Debra hissed at Drew. "I know you can take care of yourself… but," she quickly turned to Aisha, "what are you going to do? Scratch their eyes out?"

Aisha, her focus unwavering, replied, "I trained with a Mossad agent for my last movie. He taught me Krav Maga."

Just as one of the men grabbed the bloodied clothes from the corner, Drew kicked the basement door open with a loud crash. The two suspects froze, their eyes wide in shock at the sight of Drew, Debra, and Aisha storming in.

"You're done," Drew commanded, his voice steady and authoritative. "We have your conversation recorded. The cops are on their way."

"We should have killed you when we had the chance," the shorter man barked.

Aisha, maintaining awareness of Drew's position, faced the second suspect.

Drew noticed the man's eyes glance toward the only exit behind them, clearly calculating his options. Before anyone could react, Aisha lunged at the man in front of her, aiming a swift kick at his midsection. He stumbled back, winded, while Drew charged at the other man, who was already swinging a fist in his direction. Drew ducked just in time, countering with a punch that landed squarely on the man's jaw.

The room erupted into chaos. Aisha grappled with her opponent, using her agility to dodge his wild swings. She landed a few quick jabs, but he was strong and relentless. He pushed her against the table, sending the antique murder weapon toward Debra.

Using the table for support, Aisha delivered a rapid battement kick to her attacker's face, sending him reeling to the ground. Debra quickly lifted the knife from the cold floor and moved deliberately, sidestepping the assailant's flailing legs as he struggled amid Aisha's calculated assault.

Drew swiftly sidestepped his attacker's punch before delivering a powerful strike to his forearm, followed by a knee to the abdomen that left him doubled over in pain. Aisha then feinted, briefly distracting the assailant as he attempted to rise. She moved swiftly to his side, trapping his arm and applying pressure to immobilize him.

Drew caught his assailant off guard by delivering a powerful blow to his side that sent him crashing to the ground. Dazed, the man turned, reaching for his gun, which teetered precariously on the edge of a chair.

"Drew, he's going for the gun!" Debra warned.

With one quick kick to his back, Drew watched his attacker crash into the wall headfirst, knocking him out and causing the gun to fall to the floor.

Aisha swung her right knee against the back of the killer's knees, sending him once more to the floor. Then, with both fists pressed together, she delivered a final blow to the side of his neck, rendering him unconscious.

Instantly, the room fell silent, with only Aisha and Drew trying to catch their breath.

"What just happened? Who are you people?" Debra said, adrenaline coursing through her veins. "I didn't know you two had it in you!"

Aisha and Drew exchanged a glance.

"You told these guys the cops were on their way. Is that true?"

"No," Drew huffed. "I called Detective Jameson, but it went straight to voicemail."

"Now what?" Debra asked, looking around the room.

"We can use that rope," Aisha said, pointing to several pieces of art securely tied up in the corner.

"Let's tie these criminals up and lock them here for safekeeping," Drew said as he untethered the rope from the paintings. "We have a recorded confession and the murder weapon. That's our bargaining chip with Marcus Larson, who's behind all this."

The elevator to the top-floor offices moved at a glacial pace. "We look like we've been in a brawl," Debra remarked as she stared at her cohorts. "Come on, we need to freshen up." Once they reached the top floor, they darted into the restrooms.

"How are we going to play this?" Aisha asked.

"We need to know Larson's connection to City Hall," Drew said, formulating a plan designed to extract a confession from him.

"He has no idea how much we know," Debra observed.

"So, we bait him and then draw him in," Drew schemed.

Just then, Drew noticed their target—Mr. Larson—ten paces behind them.

"Our receptionist at the front told me you were looking for me. Did you need something?" he asked with a smile.

Drew sensed the pressure of Marcus Larson's burden crushing him. His impeccably polished appearance showed signs of strain—his hair was disheveled, and sweat dampened his skin.

"You got a wonderful compliment from City Hall," Drew said, offering bait.

Marcus Larson raised his eyebrows, pausing to evaluate the tone of the conversation before remaining silent.

213

"Yes, the mayor told us he loved what you did with the place," Debra followed up.

"Oh yes," Marcus replied, "I change the art out in the rotonda once a month. He's a fan of modern art." Then he changed the subject. "I hope you all are coming to the La Croix exhibit at Tavern on the Green tomorrow." As he began to walk away,

"We will all be there," Drew interrupted, gently grasping Marcus Larson's arm. He raised a finger to his nose and brushed his upper lip.

Larson froze, twitching nervously as he slowly brought his hand to his upper lip, sensing remnants of powder along the border of his nostrils.

"You missed a spot," Aisha chimed in.

Frantically, he rubbed away the remaining cocaine from his face.

"City Hall seems to have a large supply of that stuff in their basement."

"And artwork," Debra added.

"And blood," Aisha finished, pulling out her phone and hitting play.

Marcus Larson's face turned white as he listened to his two hired hands confess to killing Isandro, the security guard, and implicating him as the mastermind.

"I think we'd better go into your office, Larson," Drew said, turning him around and leading him inside.

Drew seated Larson in his own chair and rotated him to face him. "I have your three-million-dollar knife in my bag," he began.

"It also bears the blood of your henchman, Isandro," Debra exclaimed, unable to contain herself. "How could you?"

"He did your dirty work—along with Squeaky and Fromme, whom we've tied up and locked away in your basement," Aisha added.

"You have no defense, Larson. Either come clean or you'll never see the light of day again," Drew warned.

"You'll be hanging watercolors in prison for the rest of your life," Aisha remarked with a smile as she brushed lint off his jacket.

Larson recoiled at her approach. He stared up at Drew and let out a deep sigh, sweat beading on his forehead. "This is what you're going to do for us," Drew alluded.

Debra's phone rang, startling the trio. "It's Elena," she announced.

"Debra, Grace, and Detective Jameson never showed up at City Hall. Officer Martinez and I backtracked and found the detective's abandoned car by the side of FDR Drive," Elena explained.

"She's not answering her phone?" Debra asked.

"Neither of them," came the reply.

"Get Israel and Francy on the phone," Debra instructed. "Marcus Larson is on a short leash—he must be involved in this. Keep me posted." With that, Debra abruptly hung up.

Officer Martinez circled Detective Jameson's car. "This is very strange. The driver's side door is open and there are no signs of a struggle," she reported to Elena.

"Officer, look at this," Elena called from the opposite side of the car. "Do these marks seem like drag marks to you?"

Quickly, Officer Martinez moved to the back of the car, carefully avoiding the oncoming traffic. She examined the staggered marks in the dirt and hesitated, "It could be."

Elena activated speed dial on her phone. "Israel, it's Elena. Where are you right now?"

Israel answered as he scanned his surroundings. "Francy and I were about to catch the train near Fulton Street. What's up?" Then, the call abruptly disconnected.

Glancing at her phone screen, Elena studied an image that was hard to decipher. Tilting her head, she checked the sender's name. "Grace!" she exclaimed. "Office, Grace just sent me an image."

Officer Martinez inspected the picture. "That's the Wavertree!"

Elena looked at her in confusion.

"That's the ship docked at South Street Seaport—I always called it the pirate ship," Officer Martinez explained.

Instantly, Elena recalled the famous ship—a longstanding seaport attraction. She texted the image to Israel. "Come on, let's get down there!"

Martinez quickly returned to her patrol car, jumped in, buckled her seat belt, and activated the siren.

Elena slid into the passenger seat and hit redial. "Isra, we're on our way—meet us at South Street Seaport," she instructed.

"Your friend may not have been able to speak but managed to snap a photo of the ship, hoping you'd recognize the location," Martinez surmised. "What happened to Jameson?"

Elena was momentarily speechless, her mind racing with questions. How did they arrive at South Street Seaport without the car? Were those truly drag marks? Had someone forced them into another vehicle? Or—had Grace and Detective Jameson been abducted?

Martinez, having seen such reactions before, said gently, "Elena, let's not jump to conclusions. We'll assess the situation once we get there and take the necessary action."

Staring out the front window as they sped down FDR Drive, Elena watched the buildings and landmarks blur past at breakneck speed.

"Where are your other friends?" Marinez asked.

"Drew, Debra, and Aisha are questioning the director of the Whitney Museum—they seem convinced he's involved in all of this," Elena replied.

South Street Seaport bustled with tourists strolling along cobblestone pathways between shops and restaurants. A hint of salt mingled with the sweltering heat of a late summer afternoon.

Officer Martinez and Elena pulled the patrol car alongside the side street, where wooden planks welcomed seafaring adventurers along the New York coastline. "We're on foot patrol now," Martinez instructed.

Israel and Francy had arrived ahead of them, scanning for their friend as they navigated past bustling gift shops and sidewalk cafés. "There's that big boat," Francy noted, indicating the prominent black mast and furled sails dominating the skyline.

Advancing into the seaport, Officer Martinez and Elena scanned their surroundings, desperately searching for any sign of Grace. "What could have happened?" Elena murmured to herself.

# Chapter 16
## New York Harbor

"There they are, Pier 17!" Israel shouted.

Elena immediately spotted Israel sprinting toward the water. "Martinez, my friends are straight ahead... about five hundred yards!"

Martinez quickly radioed ahead, "Dispatch, this is 32-Charlie. We have a 207 in progress at Pier 17, South Street Seaport. I have visual on two male suspects in dark hoods loading a possible kidnapped victim into a speed boat. They appear to be fleeing. Requesting immediate backup and harbor patrol, over."

"They're getting into that speed boat!" Elena responded as she caught up with Francy; both were racing toward the dock.

"Come on, guys, hurry!" Israel urged while looking back over his shoulder at Elena and Francy rounding the corner. His eyes scanned for a means of escape. "We can't lose them!"

"Israel, there!" Elena yelled, pointing to a boat next to the gigantic sailboats tossing in the wake of the getaway vessel.

Israel raced ahead and leapt into a sleek black-and-red Mercury speed boat. His mind buzzed as he pulled back the key switch to reveal a jumble of colored wires. He paused, quickly studying the combination.

"That looks like a rat's nest," Francy commented as she peered over his shoulder.

"Okay, so the black-and-yellow wire grounds the switch box... and then red connects to purple," Israel murmured. Beads of sweat formed on his face as he maneuvered and twisted the adjacent wires together. Sparks flew, giving him rapid feedback as he worked.

The engine roared to life!

"You amaze me!" Elena exclaimed, straddling the back of the boat.

Francy released the mooring from the dock as the boat lurched forward. "Let's go," she called, slapping the side of the vessel.

"I'll wait for backup," Martinez instructed as she turned and dashed back to her patrol car.

"There they are!" Elena pointed, spotting their adversaries rounding the edge of the island.

Israel gripped the wheel of the commandeered speedboat; his knuckles turned white as he gauged the throttle. The girls clung to the sides, their expressions steely with determination. As the boat entered the harbor, Elena moved to the bow, her eyes fixed on the target.

"Tell me what you see!" Israel shouted over the engine's roar.

"I see Grace—she's tied up at the back of the boat with her head bowed. There are two masked men with her," Elena replied. "They're heading for the Statue of Liberty. We're closing in!"

Israel pushed the throttle forward, and the boat surged ahead. The wind whipped through his hair while spray stung his face. They tore past a slower-moving tourist boat, its passengers' faces blurring as they sped by.

"Incoming!" Francy warned, pointing to an NYPD harbor patrol boat cutting across their path.

"They must have gotten the call from Martinez," Elena observed, checking if Martinez was aboard.

Israel jerked the wheel hard to the right to avoid a collision. The speedboat tilted precariously, and the girls cried out as they slid across the sole.

"Hold on!" Israel bellowed, righting the vessel just in time to avoid a moored sailboat. "Are they still headed for the Statue of Liberty?"

"Almost in range," Elena called, spreading her legs wide for balance. "Get us a bit closer!"

"What is that?" Francy gasped as she noticed Elena's outstretched arm clutching a firearm.

"It's a flare gun. I found it among the boat's supplies," Elena replied without taking her eyes off the danger ahead.

"I hope you know how to use that thing," Israel called as the boat jumped over incoming waves from the Staten Island ferry. "You've got an audience!"

"Don't worry," Elena retorted. "I was a wild teen back in Texas."

Israel shot Francy a quick look. "That explains a lot!"

There was no response as Elena steadied herself and prepared to take aim.

"Please try not to hit Grace," Francy pleaded nervously.

Israel gritted his teeth and pushed the engine to its limits. "We're closing the gap," he shouted, though the other boat maintained its lead despite his efforts.

Suddenly, Francy pointed, "Look! The patrol boat is moving to intercept!"

The NYPD vessel veered across the waves, its lights flashing, forcing them to swing sharply to port. Israel seized the opportunity, wrenching the wheel hard to the left as their boat surged forward with renewed speed.

"Yes!" Elena cheered as she rose, balancing precariously. "I've got a bead on them… NOW!"

A loud report echoed over the water as Elena fired the flare gun. The flare zipped past Israel's ear and struck the pursuing vessel with a re-sounding clang. Its stern now sported a fiery hole, smoke billowing from the damaged side.

The NYPD boat veered right, searching for the source of the flare. Elena waved back.

"They're getting away," Francy yelled.

Israel allowed himself a grim smile, his eyes never leaving the quarry. "Not yet, they're not."

Desperately attempting to steer their boat, the kidnappers returned fire—first at the NYPD boat, then toward Israel.

"Incoming!" Israel warned as he saw the man take aim.

One of them stood up, brandishing a menacing firearm in his hands.

Israel spun the wheel hard to the right just as the bullet whizzed past. "Return fire!" Israel bellowed, noticing Elena already reloading.

Her second shot went low, striking the water and sending up a plume of spray that obscured the other boat. Israel seized the cover, steering sharply across their stern and closing the distance to his enemy.

Amid their accelerating boat, Francy yelled, "They're circling the Statue of Liberty," as it cleaved through the waves. "The NYPD vessel is tailing them," Elena called out while gripping for dear life.

"Now's our chance!" Israel exclaimed. "We'll intercept them." He turned the boat sharply, circling back and narrowly avoiding a tug boat trailing behind them.

The Statue of Liberty stood as a silent guardian over the peaceful waters of New York Harbor. However, her tranquility was disrupted by the roar of engines circling her imposing figure. Meanwhile, the boats streaked through the waves around Liberty Island, their wakes carving through the sun-scorched surface.

In the lead, a sleek black vessel with a menacing, gleaming hull still smoked heavily at the stern from where Elena had fired. The NYPD vessel followed close behind, ordering them to pull over near the island.

Israel steered his commandeered boat uncomfortably close to the island as tourists watched with interest, believing they were on a movie set. Camera phones snapped and onlookers cheered as Israel offered an encouraging smile. "They should be coming around the corner any minute!" he yelled.

"What are you going to do, play chicken with them?" Francy retorted.

"If I have to!" Israel shot back.

The boat's powerful engines screamed as they pushed it to its limits, maneuvering dangerously between the recreational vessels that were in port for a peaceful summer day in the harbor.

"There they are!" Elena shouted from the bow. "Their faces are hidden behind dark masks! And what happened to Detective Jameson?"

"Why did he leave her side?" Francy asked while watching the NYPD's pursuit boat—a formidable craft with flashing lights and sirens—

close the gap. Officers pressed forward with determination, their radios crackling with urgency. Yet the criminals' boat swerved sharply, narrowly avoiding a collision as it veered wide around the island, passing Israel in the wake of the Staten Island Ferry's wave crest before screeching ahead.

Trapped on one side of the ferry, Israel managed to circle around the large vessel, skillfully evading a cluster of anchored boats.

"Do you see them?" Elena screamed over the deafening roar of the ferry and the cheers of onlookers.

Francy and Israel scanned the vast waters as they exchanged searching glances, while the NYPD vessel pulled alongside them.

"Which way did they go?" an officer queried.

Israel didn't answer; he was too busy scanning the waters to distinguish between moving and stationary boats.

"We got bogged down behind the ferry," Francy yelled to one of the officers. Their harbor patrol boat sped ahead, conducting a wide search for the now unseen speedboat.

Israel slowed slightly, scanning every vessel in his peripheral vision, while Elena attempted to call Grace on her phone. Frustrated, she cursed and shoved her phone back into her pocket. "What are we going to do?"

Israel accelerated, maneuvering between the vessels as he searched for any clue or response from fellow boaters.

"Isra, look!" Francy called out while pointing to a large woman in a tiny bikini who was indicating the Verrazzano-Narrows Bridge in the distance, its massive span connecting Brooklyn and Staten Island.

Francy raised her hand in thanks.

"They can't be that far," Israel said, shaking his head.

Elena signaled to the woman by raising both hands as she waved and pointed toward the bridge.

The woman quickly gestured "no," raising both arms as if guiding an airplane into its hangar.

"The East River!" Elena shouted to Israel. "They've turned toward it!"

"Hold on!" Israel yelled as he pushed the throttle to the maximum, propelling the boat forward as it skimmed the water like a skipping stone.

Francy observed the NYPD vessel moving in the opposite direction. She gazed west at the painted sky, its golden hue reflecting on the water. The Lady in the Narrows stood strong and proud, her gaze fixed outward—a steadfast witness to their pursuit.

★★★

The speedboat's wake sliced through the murky East River as Grace's captors steered them north along Manhattan's East River Drive, passing the spot where Isandor—the murdered security guard—was found. Grace's wrists burned from the tight zip ties, yet she maintained a neutral expression.

With practiced precision, the driver maneuvered the boat upstream toward the Bronx.

"I think we're good," one man told the other. "We're far enough from any cameras."

Grace watched as the boat driver removed his mask. Then, her captor followed suit. "I knew it was you, Jameson," she replied dryly. "I could tell from that hunch of yours—you drugged me with that water."

"Don't worry, my sweet girl," Jameson said. "We're gonna get what we need from you and show you where the Bronx River rats feed."

The driver steered the watercraft under a series of small bridges into open waters. Grace searched desperately for any familiar landmark or building, but her efforts were in vain—her phone was no longer in her pocket.

"Why did you turn dirty? That's all I want to know," Grace demanded, locking eyes with Jameson, the sting of betrayal burning inside her.

He didn't respond.

As the boat drifted along the East River, the silhouette of Rikers Island gradually emerged—a stark, imposing presence amid the waterways.

"What is that place?" Grace asked, eyeing the menacing structure.

"Rikers," Jameson answered.

"The prison?" Grace said in a surprised tone. "You'll be there soon enough. Oh, you probably sent a lot of guys there," she paused. "Well, they'll be happy to see you."

The driver turned to stare at the massive structure. From the water, the prison complex dominated the island's surroundings. The buildings were utilitarian and fortress-like, with high concrete walls topped with coiled razor wire, emphasizing security over aesthetics.

"Where are you taking me?" Grace asked, her eyes fixed on New York passing by.

Jameson signaled the driver to veer right along the waterway. As the vessel approached the coast, the sounds of the city faded into an unsettling silence.

Grace sensed they were nearing LaGuardia Airport as planes ascended and descended overhead, their passengers oblivious to her plight. Suddenly, an idea struck her. "Are these zip ties really necessary, Jameson? I'm not going anywhere. I can't swim," she lied. "At least put my glasses on so I can appreciate the view. I took out my contacts hours ago."

Detective Jameson fixed his gaze on her, intrigue stirring within him. "It's unfortunate that our paths intersect during such a difficult time in my life," he remarked, his tone reflecting unspoken emotion.

"Tough time?" she smirked. "Come on, you're a New York detective. You have a nice apartment, you're not a beat cop or starving, and you're quite attractive."

Jameson noticed her glasses hanging around her neck and carefully placed them on the bridge of her nose.

"Thank you," she said.

Turning to the driver, Jameson pointed toward the coastline on the right.

Grace leaned forward, adjusting the glasses on her face.

"When you see the first break in the cove, turn in there," Jameson instructed.

★★★

In an instant, Israel received a notification on his phone. "Oh my God! Elena, take the wheel," he directed. "Grace is contacting us."

Francy leaped up. "What? How?" She moved to the front of the boat. With Israel positioned between Elena and Francy, the trio watched as Grace's message played on his phone.

"I gave my Ray-Ban glasses to Grace so she could read the small print on the side of the cocaine packet. I forgot she still had them," he said, his excitement contagious.

"I can't believe she thought of it," Elena remarked, a note of relief in her tone.

"That's Jameson!" Francy gasped.

"I had a bad feeling about that guy from the start," Elena replied.

"Who's driving the boat?" Israel asked, trying to identify the person from Grace's perspective.

"No idea." Francy quickly phoned Drew.

"What's up?" Drew answered on the first ring.

"Jameson kidnapped Grace. They're on a boat and appear to be heading up the East River," Francy briefed Drew.

"Can you pinpoint their exact location?" Drew asked.

"Drew, it's Elena. I just saw Riker's Island in the background."

Drew sighed. "I really don't know that area. They could be heading to the Bronx."

"I have an idea. Put Israel on the phone."

"Amigo," he responded quickly.

"Isra, can you send me a copy of that feed?"

"Sure, it records in segments."

"Our friend Fiona from the nightclub is from the Bronx. He knows that area well. I can send him the feed."

"Brilliant idea. We're near Riker's now. We'll continue the pursuit until we recover Grace."

★★★

Grace sat silently, praying that Israel's Ray Bans were recording her whereabouts. She turned her head left and right, intermittently hoping her friends would pinpoint her location.

Her captors journeyed up the river in silence, accompanied only by the hum of the boat as it meandered along the water. The boat turned along an outlet that resembled another river. As it approached an overpass, the craft made a hard right into a hidden alcove beneath a crumbling section of a highway's retaining wall. The entrance was nearly invisible from the water, concealed by decades of hanging vines and weathered concrete. Inside, the cave-like space opened into what appeared to be an abandoned docking station, complete with a small wooden dock and rusted metal rings affixed to the walls.

"The book of secrets," Jameson demanded, his voice echoing off the damp walls. "Where is it? And how do we access it?" His associate emerged from the shadows.

"Who's your friend, Jameson? Let me guess—another weasel who thinks he'll profit off others? You two are like a bad circus act."

"That's enough," Jameson barked.

"You know, I am so disappointed in you," Grace said, shaking her head. "I really thought you were an interesting man. I thought we were just beginning to get to know each other…"

"Where's the book, Grace?"

"The book isn't what you think it is," she replied, stalling. "It's not simply about finding it. There are protocols and safeguards in place. Coded messages you could never decipher because you lack the insight."

A sharp crack resonated through the chamber as Jameson slammed his hand against a rotting wooden beam. "Don't play games with me, Grace."

"Where did it all go wrong for you, Jameson?" Grace asked as she shifted, ensuring the camera on her glasses had a clear view of her surroundings. She hoped Israel was watching the live feed—perhaps the glasses already had a built-in GPS pinpointing her location. Above all, she felt confident that the two men who believed they had her trapped were now one step closer to prison.

★★★

"Sweetie," Fiona answered the phone.

"Listen, I'm in a bind. One of my team members has been kid-napped," Drew said, his voice shaking.

"How can I help?" Fiona asked, his tone shifting.

"I'm sending you some video feeds. Can you tell me where this location is?"

"Send the text. Put me on speaker. Let me take a look." Fiona sat up in his lounge chair.

"Where are you? I hope I didn't disturb you," Drew asked.

"I'm home on my balcony, enjoying the view," he replied as he waved to his well-built neighbor across the way. "Okay, I got the videos."

Drew waited while Fiona studied the footage.

"Hey, that's the Bronx. I see Rikers… and Baretto Point Park… Is she on a boat? That poor girl," Fiona remarked.

"Yes, they have her on a boat and are taking her up the East River. Once they pass Whitestone Bridge, I'm unfamiliar with that area."

"That's because you're a snobby Manhattanite!" Fiona joked.

"Guilty," Drew whispered.

"Alright, that was Hunt's Point they just passed. Does this relate to that stolen art by any chance?"

"Yes, everything is connected," Drew admitted.

"Your friends are lucky to have you in their corner."

"I'm lucky to have them in my life … and you," Drew said with uncharacteristic sincerity.

"They're moving up the Bronx River," Fiona observed.

"Any idea where they might be headed?" Drew asked, his desperation evident.

"Maybe Hunt's Point Pier," Fiona mused.

Fiona watched the kidnapping unfold in real time. "This is bizarre. What kind of glasses are these? I need to get a pair. They're nearing the Bruckner Boulevard overpass." Suddenly, Fiona noticed a detour. "That's it," he realized, understanding where they were taking Grace. "There's a secret hiding spot directly under the Bruckner overpass—a post-war storage unit. We used to play there as kids," Fiona smiled.

"Fiona, thank you so much," Drew said. Then he hung up and called Israel.

Elena answered, "It's a post-war storage unit under the Bruckner overpass," Drew repeated.

"Drew, I'm relaying the exact coordinates to Officer Martinez. She and her team are ready," Elena said confidently.

The rescue unfolded swiftly and decisively. The first sign was a series of shadows moving over the hidden entrance, followed by the soft splash of divers entering the water. Within seconds, the alcove erupted into controlled chaos: flash-bangs, officers rappelling down, and the satisfying sight of Detective Jameson and his conspirator being tackled to the ground.

While Grace was being led to safety, she caught sight of Israel, Elena, and Francy waiting on the boat, their faces etched with relief.

# Chapter 17
## Upper East Side

The following morning, Francy and Drew visited the Belltone residence.

"Bayya, Francy and I have a rather delicate matter to discuss with you." Drew looked into her deep brown eyes and sensed an undercurrent of unspoken concern.

"We wanted to come to you first, before the sensitive details reached others," Francy said with a warm smile. "Would you talk to us?"

Bayya looked up from her cup of tea and offered a willing nod.

Francy and Drew moved the kitchen chairs away from the French farm table and sat down. Drew reached into his bag and retrieved an envelope of photos, carefully placing the images before Bayya. "Bayya, is this you?"

She picked up the photo and stared at the black-and-white image for what seemed like minutes.

"This was me in Jamaica," she recalled, remembering how dramatically her life had changed. She shook her head as she relived every detail.

"And this photo?" Drew asked, pointing to the two men.

Bayya swallowed hard and closed her eyes. "This is my son. Jonathon. Jonathon Matthews ... and his father." A tear rolled down her face as she tried to brush it away before another soon followed.

"It's okay, Bayya," Francy said gently as she put an arm around her. "This is Damon Belltone, isn't it?" she whispered.

Bayya hesitated before answering, torn by loyalty to years of silence. She could no longer bear the burden of that long-kept secret. "Yes," she replied with a heavy sigh.

"And that beautiful sapphire ring on your finger is from Damon, yes?" Drew inquired.

"Originally, it was," she sighed. "But a week after giving it to me, he took it back."

"Why?" Francy interjected.

"I believe he felt it was too personal. The ring was a family heirloom from his grandmother, and because of his name and reputation, no connection could be maintained. I have never harbored jealousy or hatred," she explained, her tone and demeanor underscoring her conviction.

"That must have been very painful," Drew observed, reading the sorrow in her eyes.

"I must tell you; he paid me generously to keep our secret. He provided me with financial security and insisted that I continue working for the family as if nothing had occurred."

"You agreed to that?" Francy asked, skeptical.

"I did," she confirmed confidently. "When Jonathon was born, I gave him my mother's maiden name, Mathews. With Damon's money, I sent him to good schools, and he arranged for us to live in a small apartment in Washington Heights." The memories of those days swirled through her mind like fleeting flashes.

"After Jonathon turned four, I returned to work for the Belltone family as if nothing had happened. Damon and his wife were busy sending Richard to school and managing his significant success as a financier."

"How did this picture come about then?" Drew asked.

Bayya shifted in her seat. Her gaze drifted toward the tea kettle, and Francy recognized the cue. Francy stood up and poured tea into Bayya's cup. "Thank you, dear."

"When Jonathon was fifteen, Damon provided airline tickets for Jonathon and me to travel to Jamaica. I wanted to reconnect with my family and give Jonathon a sense of his roots. While we were there, Damon surprised us by joining us for an entire day on the beach. I explained to Jonathon that his father lived in Jamaica and that he would visit when he could."

"Wasn't Jonathon confused about why his father lived in Jamaica while you both resided in New York?" Drew asked.

"Or why his father looked so different from him?" Francy added.

"Well, he didn't ask questions until after that trip," Bayya said, frowning. "Then he had hundreds of questions—it was as if something inside him had awakened."

"I can't imagine," Drew said, striving to understand the unfolding consequences. "After Jonathon met his father, how did he react?"

"Jonathon believed that his father lived in Jamaica and was a businessman. I also tried to make him aware of the challenges of interracial relationships during the 1960s, and how we could never be together—especially since he was married." Bayya brought her hands to her face and cradled her head in sorrow.

"That must have been incredibly hard," Francy remarked as she gently placed a hand on Bayya's shoulder.

"A fifteen-year-old boy couldn't grasp such prejudice," Drew noted, thinking of his own experiences at that age.

"Did Richard Belltone know that he had an illegitimate brother?"

"To this day, Richard remains unaware," Bayya said, her face turning solemn.

"What prompted you to reintegrate Jonathon into the Belltone family years later?" Drew asked.

"Jonathon graduated from NYU with a Master's in Fine Art. Passionate about his field, he worked at several museums until I overheard Mrs. Belltone seeking an art curator. I told her I knew someone she could interview."

"Did she ask about your relationship with Jonathon or how you knew him?" Francy questioned.

"I told her he was merely an acquaintance; I would never violate my agreement with Damon." She patted her forehead with a worn handkerchief retrieved from her apron pocket.

"Damon Belltone had already passed away by that time, correct?" Drew pulled out a kitchen chair and sat beside her.

231

"Yes, years before."

"Didn't Jonathon recognize the portrait of Damon in the hallway?" Francy asked curiously.

"No. Jonathon met Damon only once in Jamaica, when Damon was much younger. Damon passed away at ninety-five, and the portrait was completed shortly before his death." Another tear welled in Bayya's eyes.

"How did you regain possession of this beautiful ring?" Drew looked down, noticing the brilliance of its stones.

"I shouldn't say this…" Bayya hesitated, lingering on the question. "I feel as if I cannot keep this information hidden any longer." She began to cry.

Francy promptly stood and fetched Bayya a glass of water.

"I knew from the moment you began investigating Phillip's death that everything would change," Bayya whimpered. "I believe I was secretly seeking this relief."

"Bayya, we will be as discreet as possible," Drew said, leaning in and placing his hand atop hers. "If your information isn't relevant to Phillip's case, it will remain confidential."

"I discovered that Richard was having an affair with one of Mrs. Belltone's friends." Bayya sat upright. "He begged me not to inform his wife and offered me money, travel…" her voice trailed off. "I told him that all I desired was the sapphire ring."

Drew and Francy exchanged astonished glances.

"Richard did not inquire about the specific choice of the ring; we simply agreed upon it. He remains unaware of my personal connection to the ring and may have considered my request unusual. However, I believe he was relieved that this was the sole condition for my discretion."

"Is this the person involved in the affair?" Drew showed Bayya one of the photographs from Phillip's envelope.

"Yes, that is her – Phillip's girlfriend."

"What?" Francy exclaimed in shock.

"Phillip was enamored with her."

"By Jeanne Lois?" Drew inquired.

"Yes," Bayya confirmed. "Although there was a significant age difference, Phillip was mature beyond his years and appreciated intelligent women."

Drew discreetly slid the photo back into the envelope.

"This explains why Phillip was so angry with his father," Bayya said, shaking her head. "The relationship between Richard and Jeanne Lois was short-lived, but it irrevocably damaged their bond."

"My dearest Bayya," Francy consoled, "you have harbored so much information."

Bayya nodded slowly as her revelations and secrets emerged.

A sudden creak at the front door alerted Bayya. "He's here!" she exclaimed, standing and wiping her eye. She swiftly tucked away her pocket handkerchief and pressed the kitchen chairs against the table. "Richard is here."

Drew and Francy rose, thanked Bayya, and entered the living room.

Richard arrived at the sanctuary of his own home. His well-fitted suit and polished shoes signified his unwavering commitment to his status. Despite his impeccable appearance, a subtle tension clung to him, as if the burden of his responsibilities and the high-stakes environment in which he operated were beginning to take their toll. "I'm sorry I'm late," Richard apologized.

"Richard, we have some astounding information that has come to light, and there is much to discuss," Drew greeted him with a handshake.

Richard's sharp eyes, usually focused and calculating, now betrayed a hint of unease, and his normally confident stride faltered slightly as he approached the duvet.

"This is the eleventh hour, Mr. Belltone. I trust you understood that some matters would eventually surface when you engaged our services," Drew began, shaking his hand.

Richard nodded knowingly.

"Phillip was not your biological son, was he?" Drew asked.

"No, our biological son died shortly after childbirth. I adopted a boy whose mother died during delivery; only I and the hospital knew the circumstances—not even my wife is aware." Richard slowly ran his fingers through his hair and shifted in his seat. "Nevertheless, we loved Phillip as if he were our own."

"I'm sorry to mention this, but I must bring it up," Drew said gently.

"You were involved with Jeanne Lois Van Italie?" Francy interrupted.

"Yes," he admitted, hanging his head. "It was short-lived. I had no idea she was involved with my son!" he exclaimed. "This turned my son against me."

"Are you being blackmailed because of this?"

"How did you know I was being blackmailed?" Richard's expression shifted. "Yes, I am being blackmailed, but I do not know by whom."

"It isn't Jeanne Lois?" Francy inquired.

"Oh heaven no, she's not capable of that! Someone is framing me for smuggling drugs through our ports." Richard stood up abruptly. "I constantly receive images of packages of cocaine routed through my facilities."

"Can you explain?" Drew asked.

"As a global estate financier, I oversee several major ports worldwide. Illicit drugs have been found in my facilities. Someone is exploiting my ports to smuggle cocaine."

"Do you know how they're getting in?"

"They must be infiltrating port operations by various means. They are probably bribing corrupt workers or taking advantage of weaknesses in the port infrastructure."

"So, they're using this as leverage for large sums of money," Drew stated.

"If illicit drugs are discovered in my ports under my management, it could lead to severe legal consequences, financial losses, and damage to my reputation. The scale and complexity of global drug trafficking make it a formidable challenge for port authorities."

"Well, we have several detainees who are providing information, and we believe we have the situation under control," Drew nodded.

"What we need to do is set a trap to resolve this matter," Francy added.

"We have the perfect place to do this," Drew smiled.

# Chapter 18
## Central Park

As the horse-drawn carriages ambled down 59th Street, the bustling cityscape of Manhattan gradually gave way to the serene expanse of Central Park. The rhythmic clip-clop of the horse's hooves on the cobblestones blended with the gentle rustle of leaves overhead, forming a symphony of urban calm in the early summer evensong.

Debra, Elena, and Francy relaxed, savoring the cool breeze on their faces. Sitting opposite them, Drew could only smile as he took in the three of them, enjoying the evening ride. Debra, Aisha, and Israel followed closely behind in another carriage, their horse striding proudly along the first carriage. The girls were elegantly dressed—their beaded gowns catching the light from the antique street lamps just beginning to glow in the setting sun. The carriages, adorned with plush velvet cushions and gleaming brass fittings, provided a comfortable vantage point from which to appreciate the park's natural beauty. Towering oaks and elms lined the path, their branches forming a canopy that broke the sunset into dappled patterns on the ground. Squirrels played among the trees while a saxophonist's distant melody added a gentle counterpoint to their peaceful ride.

Approaching Tavern on the Green, the iconic restaurant emerged from lush surroundings. Its historic stone façade, bathed in soft, ambient lighting, radiated a warm and inviting glow. The main entrance, bordered by elegant wrought-iron gates, opened to reveal a courtyard adorned with twinkling fairy lights and abundant greenery. A light mist rose from the nearby fountain, lending an unusual mystique to the scene. The aroma of midsummer roses mingled with hints of gourmet cuisine, enticing every sense.

"Man, I'm hungry," Israel commented as he helped Debra and Aisha down from the carriage.

"Something smells absolutely amazing," Debra agreed.

As they disembarked, paparazzi immediately recognized Aisha and rushed to capture photos. She dismissed them with a polite nod and hurried into the restaurant. The remaining four friends followed closely, and the group of seven was greeted by attentive staff who led them through the grand entrance into the restaurant's opulent interior.

Crystal chandeliers hung from the vaulted ceilings, casting a soft amber glow over the polished hardwood floors. The walls displayed modern artwork and ornate wall hangings from the Whitney Museum, creating a striking contrast. The tables were set with fine china, gleaming silverware, and crystal glassware, each meticulously arranged for the evening's event.

"Crowded!" Mr. Belltone's executive assistant, Candela, beamed with delight at the sight of the entire team. "We are all set and ready," she confirmed to Drew. "Come, I'll show you to your seats." She then escorted the crew to a large table overlooking the restaurant's beautiful gardens.

The Whitney Museum of American Art had transformed the space into a living work of contemporary art, reflecting its commitment to showcasing the modern creations of the elusive artist La Croix. Drew watched as distinguished patrons mingled among the installations, engaging in lively conversation and sampling curated hors d'oeuvres.

Debra grasped Drew's arm as Tchaikovsky's "Waltz of the Flowers" filled the room, the gentle strains of a string quartet enhancing the ambiance.

"It looks like all our players are here," Francy whispered as she leaned in close.

"They have many of La Croix's most important works displayed in this dining room. Mr. Larson knew exactly what he was doing," Drew nodded.

"It's incredible what a person can do with their back up against a wall," Elena chimed in.

"It feels like we're going fishing," Grace added, joining Elena in a toast.

Smiling warmly, Drew slowly rose to address the crowded room. "Ladies and gentlemen, thank you for joining us this evening to celebrate what promises to be a spectacular exhibition. As many of you know, art is more than just color on a canvas—it is a reflection of our deepest truths. Sometimes, those truths lie hidden beneath the surface, waiting to be revealed."

Feeling a surge of nervous tension, Drew prepared to introduce the next speaker. "With that said, I would like to introduce you to the former curator of the Whitney Museum, Marcus Larson."

The crowd quieted, intrigued by his words. Marcus stepped forward—his tall, lanky frame moving slowly to the podium. He spoke with earnest intensity. "We are here to celebrate some of La Croix's most renowned works. Please take a moment to admire this piece—'The Sweetest Deception.' Beautiful, isn't it? But what if I told you that it isn't just a painting? That it stands as a symbol of something far darker... something significantly more dangerous?"

Marcus then gestured toward a large, colorful painting hanging in the center of the room—a vibrant abstract composition of swirling confections and bold shapes. "This painting, along with several others in the collection, tells a hidden story. A tale of smuggling, secrets, and power used to alter the very core of people's lives. You see, the artist behind these works has also become entangled in something far more illicit—an enterprise they were coerced into."

Marcus showcased the painting with a deliberate gesture. In a swift moment, he used a fine knife to carefully cut along the canvas seam, ensuring the artwork remained intact. As the incision deepened, the canvas separated to reveal hidden compartments within its layers. Hundreds of precisely wrapped drug packets, concealed in the canvas folds, cascaded onto the floor.

At the crowded restaurant, gasps echoed as diners leaped from their seats to witness the shower of drugs. Many froze in shock, their faces etched with disbelief as whispers spread rapidly throughout the room, each person struggling to comprehend what was unfolding.

"La Croix had ensured that the packets were artfully concealed within the painting's structure, thwarting detection through conventional methods." His voice trembled, reflecting not only his sense of self-betrayal but also the deep remorse he now felt.

Marcus moved toward one of La Croix's renowned obelisks and, with precise intent, struck its apex with a hammer. When he tilted the structure, an unanticipated cascade of identical drug packets tumbled out, affirming the grim truth.

Several onlookers instinctively stepped back, their faces drawn in fear as the unexpected drug display intensified public unease.

A line of New York City policemen entered, forming a secure barrier between the scattered packets and the stunned crowd.

"Ladies and gentlemen, please, please, take a seat," Drew pleaded. "I need your complete cooperation. The show is just getting started."

Debra slowly stood in the center of the dining room, quietly scanning the room until her gaze fixed on one person. "Ton destin est entre tes mains," she declared. The room fell silent as she repeated the phrase in French,

"Your fate is in your hands," prompting Jeanne Lois to murmur the words while rising slowly.

"Your own words—from your first public work of art spray-painted on a wall in Montmartre." Lowering her head, Jeanne Lois replied, "My fate is in my hands."

"You are La Croix," Debra proclaimed above the commotion.

After a drawn-out pause, she simply admitted, "I am." At these words, Jeanne Lois broke down in tears, her anguished sobs betraying the burden of a long-held secret finally released.

Jeanne Lois's sudden admission plunged the room into stunned silence as onlookers exchanged uneasy glances, uncertain how to respond to her raw confession.

Moved by the vulnerability on display, Debra was overcome with empathy. Drew placed an arm around her and said, "It had to be done."

The room grew dense with compassion, doubt, and discomfort as the crowd grappled with the impact of her revelations.

Suddenly, a commotion erupted at the entrance when a voice commanded, "Let me through here right now." Katherine Goossens pushed her way through the crowd with fierce determination. Her heels clicked against the polished floor, each step echoing like the drumbeat of an imminent revelation. She bypassed the onlookers clustered near the exposed artist and halted to scan the room. Clad in a simple black dress that accentuated her showgirl figure, her face flushed with anger, Katherine fixed her gaze on Debra and offered a curt nod of approval. Then her eyes, burning with betrayal, fell on Jonathon and Jeanne Lois, seated together with their hands entwined—a sight that confirmed her worst suspicions and ignited a furious storm within her.

Drew signaled to a nearby policeman as one lunged toward Katherine in an effort to shield the couple.

With trembling rage, Katherine declared, "So, this is how it ends. Jeanne Lois, my own cousin, engaged to Jonathon—the man I loved and trusted." Turning to Jonathon with narrowing eyes, she continued, "You, who promised me everything, have betrayed me in the most deplorable way." Lifting her hand, she revealed a diamond engagement ring that sparkled in the light.

The room fell silent as the impact of her words settled over everyone. Katherine's chest heaved as she continued, her voice growing louder with each word. Pointing an accusing finger at Jeanne Lois, she demanded, "Jeanne Lois, you were in love with Phillip! He adored you so much that he had your signature permanently inked on his skin. What happened? What did you do?" Her accusation lingered in the air, focusing every eye on Jeanne Lois and leaving the room in palpable suspense.

Then, locking eyes with as many shocked patrons as she could, her gaze burning with dangerous fire, she declared, "But you haven't heard the worst of it. I loved you so deeply, Jonathon, that I was prepared to do anything to secure our future together." Pausing for effect, she continued, "I even killed for you."

A collective gasp swept through the onlookers. Jonathon recoiled, his face paling, while Jeanne Lois exchanged confused and fearful glances.

Katherine's lips curled into a bitter smile as she coldly confessed to the crowd, "It was I who poisoned Phillip," extending her hands in a gesture of finality.

Drew suddenly noticed the neurotoxin burn on her right thumb and index finger.

Jonathon staggered backward as he struggled to stand, his face contorted in horror. "You... you killed Phillip?"

Drew and Francy turned to Mrs. Belltone, whose capacity for enduring further revelations appeared spent. She trembled, head cradled in her hands, her life in ruins once more.

"No need to play dumb, my darling," Katherine replied evenly. "It was you who proposed it—saying it would liberate us and bond us together. I accepted the lie without question. And now, I've unmasked you as the fraud you are."

Jonathon raised one hand to halt Katherine's advance while using the other to shield Jeanne Lois.

Two policemen immediately moved to detain Katherine. She resisted, pulling her arm free. Incensed, she shouted, "I caused his death so you could inherit his wealth, and so we could escape to Europe and live as planned."

Chaos erupted in the room. Standing resolutely, Katherine's labored breaths betrayed her rage as she screamed at Jeanne Lois, "You're going to pay for this!"

The officers cuffed Katherine and escorted her from the restaurant. Two additional officers approached Jeanne Lois, who slowly rose to her feet. She carefully freed her entwined fingers from Jonathon's grasp. As he reached for her, the officers guided her out of the establishment, her head bowed in shame.

Suddenly, a plate shattered on the floor, startling everyone. "Ladies and gentlemen," Mr. Belltone declared, "I need your full attention. Please, Drew, continue."

Drew glanced at his team for support and stepped to the front. "A functioning sociopath can often be charming, intelligent, and successful—holding down a job, maintaining relationships, or appearing normal on the surface. However, they may disregard the feelings of others and flout social rules while expertly concealing this fact. Isn't that right, Jonathon?"

Jonathon cast a defiant glance at Drew and slowly resumed his seat.

"They excel at feigning care when it serves their purposes. They may treat people as instruments, using them to achieve their ends rather than acknowledging them as individuals with their own needs and emotions."

Israel rose and joined Drew at the front. "Jonathon, you manipulated Marcus Larson, your former boss at the Whitney, for your own gain. In exchange for large sums of money, you forced him to perform your illicit activities. Together with Isandor—killed by Marcus—and your two accomplices at the museum, now accused of attempted murder of my dear friends, you executed your crimes. We have their confessions."

Jonathon smirked. "It sounds like they were the criminals, not me."

"Yes, Jonathon—a man who has exploited his position and influence to manipulate others and ruin lives for power and profit." Grace rose and stepped forward.

"You even had Detective Jameson in your pocket. Unsatisfied with his earnings, he was lured by your promises of greater power and financial gain." Grace's simmering anger was evident.

Jonathon averted her gaze.

"He believed he was above the law, free to act as he wished. Now facing charges that include kidnapping and obstruction of justice—and with evidence tampering, destruction, and concealment added—he risks a lifetime in prison. And he did all this foolishly for you," she explained.

Jonathon crossed his legs. "It sounds like he's responsible for his actions."

"And you're responsible for yours," Drew remarked with a smile as he faced Jonathon. "Ladies and gentlemen, Jonathon Matthews is about to be unmasked. The Belltone family's legacy relies on an illicit affair that unfolded three generations ago between Damon Belltone, Richard's father, and their maid, Bayya Jenkins. Their affair produced a son—a scandal hidden for decades that could have destroyed the family's reputation. Jonathon is the product of Damon Belltone and Bayya Jenkins."

A deep murmur swept through the room like a wave.

"Unbeknownst to all, Jonathon had been pursuing his own hidden agenda. Behind meticulously planned schemes and manipulations, he aimed to seize control of the Belltone family empire." Drew turned to Jonathon. "Your nephew, Phillip, uncovered this truth—a surprise you never intended. So, true to your nature, you forced someone else to do your dirty work, persuading Katherine to serve your interests with the promise of love and a shared escape with the Belltone fortune."

Jonathon remained silent.

Elena whispered to Aisha, "It's almost as if he's gloating."

"Phillip's murder was merely a stepping stone toward your blackmail scheme. Unbeknownst to you, Phillip outsmarted you by recording everything!" Drew smirked at Jonathon, emphasizing that he was contending with an adversary within his own family.

"What you failed to realize was that your nephew had been secretly leaving clues and concealing documents to undermine your plan," Drew continued, pointing toward Elena, who held up Phillip's book of secrets.

Elena made her way to the front of the room. She cleared her throat and held up the book.

"Phillip was a man of consequence. He harnessed his raw talent to become a respected artist. Although Phillip was strong, his love for Jeanne Lois was his vulnerability. You exploited that by turning her relationship against him. Alongside Marcus Larson, you discovered that Jeanne Lois was the renowned 'La Croix.' Together, you blackmailed her. In exchange for keeping her secret identity hidden, you staged an affair between

Richard Belltone and Jeanne Lois, using that leverage to make her fall in love with you. That is pure manipulation." Elena nodded. "This pitted father against son."

Jonathon's smile grew darker.

"You exploited Jeanne Lois' art to traffic drugs through Richard Belltone's ports, bribing port authorities with the money you defrauded from him," Elena added.

"Jonathon has been blackmailing several individuals, including his stepbrother," Drew announced, gesturing toward Richard Belltone, who maintained a stoic expression. "With the help of Weston, your accountant, both he and Jonathon orchestrated your every move, Mr. Belltone," Drew continued, nodding toward the sweating man in the corner.

Weston rose and pointed accusingly at Jonathon. "I knew this would collapse. You assured me everything would be fine!"

Grace rose and strode across the room with determination. Locking eyes with Weston, she slapped him forcefully.

Weston slowly regained his composure.

"That's for kidnapping me," Grace shouted as she delivered another slap. "And for your friend, Detective Jameson." She swept her vibrant emerald braids behind her and returned to her seat.

Weston adjusted his slacks over his ankle monitor and composed himself. He was there for a single purpose.

"Jonathon, I was the one at the private auction who won the bid on La Croix's 'Hidden Places' painting. Marcus Larson and I planned to take it to City Hall and offload the cocaine concealed within it. We ran our own side business because we knew we couldn't trust you."

"You're such a fool," Jonathon laughed.

Humiliated and enraged, the accountant grabbed a knife from the table and advanced toward Jonathon. Two officers moved in cautiously, keeping a safe distance from Weston as his grip tightened on the knife. Sensing imminent danger, they ordered, "Lower your weapon now."

"Your arrogance has consequences!" Weston spat, each word underscored by the crushing burden of a thousand grievances.

Before Jonathon could retort, an officer with steely resolve brandished his taser. With a swift motion of his wrist, the device discharged twin prongs that struck Weston squarely in the chest.

In an instant, sparks exploded around his body, leaving him caught between excruciating pain and paralyzing electricity as the current surged through him. The room fell silent, every eye fixed on the gruesome spectacle. Weston's defiance evaporated as he crumpled to the floor, convulsing in a fatal, rhythmic dance.

Horrified gasps gave way to panicked screams as guests stumbled toward the exit in a desperate bid to escape the unfolding nightmare. Yet most remained rooted to the spot, morbidly fascinated by the chaos, their hearts pounding in a maddening rhythm as they awaited the ultimate climax of this twisted spectacle.

"Ladies and gentlemen, please settle down," Drew commanded, urging the guests to be seated. "Jonathon and Weston exploited the alleged affair involving your stepbrother, Robert Belltone, to blackmail him, while Weston manipulated drug shipments worldwide using Belltone's port connections. All of this was concealed within these paintings, smuggled across borders under the guise of art."

"You have no proof," Jonathon declared, though a hint of concern crossed his smug expression.

"Oh, we have plenty of proof," Israel said, brandishing a hard drive. "Before Isandro could burn Mr. Belltone's servers down, I downloaded all the evidence we needed. It may be deleted from their system, but it's rarely truly erased." Israel's smile radiated pride.

"Each payment you received from Robert Belltone as blackmail was later used to advance your plot—to tarnish his reputation and eliminate your rivals." Israel merely shook his head at Jonathon.

"And let's not forget the artist coerced into this scheme. La Croix is not a criminal; she's a victim, like everyone else you have blackmailed, Jonathon. She never asked for this, yet you forced her hand," Debra said, gesturing toward the artwork displayed across the room.

"We also have all the forensic evidence," Elena interjected. "Thanks to Dr. Stevens's exceptional detective work, he identified the poison taken from La Croix's art studio—stolen by her cousin Katherine—using your manipulations, Jonathon. Dr. Stevens traced the delivery method of the poison through Phillip's water and Dr. Foster's coffee, linking these two murders directly to you."

"Ladies and gentlemen," Drew announced. "Robert Belltone has been nothing but a pawn in Jonathon Matthew's game for far too long—held hostage by his own shame and fear of losing everything. But no one should live in constant fear or be blackmailed into compromising their values, relationships, or integrity."

Jonathon finally broke. "This is absurd! You don't know what you're talking about."

"But it didn't end there; Jonathon believed he could hide behind layers of deceit, twisting the truth to control those around him. Yet tonight, everything is revealed—no more secrets, no more lies. The game is over," Drew declared as he motioned to the police.

Instantly, Jonathon sprang to his feet, ready to act. The police staff, on edge since Drew's speech began, moved quickly to apprehend him. Realizing the gravity of the situation, Jonathon attempted to run for the front door, but his escape was short-lived. A few dinner guests—now fully aware of his crimes—shouted to block his path. Trapped by several nearby men, he found no way to slip away.

Panicked, Jonathon shouted as the crowd held him back. "You don't know what you're doing! You can't do this! I'll ruin you all! You'll regret this!"

Suddenly, the crowd at the front of the room parted. Aisha, who had been sitting quietly at the table, made her way through the bewildered guests. She approached Jonathon and produced the long silver key from her purse. Drew appeared behind her with the Tinker Box obtained at the underground auction.

"We have one more bombshell to deliver," Aisha purred. "It was La Croix—disguised as the lady in black at the underground auction—who outbid everyone for this box. It was her intention that you never get your hands on it."

"This box belonged to your father, Damon Belltone. That was the reason you wanted to buy it back so badly, isn't it?" Drew knew the answer well.

"But what you didn't know about were its contents," Aisha smiled wickedly.

"There is nothing in that box!" Jonathon yelled back.

Aisha turned to Drew and inserted the ancient key into the lock, turning it gently until it clicked. Placing both hands on the lid, she opened the box.

Jonathon stepped forward from his restraints and looked squarely into the box. "I told you it was empty!" A smug, defiant look crossed his face.

Drew reached into the box and pushed down the front two corners, triggering a false bottom that popped up. Richard Belltone then moved up behind Drew and withdrew the contents. "Hundreds of stocks and bonds," he announced, waving them in Jonathon's face. "Every one bears your name. My father, perhaps overcome by remorse later in life for denying you and your mother, left these for you—to mature over the years—a fortune!"

A sickened expression spread across Jonathon's face as shock overtook him.

"Officer Martinez, get him out of here," Belltone commanded.

Officer Martinez, dressed in full uniform, marched up behind Jonathon Matthews, handcuffed him, and escorted him straight out the front door.

The audience stood in stunned silence, overwhelmed by the revelations. They had braced themselves for more bombshells, yet the intensity of the moment exceeded their expectations. Drew signaled the waitstaff to begin serving as the room settled into whispered conversations, gentle music, and the clinking of silverware, though an undercurrent of disbelief lingered—as if the gravity of the revelations still held them captive.

Drew observed the room with an unreadable expression as the evening simmered with unspoken tension. Richard Belltone then approached him, his voice shaky. "I—I didn't know how to stop it. I thought it would end, but it just kept escalating. The blackmail, the shipments—all of it. I believed I could control and hide it, but now it's all exposed, and I—I never meant to hurt anyone."

Drew placed a reassuring hand on his shoulder. "You never asked for this, Robert, but now you have a chance to regain control and make things right."

"But what about the press?" he asked.

"The press will exploit the sensationalism, yet the truth is now public. People know what Jonathon Matthews was capable of, and it's going to be hard for him to escape this one. We have every piece of evidence—his blackmail tactics, the smuggling operation, the killings. He's finished," Drew reassured him.

Mr. Belltone felt a wave of shame, yet a new resolve shone in his eyes. "I've ruined everything—my marriage, my career. I...I don't know how to fix this."

"Sir, listen to me," Drew replied calmly, "the first step in fixing anything is being honest. The public knows now, and once you confess your part, people will respect you more. You'll have to make amends with your wife and anyone else you've hurt, but you can rebuild from here," he promised.

"I'll do whatever it takes."

"It won't be easy, but you can make amends. The affair? It's over now. The blackmail? Ended. The smuggling? That will take time to unravel, but you're no longer bound by Jonathon's influence. You have a chance to move forward," Drew said confidently.

Mrs. Belltone walked up to the table. She slipped her arm around her husband's waist and gave him a kiss on the cheek. "You've done something outstanding tonight, Drew. You didn't just expose the criminal—you freed everyone caught in Jonathon's grip."

Drew nodded thoughtfully. "I didn't do it alone. My friends have been my strength. The truth always comes out, no matter how well it's hidden. It's simply a matter of waiting for the right moment."

Mrs. Belltone blew a kiss to the entire table. "I always knew the seven of you had magic together. If there's ever anything we can do for you, just let us know."

The group rose and thanked the Belltones for the opportunity. With a final expression of gratitude, New York's power couple turned and left the restaurant arm in arm.

The following day, the city's sounds began to seep into the morning calm—just like any other New York morning. The soft rumble of an awakening subway sent its early warriors on their way, but today, their daily news carried a fresh headline:

**New York's Hometown Paper**

# NEW YORK POST

---

## High Stakes Homicide: Miami's Sexy Seven Solve NYC Heir's Death

**New York, New York-** In New York, scandals rise with the sun. Today was no different. Called to assist New York's power couple, Drew and the Detectives were summoned to the Big Apple for another high profile case.

The crew received an invitation to Café Vivaldi in the East Village. Doris called Elena and insisted that she and her friends make a morning appearance at the café, promising a special surprise before they headed back to Miami. Drew, Elena, Debra, Aisha, Grace, Francy, and Israel headed downtown to meet the effervescent Doris in her element.

"Well, well," Doris greeted, raising her voice so that everyone in the coffee shop could hear. "Let's welcome our very own New York celebrities," she said, gently bowing before Elena and Drew as the crowd applauded. They blushed at the unexpected recognition.

Turning to the rest of the crew, Doris said, "Francy, if I had a body like yours, I wouldn't be working in this dump," smiling as she spoke.

Doris blushed as she added, "Aisha, you look beautiful—you're better than a Bond girl!"

Doris bowed to Israel. "Israel, gorgeous! Are you single?"

She then turned to Debra and murmured, pursing her lips, "You must be Debra. Brains and beauty, of course."

"And you must be Grace…" Doris removed her wool beanie and teased, "Do you think I could rock green braids too?" Rising from her nearly flawless curtsy and adjusting her perpetually shifting apron, she gestured toward the front of the shop's menu.

"We've created a new drink in your honor," she smirked. "I'm proud to present Sleuth Tea!" Leaning in close, she whispered into Elena's ear, "It's selling like hotcakes."

"That's amazing," Elena said with a smile, acknowledging the crowd's applause.

Doris smiled and snapped her wrist. "Honey, everyone wants to be a detective!"

Be sure to

Follow Drew and the Detectives as they tackle their next thrilling case in the dazzling city of Los Angeles in *Hollywood Fame and Foul Play.*

# Drew: The Puzzler

- Consummate New Yorker, dancer, and gifted puzzler.
- He interprets body language and reads others' emotions like a barometer.
- His intense curiosity about human decision-making enhances his detective work.

# Elena: The Rocker

- Street-smart New Yorker.
- Talented singer, dancer, and rocker.
- Her obsessive nature keeps everyone in check.

## Aisha: The Movie Star

- Spain's most beloved actress.
- A natural beauty with an eye for intrigue.
- She sees life as an adventure to tackle head-on.

## Grace: The Empathic Caregiver

- Sultry African beauty with moves to match.
- The empathetic caregiver of the group.
- Her innocent meddling makes her the team's instigator.

# Israel: The Whiz Kid

- Actor, dancer, and tech-savvy genius.
- Inquisitive, always thinking two steps ahead.
- His adventurous spirit guides the team forward.

# Debra: The Fashionista

- Argentinean heiress, fashionista, and "petite ballerina."
- Her strong will and distinct outlook on life give her a suave detective's edge.
- With a heart of gold, she serves as the enlightened guardian of the group.

# Francy: The Fitness Star

- Classic Italian beauty.
- A top fitness star driven by strong determination.
- She leads the team through their toughest challenges.

# About the Author

Andrew Pacholyk is an international best-selling author who captivates his audience with skillful storytelling and intriguing characters. His award-winning work has earned critical acclaim for blending life lessons, humor, and suspense with deeply human narratives. Andrew's notable achievements include the prestigious Literary Titan Gold Book Award and a 2022 Ommie Award nomination for Best Spiritual Memoir for his work "Barefoot: A Surfer's View of the Universe." His creative work has also been featured in esteemed media outlets such as The New York Times, The Huffington Post, OM Times, and CBS News.

Connect with Andrew: https://www.peacefulmind.com/about-us

# Don't forget to read the 1st book that started it all!

Lie. Betray. Murder. Repeat.

Drew and his talented friends are the highlight of Miami, mesmerizing crowds with their dynamic performances. However, their carefree lives shatter when a wealthy shipping tycoon is brutally murdered, sending shockwaves throughout the city.

Suspicion quickly falls on several family members, including Drew and his crew, after incriminating evidence links them to the tycoon's daughter in the wake of the murder. Now, unwittingly caught in the grip of this sinister plot, the dancers must race against time to prove their innocence and expose the true killer.

They embark on a gripping quest across Miami, uncovering a conspiracy darker than they ever imagined. Drew and his friends must unearth the truth and clear their names before the killer strikes again. Every second counts in The Rhythm of Betrayal.

https://www.peacefulmind.com/drew/

★Rated top 25 mystery audiobooks for 2024 - **Reuters**

★Why the Rhythm of Betrayal Can be the Next Hollywood Blockbuster - **Fox News**

★Top 10 Whodunits in 2024 – **Mysteries Inc.**

★Rate #1 best book of ensemble characters
– **Madness + Murder Magazine**

★The New Detectives – different, unique, great premise. Already a cult classic – **Time Out Magazine**

★A proper American murder mystery – **Foyles**

★The Miami setting is described so well that you can almost feel the heat and hear the music – **Barnes and Noble**

★A fast-paced page turner – **Mystery Lovers Inc.**